Christmas Island

MARY SHOTWELL

CITY OWL
PRESS

CHRISTMAS ISLAND
Waverly Lake, Book 3

CITY OWL PRESS
www.cityowlpress.com

Cover Design by Tina Moss. All stock photos licensed appropriately.

Edited by Tee Tate.

For information on subsidiary rights, please contact the publisher at info@cityowlpress.com.

Print Edition ISBN: 978-1-64898-260-6

Digital Edition ISBN: 978-1-64898-261-3

Printed in the United States of America

To my Tennessee book club

Chapter One

Thursday, December 15

LAURA CRAWFORD STEPPED ONTO THE SIDEWALK IN front of her apartment in South End, a tidy, chic two-bedroom in a comfortable nook of Charlotte, North Carolina. Technically, it wasn't her apartment, but rather *their* apartment. Hers and Logan's. The harder she tried not to think about Logan Ainsworth and his misdeeds, the more he popped up in her thoughts.

Just move on. He's never coming back.

He'll come crawling back, begging for forgiveness.

Once a cheater, always a cheater.

He'll see the error of his ways.

Everyone had something to say about her fiancé leaving her for another woman. The cheating itself was terrible enough. Not knowing where to go and what to do about their shared apartment was almost as bad.

She grazed her thumb over her ring finger. The diamond adorned on the gold ring had been a staple of her wardrobe, a part of her hand, that she continued to forget she no longer wore it. She kept it in her purse, not quite ready to lock it away. For whatever reason, keeping it with her, but not on her, felt right.

She walked in her comfortable flats, her stretchy, gray work pants, and a pink blouse under her knee-length wool coat, the dressiest she'd get for her job. Heels were not an option, even though the non-profit office was one neighborhood away in Dilworth. Who really enjoyed wearing heels all day? If Laura had to describe herself in one word, it would be practical. Practicality saved money, time, and like flats, provided the more comfortable choice.

If anything, she wished she had added her knit headband—her pulled back, highlighted hair doing nothing to shield her ears from the stiff morning breeze. She raised her shoulders and clenched her coat, passing by the second of three murals on the workday walk. More than half of the nearly dozen murals along these brick facades were likely there purely for social media attention. Now that Christmas swiftly approached, lighted metal ornaments of candy canes and snowflakes hung off lampposts and facades of businesses willing to participate in the ambiance. The neighborhood was Instagram-worthy; a menagerie of coffee shops, art studios, craft breweries, and modern apartments.

Ugh. That shared apartment. What was she going to do? She couldn't afford the rent so close to work on her own. If Logan didn't have a problem with her staying there—why should he, considering he was nowhere to be found and had cut off communication some three weeks ago—then was it necessary to go through moving stress?

Practicality, Laura.

The Learning Center for Autism Spectrum Disorder sat wedged between a children's boutique and cafe, a first-floor, twelve hundred square-foot space with a classroom, three offices, and front desk. The naming wasn't coincidental. The founder came up with the acronym before the full title—TLC for ASD. Laura and all the employees called it TLC for short.

Laura stepped inside and found the front desk unoccupied. Generally, they left it that way until after school when the majority of clients came by. She walked past the desk and the sign on the wall displaying the logo—a hand lifting an infinity symbol.

"There she is." Cindy stood next to a familiar mother with her son.

"Good morning, Cindy." Laura smiled back, wishing it came as effortless as Cindy's cheerfulness. Not that it pained her to smile. It was just that Cindy became an orientation leader fresh out of college, and her small frame, short, fun bob and undying positivity made Laura's twenty-six years of age seem two generations older. Less peppy.

"I didn't expect to see you here, Ryan. Mrs. Faye."

"We wanted to stop by this morning, since it's a Power Monday for the school. I don't really understand how much an extra hour or two for the kids once a month helps them in any way, but what do I know?"

"Mom." Ryan, wearing a faded Nirvana T-shirt, nudged his mother's shoulder. He held a jacket in one hand, and hid his other hand behind his back.

"Sorry. Show her, honey."

He proudly revealed his secret—a printed book report clearly showing a grade of 'A' on the front.

"That's amazing!" Laura high-fived the teenager. Such a success was the reason she had taken the job in the first place at TLC.

"It's a testament to the work you all do here," Mrs. Faye said.

Laura took the compliment in stride, reaching to tuck her hair behind her ear before remembering it was pulled back in a ponytail. "It's also because of the hard work Ryan has put in."

Ryan had been her first consultation since starting the position as community and regional outreach planner at TLC. A year ago, she'd held a community information night at his high school, one of many schools she visited throughout the greater Charlotte area. He and his mother came in the following morning. Ryan wasn't too keen on being there and kept staring at the door and standing, only for Mrs. Faye to sit him down again. He wore that same Nirvana T-shirt and Laura quoted Kurt Cobain, which promptly won not only his attention but his willingness to participate. Laura came up with a plan that included after-school sessions for academics along with hands-on simulations and field trips to alleviate his social discomfort.

Now here were Ryan and Mrs. Faye a year down the road, showing tangible results. TLC had doubled its employees in that time, and Laura no longer focused on creating and implementing personal plans of action. She didn't miss wearing several hats at once but missed the deeper connections with the students.

"Keep that up and I'm going to have to attend your graduation."

"Mom said I don't have to walk in one of those stupid dresses and hats."

"We're working on it." Mrs. Faye winked.

Ryan turned to his mother. "We'll be late."

"That's my cue." Mrs. Faye led her son towards the front door, and Laura followed.

"Don't take 160," Ryan said. "We have to go to Clanton Road, then right on—"

"I know, I know." Mrs. Faye patted his shoulder as Laura held the door for them.

"Have a great day at school, Ryan."

He walked out to the sidewalk and his mother looked back.

Laura lowered her voice. "Sounds like you'd better take Clanton."

Mrs. Faye smiled. "Who needs a GPS? I keep telling him he needs to be a traffic reporter."

"No cameras." Ryan shook his head.

The two left, and Laura held the door as a young man carrying a package approached. He read the label. "For...Pham Kim-Anh."

"I'll take it to Kim."

"You do work here, right?" He couldn't have been a day over twenty.

"I do. Where's Sam? He usually has this route."

His apprehension disappeared. "I'm covering him the rest of the week."

"And your name is?"

"Trey."

"Nice to meet you, Trey. I'm Laura. You'd better get going. Sam sets the bar high for reliable delivery people."

Trey smiled. "Understood."

"I'll see you around, then."

Trey nodded, and Laura went back inside the office.

"Wasn't that amazing?" Cindy leaned on the front desk. "His first A on an essay, can you believe it?"

"It was amazing." The full circle Ryan took hit her again.

"What do you have there?"

Laura looked at the package in her hand. "It's for Kim. I'm assuming she's back there?"

"Yep. She was here on the phone before I got here. I don't even know who she could be talking to so early."

"You know Kim." Laura walked down the hallway. The multimedia classroom took up most of the space to her left, while storage, a restroom, and an office took up the right. The other two offices sat in the back, the right corner office her boss, Kim's, headquarters.

Laura knocked on the frame of the office's open door.. Laura always knocked because Kim could get so focused on a task people suddenly appearing in front of her scared the bejesus out of her.

"Morning." Kim's dark hair curled under at her shoulders and simple diamond studs gleamed on her pierced ears. Although twenty years older than Laura, hardly a gray streak of hair shone through Kim's black locks. Meanwhile, Laura had been highlighting her hair since twenty-one. Her brunette hair was losing the fight, and the blond streaks disguised the gray and subsequent root growth better than her natural color. It was a little annoying to be sandwiched between two coworkers whose looks defied their ages.

"Got a package for you." Laura set it on her desk.

"Any word from Logan?" Kim had a tendency to ask every Monday, but seeing as she led a three-day short course this week, it was the first chance she'd had to ask.

Laura sighed. "So much for work getting my mind off of him."

"I'm sorry. I just thought he had another week to realize what an idiot he is."

"Unfortunately, he is still unaware of that fact."

Kim's shoulders sagged, clearly disappointed in Logan's lack of self-reflection.

"You know, I don't even know if he's told his friends or family?" Breakups were tough enough. But it thickened the hurt when his work friends, and even his family, had accepted her as one of them. Laura had especially bonded with his mother throughout her battle with cancer. It pained her not knowing how she was doing. "I'm guessing the fact they haven't contacted me means they do know."

"They're probably wincing at his behavior, too embarrassed to admit their poor choice in friends." Kim winked. "If it makes you feel better, I do have something to keep your mind off of Buttface McGee."

Laura half chuckled. Kim's straightforward attitude could be a shocker at times. But Laura also worried what could be up her sleeve.

Kim gestured to take a seat.

Laura obliged, bracing for whatever project Kim had on her mind.

"Beverly and James Bennett contacted me. Apparently, they had a chat over Thanksgiving weekend. Long story short, they came up with the idea of a Holiday Fundraiser."

"Oh?"

"To benefit the organization."

"Well, that's good news, right?"

"I believe so. The Bennetts know a lot of families and have really embraced the ASD community the past few months, ever since introducing us to their granddaughter, Hannah."

Laura nodded. Hannah had attended a few regional events with her father and sometimes her grandparents. She was a sweet girl; seven or eight years old.

"They want to have a fundraiser here in Charlotte? Let me guess, you're freaking out because that's incredibly short notice."

Kim's lips curled in a smirk. "*I'm* not freaking out."

Laura jumped from her seat. "You want me to do this? Organize a fundraiser? Isn't that the job of the event manager?"

"You're right, it is. But seeing as Sophie is currently on maternity leave, our community and regional outreach manager is the next best thing."

Laura tipped her head back and closed her eyes. It would be short notice, and to get a venue in Charlotte—

"Wait. The Bennetts aren't from Charlotte. They do mean to have it here, though, right?"

Kim grabbed a folder off her desk and handed it over. "If you head out of here early tomorrow, you should miss the city traffic and get to Waverly Lake in three hours."

"Are you serious? You're giving me a day's notice on this?" Technically, not even a day if she had to leave early tomorrow morning.

"Did you have plans for this weekend?" Kim blinked, hand on her hip.

Laura's mind reeled. Did Kim even care whether Logan called, or was she just asking to know if Laura's weekend would be open? No, Kim cared. And she'd also known no plans existed before asking. That was what happened when the boss-employee relationship crossed into friendship.

Laura groaned, flipping through the file folder.

"They're expecting you tomorrow. The address is in there, as well as your hotel info, along with the groups Beverly Bennett suggested contacting for attendance and spreading the word."

"Hotel? I can't drive out and drive back?"

"I have you staying the night. You'll have to discuss scope and logistics with them so you can help find a venue. Plus, I figured you could use a night away from that apartment. I mean, aren't you reminded of him with every piece of furniture, every decoration?"

"Of course, I am. It's just that I don't have an alternative yet."

"You do now. At least for one night." Kim raised her eyebrows.

Laura nodded. "I didn't get a chance to tell Trey goodbye."

"Trey? Who is Trey?"

"Sam's replacement for this week."

"Who is Sam?"

Laura rolled her eyes. "Our delivery guy. Trey is covering him this week. Poor kid was nervous I didn't work here and was going to steal your package, but we sorted it out."

"Your fiancé is nowhere to be found with his lover, you're still living in his apartment, and you're worried about not saying goodbye to the temporary delivery boy." Kim chuckled and shook her head. "You definitely need a night away."

"Fine, fine." Laura walked to the door and turned around. "I'll have you know that befriending people you see in your neighborhood every day is a good trait to have."

"Go." Kim waved her out. "Before I make it two nights away."

Chapter Two

Friday, December 16

STEVE ALBERTSON LOOKED AT HIS WATCH, A SHARP, clean-faced dress watch he had purchased at a boutique store in Asheville, North Carolina. He was sold on the environmentally conscious angle in its manufacturing, although the price tag rivaled that of a Rolex. Not to mention the gas he used to commute there from Waverly Lake probably negated the pollution he had averted by buying the thing.

"So, tell him, Steve."

Steve looked up, not having processed the time. It was more of an escape from the two locals bickering in his office of Albertson Law, PLLC. Jerry Connelly owned a craft store, next door to Brad Eubanks, whose dentistry office abutted their shared wall.

"It's my shop, I can play what I want. It puts the customers in a good mood. Hence, they buy more."

"I'd be shocked to see evidence of that. If I have to hear *Run Rudolph Run* one more time..." Brad clenched his hand into a fist, jaw locked.

"First of all, it's technically *Run Rudolph Run*."

Brad stepped toward Jerry. Steve rushed between the two men, holding up his hands, which met Brad's chest. "Cool it, you two." He separated them, his hands on their chests until he felt they weren't going to have at it. His paralegal coworker Margaret raised from her seat at the front desk, perhaps afraid of a brawl. Knowing Margaret, it was more likely to give Steve a hand in fending them off.

"This is a law office. *My* law office. Now unless one of you wants to hire me as your legal counsel, which you won't since this is not something either of you would find worthwhile to sue over, I need you to leave."

"You saw how he is," Jerry said. "How are my customers supposed to feel safe with that attitude next door?"

"Keep playing that music and you won't have any customers."

Steve waved his hands. "All right. Stop it. This is how it's going to go." He turned to Jerry. "After five o'clock, you can play whatever music you'd like. That way, it won't coincide with Brad's patients in the office."

Steve turned to Brad. "However, Jerry can play Christmas music during regular hours, *if* it's instrumental. If you can't work with soft elevator music on the other side of your office wall, I suggest you find a new location, or install some speakers in your place. Got it?" He stared down both men. "Do we have an understanding?"

"Yes."

"Fine."

"Now shake on it and get out of here." The men looked at each other as if doing so took a year off their lives. "Shake on it, or I'm going to sue you both for wasting my time."

Margaret swiveled around, hiding her chuckling.

Steve was somewhere between laughing at the grown men and pushing them out the door.

They shook hands, albeit a sorry attempt, and Steve guided them out the door. He kept his eye on them as Jerry walked down the sidewalk, and Brad crossed Dowager Street, headed in the same direction.

"You'd make a good dad someday." Margaret smiled.

Steve instinctively looked at the picture on her desk of her and her son at the beach. Her brown skin glistened in the sunshine, her son squinting, his smile bigger than the ocean.

"Some days I think it might be easier to deal with children."

Margaret laughed. "You may be right. It's harder than anything I've ever done, but I've never had to mitigate two men acting like babies."

"It seems to be getting worse." Steve shook his head. "Not just with Jerry and Brad. The other day I was grabbing coffee and Mrs. MacMayer brought me outside where she had been fighting Cameron Pulaski over a parking spot."

"Don't forget Mr. Garrett popping by on his way to cut down a Virginia pine from Lakeshore Park for his Christmas tree. If he hadn't come inside to sign those documents on his way you would've had a holiday nightmare on your hands."

Steve closed his eyes and pinched the bridge of his nose. It was exhausting having to always play the attorney even when out getting coffee.

"I'm telling you, I've just about had it. It's like the holidays bring out the worst in people. It's an elevated level of anxiety and irritability that makes for a storm. And on top of that, we're in Waverly Lake. Where everyone thinks I dish out legal advice over every little thing."

Margaret sighed. She had a habit of doing so right before dispelling her wisdom. "I know it can be frustrating. Trust me, I've had my share of 'Do you have a minute?' conversations with folks around here. Just remember there was a time when people were hesitant to trust you taking over Mr. Hackford's law firm. You told me once that there was a time when you were scared it wasn't going to work out here. Now you're Waverly Lake's own Thomas Gibson."

"What does that mean?"

"You know, lean nose, chiseled chin, clean-cut hair parted on the side. It's easy to see you as a lawyer since you look like a

Hollywood movie attorney."

"I don't know about that."

"Okay. You think what you want. The fact is, after all that worrying, everyone in town trusts you with their secrets. With their lives."

She had a point, as usual. It was one of the reasons he loved working with her. She had a way of altering his perspective, of calming him down as he had to do many times with the locals. "When did I ever tell you that? About being scared and all?"

She smirked, knowing his changing-the-subject move all too well. "When I first started, at that party for the Weismans. You may have had a drink."

"See. That's why it's great we work together. Because you know all it takes is one glass to get all sentimental, and you talk me out of it at gatherings, every time."

"If only you knew what it's like babysitting a grown adult." She shook her head.

"You're so funny." Steve chuckled. "A drink is just what I need. Soon enough, on the beach, with the sun and the water. I can't even remember the last time I had a vacation." His last "break" was a long weekend in October, and that wasn't even close to a vacation. He participated in Lovetoberfest, a marathon of blind dates he'd agreed to—how he wasn't drinking to make that decision, who knew— that had led to Rachel. Their one amazing date led to exchanging numbers, but the fall romance died off with distance. At least for her. Why wasn't anyone willing to make an effort for a relationship? Was he that off-putting?

"Thanks again for connecting me with the condo." Margaret's aunt owned a two-bedroom condo in a high-rise on the beach in Florida, along the Gulf. It was where that picture on her desk had been taken.

"You sure I'm not imposing, with it being the holidays and all?"

"It's not imposing if she doesn't have renters." Margaret typed in her phone then showed the screen to Steve. "See? Not a soul the next two weeks, and then it's booked through New Year's. I thought as much." Margaret looked up at him. "Usually, people want to spend the holidays with their families, then head south before returning for school or work."

He nodded. The fact he had considered it was shocking enough. To drive to Florida and spend the holidays there? What would his parents say, missing out on Christmas in Waverly Lake? Could he leave his clients alone for that long? Better yet, could they leave him alone? But now that it was here, he couldn't leave fast enough.

"I can always postpone it, you know. I feel bad leaving you with the craziness to deal with by yourself."

"Outside of the meeting with the Bennetts this morning, there's nothing I can't take care of in your place."

"You know I owe you one, right?"

"Think of it as my Christmas gift to you."

"Are you sure you're okay—?" He stopped. Of course, she'd be okay. He wouldn't leave his practice with anyone else. Margaret was perfectly capable of the day-to-day management of the office. As a paralegal, she could handle the paperwork. Besides, the closer they got to the holidays the less amount of work the courts pushed through, which was why he had zero hearings the rest of December. If there was anything he needed to sign, she could overnight it. This was the perfect time to get away.

"You know I don't need to answer that."

"I know. What time is that meeting with the Bennetts?"

She checked her cell phone for the time. "Half an hour. That should give you enough time to pack your things."

"How did you know I haven't packed yet?"

Because she knew you'd leave room to chicken out.

Packing was one step closer to having to go. Why was he looking for excuses? If he stayed longer in Waverly Lake, he'd encounter more people bickering over the smallest thing. They'd invade his office, invade his personal space whenever he went out.

"I'm not backing out, you know." He smiled, a nervous laugh escaping.

"Your confidence needs some work, but okay. Everything will be all right."

"Okay. I'll be leaving after this meeting."

"Do you mind briefing me what it's about? In case it carries over into your trip. I just want to make sure I'm as prepared as I can be."

"You know, Beverly didn't say much over the phone. I got the sense it was something more personal than professional so I'm not billing hours or anything for it. I figured since it's at the community center it may have something to do with Ben Phillips or Beverly's daughter Tracy?" Ben and Tracy had taken over Phillips Manor two months ago, transforming it in a short amount of time from an aging house to a community center. Steve helped Ben legally claim his inheritance after the custodian of the account passed away. Since then, he had helped Ben with a few legal matters here and there on what he could and couldn't do with the property.

"Regardless of what it is, I'll let you know."

"Call me on your way to Florida."

He stood for a second, quite still in the lobby of the law office bearing his name. Waverly Lake was his hometown, his homebase, his world. For all its small-town charm that crossed over into claustrophobia and monotony and lack of privacy, he couldn't imagine living anywhere else. But the thought of getting out of Waverly Lake during one of its peak tourist seasons already felt like salt air in his lungs. "I like the sound of that."

He walked to his office in the back of the building and grabbed his suit jacket—yes, he was the only citizen of Waverly Lake to wear a suit and tie to work, but a man has his scruples—and briefcase, and waved to Margaret, then walked out the front door. The promise of privacy at the beach was so powerful, his common sense had gone down the street with Jerry and Brad.

He cracked open the front door and popped his head in the office.

Margaret stared at him as if he had lost his mind. "I was

wondering when you'd realize. I figured when you got in your car to enter directions."

"It's frightening how well you know me."

She handed him his cell phone.

"Thanks."

"You're welcome. Now go enjoy your trip, will ya?"

Chapter Three

Laura blew into the hole of a coffee cup lid, holding the brew in one hand while bracing the steering wheel of her fifteen-year-old gray Toyota Corolla with the other. Although Charlotte was a decent-size city, there were obstacles in public transportation. Plus, her job required her to visit school districts crossing into different counties, which was not feasible without a car. She didn't often take it out for journeys this far, and hoped it wasn't pushed to its limits.

She had left Charlotte early enough, dying for a cup of joe, but she didn't want to have to stop an hour later for a restroom break. Instead, she drove all the way through to Asheville, which paid off. Asheville had a bounty of gourmet coffee shops, and her choice didn't disappoint. Now if only the roadways weren't so winding, she'd be able to drink it without the threat of spilling.

As the initial scorch died down on her tongue, a few flurries danced about in the wind. Charlotte saw the occasional snowfall in the winter, but nothing to stay on the ground for long. Here though, snowstorms could be bigger events, and back-to-back, the elevation affecting the temperature and humidity. She drove by valleys and nooks in the hills graced by a few hours of daylight at most.

Luckily, the roads were fairly dry so far. She shook her head at feeling lucky. This wasn't even in her job duties. Fundraising events fell under Sophie's jurisdiction, but she was on maternity leave. Something Laura anticipated a year or two down the road for herself. At least that was the pathway she'd seen for her life with Logan just last month. Funny how an event could alter the course of the future. But calling off the engagement was the right thing to do, even if it did upend her plans. Even if it was the cheating liar's fault.

No matter. This was a weekend for her to get away. A weekend to forget about Logan and focus on her job. If she put everything she had into this project, maybe she'd impress Kim and gain more responsibility, more power to make positive changes in families' lives. It was time to embrace her independence, and Waverly Lake was just as good a place as any.

She had never been to Waverly Lake, although the lake held a notoriety from visitors she encountered here and there. It competed with Lake Norman for the best regatta, something she'd grown up with while living along Lake Norman's shoreline. It was no surprise Waverly Lake hadn't been on her family's radar for vacation, considering it took several twists and turns to navigate into town. Ironically that may have also been the appeal to locals.

As she turned south onto Dowager Street, the lake offered its first view to her right. She passed a cute park along the shoreline followed by Bingham Station, a gas station with old pumps and a front porch, reminiscent of another time. The roadside greeted her. *Welcome to Waverly Lake, population 4,382.* And she thought her hometown was small. Waverly Lake was under half the size.

The road weaved around a square, remnants of snowmen in the green space all but melted. Green wreaths decorated storefront shops, a pharmacy, hardware store, souvenir shop, salon; just about everything a small town needed to be called a small town. The flagpoles lining the street flew red and green flags with emblems of snowflakes and hollies and candy canes. A few people walked the sidewalks, coat collars and shoulders held high to block the brisk crosswinds. The radio station on the way announced another round of cold weather, bringing with it plenty of moisture. Hopefully she'd be up and out of here by then.

The GPS dinged and alerted her to turn left up ahead. She analyzed the screen on her phone, positioned in a suction cup holder over the dashboard. She was supposed to be meeting with Mr. and Mrs. Bennett at the community center, but as she turned onto Dorset Drive, she was certain she had typed in the wrong address. There weren't businesses down this way, but rather homes. Large homes with gated yards.

"You have arrived at your destination."

She stopped in the middle of the street, scanning for the address number. She located the white sign with black lettering softly lit by landscaping lights. *Phillips Community Center.* In smaller font below it, *Where you're a part of Waverly Lake's family.*

"I guess you were right, map."

A car horn honked. She looked in the rearview mirror. The driver of a black sedan waved his arms with impatience. She shook her head. "He should see Charlotte at five o'clock."

She crossed the street and pulled up beside an available spot along the curb. She backed in, the black sedan waiting on her, as if the driver wanted to see if she could pull off the parallel parking job. Of course, she could pull it off. She was a city girl. She hadn't had to drive to work since the move to the apartment, but once a parallel parker...

She made sure to have an even distance between the two cars, all the while feeling the burning stare of the other driver on the back of her head. "Stop being paranoid." She put the car in park and took a breath. *He's probably upset you took the last spot on the road.*

She grabbed her purse and folder, leaving her luggage in the trunk. There wasn't time to check in before the meeting, but that didn't matter since check-in wasn't until after noon. She grabbed her phone from the dash and texted Kim. *Arrived safely. On my way into the meeting. Will update you after.*

Laura got out of the car and shut the door behind her.

"You can't park there."

Laura looked over her car, to the man crossing the street. "Excuse me?"

He clicked his key fob and the black car—she now recognized as a BMW—a block further down beeped. Of course, it was the impatient driver. He was lean and tall, his dark hair parted to the side neatly. The breeze did little to dishevel it, while her hair kept licking her face. She pulled the strands back behind her ear.

"I said you can't park there."

She looked behind her and up and down the street. The neighborhood, even with the street parking, was tidy and well-kept, with red maple trees lining the sidewalks. The only *No Parking* sign stood at the next intersection by a fire hydrant. "I don't see a sign that says I can't."

He held up his hands in frustration.

Yep. Upset I took his parking spot.

"It's understood you can't parallel park in the wrong direction."

She snarked. The audacity of this man, in his tailored suit and clean-shaven face, who would otherwise be handsome were it not for his ugly attitude. He looked as if he was on his way to Wall Street and got sucked into a Waverly Lake vortex in his own Twilight Zone episode.

"I get the feeling this isn't a very busy street." *I get the feeling that no streets in Waverly Lake are busy.* "People do it in my neighborhood all the time." She purposely left out the fact there was a fifty-fifty chance of getting a ticket for doing it.

"Doesn't mean it's right."

"You're just upset I made you walk an extra thirty steps." She shifted her weight on one foot, phone-holding hand on her hip. "Wouldn't want to wrinkle the suit or dirty those leather shoes."

He jolted, bewilderment and shock clear on in his face.

She winced. It wasn't like her to lash out at a stranger. Just something about him got under her skin. She touched her ring finger out of habit and realized the connection.

The expensive car, the suit, the fancy shoes. Perfect hair. He was another Logan. It all signaled *cheater, liar, bad person* in her head. Which wasn't fair. Although she could be right.

"You also can't be driving with a burnt-out taillight like that."

And to think she was on the verge of apologizing. "Are you a cop? I'll admit, it's my first time in Waverly Lake, but I'm pretty sure cops don't wear *that* as a uniform."

"No." He stiffened, straightening his jacket. "I'm a lawyer."

She held back the laughter. *He is like Logan.* Did all lawyers have to wield a certain disdainful personality to be successful? Or did having that personality lead them to be lawyers? *Chicken and egg, Laura. Chicken and egg.* "That explains it."

"Explains what?" He moved to the sidewalk, still a good six feet away from her, but somehow it felt more hostile.

"The impatient attitude. The fancy car. The fancy everything. I know your type."

"My type? I'm not sure I've ever been more insulted and intrigued at the same time."

"Never mind. What is your name?"

"I'm not so sure I want to give it to you after all this." He looked to his left, staring into nothing, then back to her. "Steve. Albertson."

"Good, Steve Albertson. Now I know who not to call if I get a ticket for my illegal parking."

"Don't forget about the taillight."

She huffed. Never had she met a man who could so easily get under her skin. Even though she wholeheartedly believed he wasn't even trying. What did that say about him? Or worse, her?

"And your name? I trusted you with mine. Or is that not how they operate in the big city? No one gets to know anyone around them."

She was slightly shocked at the insinuation of her origins, although it was correct.

"Oh, come on, it's Waverly Lake," he said. "I've only lived here my whole life. I know who is from around here and who isn't, not to mention you said it's your first visit. When someone isn't from here, they're from a big city. Because anywhere else is bigger than here."

She chuckled, though kept it muted as much as possible. "I had assumed *you* were from a big city. You don't exactly fit the small-town type."

"Maybe you need to spend more time in a small town."

She didn't know if she found him insanely agitating or if he crossed into charming in some weird, warped way. "Laura," she said. "Crawford."

"Well, Laura Crawford, I'd say nice to meet you, but I think we both know that's not how it went down."

She gave him a nod. "If you don't mind, I have a meeting to get to."

"Same." He cleared his throat. "I hope to not see a ticket—or two—on your car when I leave."

Laura took a few steps before swiveling around again. "You're not going to call the police on me, are you? Just to prove your point?"

He smirked and looked down at his oxford dress shoes.

"Are you seriously—"

"No." He chuckled. "I'm not that kind of person."

"I couldn't be so sure."

"Well, I'm telling you now, I'm not. I guess you're just going to have to believe me."

"I'll believe you when I come out to my car and see no tickets."

"Now wait a minute." He held up a hand. "I can't help it if someone else did report it, or an officer on patrol saw it."

It was her turn to smirk. "Nope. If I see a ticket on there, I'll know you're not a man of your word."

"That's not fair."

"You know everyone, right? You said so yourself."

"But—"

"Then I'm sure you could talk to someone down at the station to explain how a naive, innocent out-of-town woman, who is probably now late for her meeting, didn't mean to break any rules."

"Now that would be a lie."

"Would it?" She turned back around and walked toward the community center.

"I mean the innocent part."

She powered through the insult, keeping her stride. An older woman, walking two cocker spaniels wearing little booties and matching sweaters, walked toward her.

"Good morning," Laura said, with her energized confidence.

"Morning."

The lady walked past and yelled back. "If that's your car, you can't park there."

Laura paused in her deflated march to the community center, closing her eyes. Perhaps the oncoming winter storm wasn't the only reason to get out of here as soon as possible.

Chapter Four

Steve watched as Laura Crawford headed to Phillips Community Center. Her flippant attitude toward the law vexed him, but as he approached, her sheer beauty knocked the wind out of him. Her blond-streaked, wavy brunette hair blew in the near-winter wind, delicate hands holding it off her round face. She wore dark jeans and black flats over tiny feet, and her belted winter coat hinted at her lean, fit physique. He had almost forgotten why he was mad at her in the first place.

Then she spoke.

Under almost any other circumstance he would've flirted with her. Okay, some of their discussion was flirtation, at least on his side. It didn't matter. The encounter did not start, progress, or end well. And now he seemed like a crazy stalker, following her into the community center. It wasn't his fault that was the location of his meeting.

Just one meeting, that's all. Then he could feel the Florida sunshine warm his face.

The building looked anything but a community center. That was because Ben Phillips, the inheritor of the grand house, restored and converted it to a community center. After his parents passed away when he was young, he roamed the southeast through the foster system. When he finally returned to Waverly Lake, he claimed his inheritance and dedicated the space as a home anyone could come to for activities, socializing, and meals. He and his girlfriend Tracy acted as family to everyone.

Steve walked up the steps amid the grand white columns and through the front door. He stood in a great marble foyer with a high ceiling and double staircase. The chandelier alone had to have cost a fortune back in the day. The restoration would've been a feat. Somehow its resplendence worked for the center, a piece of Waverly Lake history that sparked conversation between new visitors and volunteers.

He walked past Laura, who was chatting with a volunteer at an informal setup of a simple desk and chair. A brochure stand displayed pamphlets of things to do and places to stay around town, and a large rolling bulletin board behind that showcased a calendar of upcoming events at the center.

"Steve! Good morning." Ben greeted him with a handshake and smile. The two men stood about equal in height. Although they were both twenty-eight years old, Ben's skin was more like an outdoorsman—always more weathered and a little tanner than Steve's paleness. Not wrinkled or haggard, but as if his skin experienced more adventure than most his age. Steve knew he looked like he hadn't worked a day outside, and that was because he hadn't. Sometimes people assumed he was younger than he was or unappreciative of where he lived. It wasn't for a lack of interest. He'd love to get out on the water more than just during the regatta, but he barely had time for a vacation every few years.

"I have to say, every time I walk into this place, I'm amazed with what you've done," Steve said. "It never gets old."

"A bit of elbow grease goes a long way. You're here for the meeting?"

"Yep. Then I'm off to Florida for a little vacation."

"You? On vacation?"

"I know. It sounds crazy to me too."

"Well, they're all back there." He pointed behind himself, off to a room unseen from the foyer. "Help yourself to some coffee, then turn left. I'm sure you'll hear them before you see them."

"You're not participating in it?"

Ben grinned and shook his head. "I've had enough of my own family drama to deal with this year. I'll leave Tracy's family to themselves."

"I get the feeling that's a wise move." Steve patted Ben's shoulder, then walked through the hallway between the double stairs and reached a small table with coffee pods and tea bags laid out. He took a minute to fill up a mug with dark roast, then followed the clamor of voices into a side room.

"Good morning, Bennetts." His greeting halted their loud discussion. "Beverly, James." He nodded his head to the couple in their sixties. Beverly Bennett wore a pink-and-black striped blouse with black pants, pearl earrings and necklace completing the pageantry—as if Steve could talk—while her husband sported his usual khakis and a brown sweater.

"Nice to see you, Danny." Steve had graduated high school with their son, Daniel Bennett, who now worked as a marine mechanic down at Pearson's Wharf. Danny nodded and sipped his coffee, his hair as jet-black as marine oil. His presence meant his daughter had something to do with this meeting. Danny generally didn't get muddled up with his parents' affairs unless it related to Hannah.

Steve took a seat by Danny, across from Beverly and James. "What can I help you all with this morning?"

Beverly opened her mouth to speak when Tracy Bennett, her daughter, entered the room.

With Laura.

Steve's coffee caught in his throat at the sight, tickling him in a coughing spasm. He held it back until he couldn't anymore, letting out two, three coughs that left his eyes watery and face red.

Laura smiled at the gathering until she spotted Steve.

"I'll let Laura introduce herself so we can get started. She'll do herself more justice than I could." Tracy sat at the head of the table, near the back window, the light catching her dark blond, curly hair.

Back in high school, Tracy was never afraid of speaking her mind. It had annoyed him back then, but these days he found it refreshing.

"Hello, I'm Laura Crawford." She shook hands with the attendees as she spoke. "I'm the community and regional outreach planner at the Learning Center for ASD. I'm filling in for our event manager, Sophie, but I can assure you everything we do is a team effort, and you'll get the same service and attention to detail with me as you would have with her."

Steve gripped the handle of his coffee mug. He couldn't lift it to his mouth because his jaw was wired shut by a mix of surprise and anguish.

"See, I would've gotten all those titles mixed up." Tracy smirked.

"How about we get right to it?" Laura smiled and opened a manila folder. "Beverly, you contacted us to plan an event. Why don't you tell me what you've been thinking about, and we can start from there?"

Beverly straightened in her seat, hands together with fingers interlaced atop the table. "Yes. Well, I've been thinking about doing something for charity for ASD. You remember meeting my granddaughter, Hannah?"

Laura nodded.

Steve was still speechless. This big-city stranger knew the Bennetts and had met Hannah?

"I don't think we're in the position to start a charity ourselves. Plus, there are perfectly good ones that exist already, like yours. So, I thought, what if we do something to raise money for your organization, like a fundraising event?"

"Great," Laura said. "Of course, we welcome donations, but an event is a great way not only to raise money but to get the word out about what we do and how we service children and teens with ASD. In the past we've held galas, Fourth of July picnics, local wine tastings. Are those along the lines you were thinking of?"

Beverly's smile grew. "I was thinking something for the holidays. Something to evoke Christmas spirit, you know, that holly-jolly feeling. It's my favorite holiday." She met her son Danny's eyes. "I think it's Hannah's favorite too."

Danny nodded and returned his attention to Laura.

"A Christmas event this season is a tight ask." She cleared her throat and played with her pen. "May I ask before we continue, what's his role in this?" She pointed to Steve, who suddenly had all eyes on him.

"Oh, I know your non-profit offered an attorney, but I insisted on using ours. This is Steve Albertson. He knows all about the town and everyone in it."

"I don't think that's necessary."

"Good," Steve blurted. It was the first thing he had said since Laura entered the room. He softened his tone to make up for the unexpected outburst. "What I mean to say, is that I'm headed out of town for the holidays."

"Vacation home?" Laura raised her eyebrows in an I-know-your-type expression.

Steve's stomach churned. The assumptions this woman placed on him, whether she did so to all lawyers, or singled him out, who knew. "It's a condo, but I'll have you know it's not mi—"

"Of course. Condo. Should've known." She eyed him, and they had an eternity of a stare down.

"I'm gonna go out on a limb here and say there's something here we don't know about." Tracy pointed at Steve, then at Laura.

"It's nothing." Laura's peppy expression returned. "How about a venue? That's probably the limiting factor right now in terms of scheduling. Maybe knowing where it will be held can help determine what type of event we should have. Should we have it here at the community center?"

Tracy leaned over the table. "Ben and I would love to have it here. Unfortunately, we're already scheduled through the month with events. Maybe if it were held off until next Christmas."

"No." Beverly held up her hand. "I don't want to wait a year to have it. Do you think the children should wait a year for help? Just imagine what programs we could support during the school year or next summer."

"We are always on the lookout for donors to support our summer camp," Laura said. Beverly's canned smile served as a solid veto. "Okay, where else could we have it?"

James slapped the table in his first move of the meeting. "That's why we have Steve."

"Exactly!" Beverly somehow gained energy from her husband's input. "Steve can help in finding a venue, along with any permits we'd need or ordinances to be mindful of. He's perfect for it."

"So now I'm a location scout?" Steve couldn't believe his ears.

"I really don't think that's necessary." Laura shook her head.

"I insist," Beverly said. "Steve, please. You know all the regulations and rules around these things. Plus, you know the town, you know where people would want to go and how'd they feel about this. We need you on this." Her eyes pleaded with him. "It's for charity, of all things."

How could he say no?

By just saying it. *No.*

And be the bah-humbug lawyer who chose Florida over helping the most prominent family in Waverly Lake organize a charity fundraiser. Surely, his clientele would have something to say about that.

This is a bad time. Not this year. I already have plans.

Only one response was acceptable.

He held off the moan. "Fine."

"There." Beverly clapped her hands together. "It's settled."

Laura cleared her throat and adjusted her posture in the seat. "Not to rain on your parade in roping the town lawyer into this, but we don't have a venue or an event. Yet you want to hold it within the coming weeks."

"Where are you staying?" Tracy asked. "You are staying overnight in town, right?"

"Yes. I'm at—" She shuffled papers within the folder. "Waverly

Lake Bed and Breakfast. Guess that was easy enough to remember," she whispered as she closed the folder. "Why do you ask?"

"Oh." Tracy's shoulders sank and her lips pressed into a straight line of semi-disappointment. "My aunt has a lodge across the lake. It's not as convenient as the B and B, but it's a great place, if you end up changing your mind. I'm sure I could finagle a room for you."

"I appreciate that, but hopefully we can get the major details finalized this afternoon."

"I've gotta get back to Pearson's." Danny stood and shook Laura's hand. "Thank you for meeting with us. I'm sure my mother will fill me in on whatever you all decide to do. Let me know how I can help."

"Thank you."

The Bennetts cleared out of the room, leaving Steve alone with Laura.

For the second time today.

"I guess we'll be working together," he said.

"I guess so." Laura organized her papers and closed the manila folder. "You don't have to come with me to find venues."

"If you know Beverly Bennett like I do, then you know that's not true." He broke a smile, yet Laura didn't return it. He wanted to be here as much as she did. Maybe less. But fighting it wasn't going to get them anywhere. "Perhaps I should take you around town, scope out the few places we could have a big gathering?"

"I'd like to check in first." She met his eyes. "That is, if you don't mind."

It was the first glimpse of politeness from her. Surely, she was as uncomfortable with all this as he was, but maybe they could tackle this task and move on. It'd be easier if they hadn't had the argument outside right before the meeting. It didn't help she was gorgeous, even in the heat of anger. Not wanting to meet her eyes too long but not wanting to seem rude avoiding them added another layer of discomfort.

"No, go ahead and check in. How about I meet you there in"—

he checked his watch, self-conscious she'd have guessed he indeed wore an expensive one—"thirty minutes?"

"That should work. See you then."

It was the longest amount of time he was willing to wait, yet the bare minimum it would take her to head on over there, check in, freshen up. Not that she'd freshen up for him. She'd made it clear in her actions this morning, in her cold looks at the meeting, she had no interest in him being around.

He had no interest in sticking around either. Maybe their dislike for each other was a good thing.

Because the sooner they could be done with this, the better.

Chapter Five

LAURA GOT IN HER COROLLA, WHICH THANKFULLY DID not receive a parking ticket over the course of the meeting, and drove east on Dowager Street. She crossed the square again, then turned right. A gravel road led to Waverly Lake Bed and Breakfast, a white three-story building with a wrap-around porch and enough ornateness to require way too much maintenance for Laura's taste. Although a hedge of pines separated it from the surrounding buildings to the north, it received direct sunlight, which meant a coat or two of paint annually. The spindles of the porch alone would take days to paint.

She parked the car and carried her suitcase across the gravel lot and up the stairs. Dark green garland swept across the porch railings, red felt bows tied at each highpoint. A wreath hung on the front door, plaid ribbons weaving around the needles, crescendoing into a large bow at the bottom.

She opened the door and stepped into the lobby. Generally, Victorian homes like this had distinct rooms with clear separation, so she was surprised to see a more open floor plan. The front desk sat to her left, behind it square tables and chairs. Ahead of her a hallway led straight into the belly of the house. To her right, a living room area with piano, full Christmas tree whose fresh smell permeated the air, and two armchairs and a sofa situated around a coffee table. A Percy Faith Christmas arrangement played at a low volume.

A man in a maroon sweater greeted her warmly at the front desk.

"Laura Crawford."

He nodded, typing into the computer. "Single room, king bed."

"That's me." It hit her that she hadn't had her own room for quite some time. Technically, with Logan out of the apartment, she was alone. But alone and having something to herself were different things.

"Here you are," the gentleman said, handing over her key card. She had stayed at a handful of bed and breakfasts in her lifetime, and all had still used actual keys. Although it probably appealed to the guests in terms of charm, it did seem more difficult to keep track of the key than a hotel key card. Plus, it seemed safer with a key card. Maybe it was a touch of the city that guided her preference. "Just one night with us?"

"Yes. Here for business." She pictured Kim lecturing her about enjoying her time here beyond work. "Hopefully, I can explore the town while I'm at it."

"You're in room six. All the rooms are upstairs. If you walk down that hallway, you'll see the stairs to your right. If you continue walking straight, you'll enter the ballroom, and the service elevator is to your left. Our coffee, tea and cocoa bar are located just over here in our sitting area."

"You have a ballroom?"

"That's what we call it. But it's mainly for conferences, parties, that sort of thing. It's where the grand finale of the Dead and Breakfast is."

She raised an eyebrow.

"We convert the place into a haunted house in October."

"That sounds interesting." She didn't know what to say. How much work went into that?

"In a small town, you have to find creative ways to keep people coming through the doors."

"Hey, I can appreciate the entrepreneurial spirit." She leaned a hand on the desk. "This ballroom, anyone can rent it out for an event?"

He nodded.

"What's the capacity of the space?"

"Max of forty occupants."

Her hope receded. How perfect that would've been to have an event right here, but the space would've been too small. At least, she hoped more than forty people would show up to a fundraiser sponsored by the Bennetts. "Thank you."

"No problem. Just up the stairs and follow the signs to room six."

She wheeled her bag down the hallway and lugged it up the stairs, a dozen steps or so split into a switchback halfway. The second floor was more like what she'd expected. She passed by a bathroom with a clawfoot tub and shower curtain, the toilet with a pull-chain flusher. Flowery wallpaper and thin maroon carpet lined the hallway. Room six was at the corner of the hall. She opened the door, surprised to see her room was in the turret, long rectangular windows overlooking the parking lot and Dowager Street a block or two beyond the trees.

Her room had a four-poster mahogany bed, corner vanity, dresser, and fireplace. A note hung next to the fireplace, directing guests to call downstairs if they wished for a fire to be lit. While it was drafty, and she would've loved to sit by a fire and curl up with a book and some hot cocoa, she had a mission to complete.

The cheerful coziness of the place lulled her into forgetting what came next. She sighed and opened her suitcase, staring at the contents. While she liked to unpack during a stay, she had to meet Steve downstairs in a few minutes. Plus, it was only one night.

She reluctantly zipped the bag back up, grabbed her purse, and briefly checked herself in the mirror on the vanity. Her stomach gurgled as she checked her teeth. Of course, nothing was in her teeth because she hadn't had a meal today.

She left the room and walked down the stairs. *Be positive.* It made no sense to make enemies here. She needed local input, and the Bennetts had assigned Steve to that task. She just had to deal with it. *It's all for charity.*

The receptionist waved as she walked by, and she waved back. The cold air greeted her once again, a refreshing breeze she would've enjoyed more had it not been for her stomach nagging to be fed.

Steve stood in the parking lot, black BMW running. He waved his hand from inside the vehicle. Of course. Why would he get out? That's what gentlemen did. Besides, this wasn't a date. What did she expect?

She got in on the passenger side and buckled up.

"I figured I'd drive since I know the town. It's easier than having to give directions everywhere."

"It's okay." She kept it cordial. That way he may be more agreeable with what she requested. "I was wondering if we could stop for lunch? I didn't get to eat on the drive in from Charlotte."

"Is that something we could do maybe on the way to a possible venue, or..." He looked at Laura, who made every effort to contain her hanger. He cleared his throat and put the car in drive. "There's a place two blocks away."

"I'd appreciate it." She toughed through a seconds-long smile.

Steve drove carefully, almost at a crawling pace. She didn't know if it was because he was protective of his precious car, or if he saw it as a way to irritate her. He parked on Dowager Street, and she followed him along the sidewalk to a shop, a sign on the door reading *The Cake Zone.*

"It's a bakery?" she asked.

"Yeah, but they make amazing sandwiches with their gourmet breads. I also have a thing about supporting local businesses. The owner graduated high school two years behind me. Always brought the best baked goods at lunch." He opened the door and awaited her entry.

Perhaps he had an ounce of chivalry in him after all. The sweetness of the air loudened her stomach. At this point she didn't really care if they had lunch food or not. She would've made cake her main course both based on her hunger and the decadent smells —warm vanilla and almond, spicy cinnamon and ginger.

The woman behind the counter wore a red-and-white Santa hat and greeted her with a smile. "Hey, Steve. Who do we have with you today?"

"Hi Jessica. This is Laura. She's...helping out on a project."

"Well, welcome. What are you hungry for today?"

Laura panicked, looking at the treats behind the glass panels. She turned to Steve. "What's good here?"

He shrugged. "Anything, really."

"Hm. I hope you're that helpful when it comes to picking venues." It came out snappy, and she immediately regretted it. It was the hunger talking.

She turned back to the counter. "I'll take one of those chicken salad croissants, and half an egg salad on toast, oh, and one of those ham and cheese wedges."

"Anything else?" Jessica asked.

"Is there anything else?" Steve said, not low enough to not hear.

She twirled around to Steve. "Did you want anything?"

"Me? No, I'm good."

"You're not getting anything?" She met his hazel eyes. Something about them softened her shell. "My treat."

"No. Thank you, though." He sat at a high counter along the wall as she waited for her food. The owner brought it around on a tray, and Laura followed.

"Enjoy and come back if you're staying for a while."

"Thank you." Laura took off her coat and laid it on the stool next to her. "You sure you don't want any of this?"

"I'm sure."

"Why don't you tell me what kind of people we can round up for this fundraiser. What would people like to see or do around here?"

He shook his head. "To be honest, I'm not really sure."

"Aren't you the Waverly Lake expert?" She wiped the egg salad off her mouth with a napkin. It was delicious. Of course, dirt would've been delicious at this point, but this was genuinely a thousand levels above dirt.

"That's the problem. I don't think you want my expertise."

"I don't?"

He shifted in his seat, leaning an elbow on the counter. "You know, there's a reason I was heading out of town for the holidays. Folks at this time of year...always seem to be on short fuses. They bicker over petty things, and it gets worse the closer it gets to Christmas. I just don't know what you could possibly do to channel that energy in a positive way to raise money."

"Wow." She covered her mouth and swallowed the ham and cheese bite, gooey cheddar goodness a taste of heaven. "That's a gloomy way to view people."

"You asked." He folded his arms over his chest. "What I can help with is a venue. I do know every place you could possibly host an event. What are you looking for?"

She nodded. "I originally thought indoors, but when I spoke with the employee at the bed and breakfast, it made me think of capacity. I don't want to be limited based on that. I thought, if it's a Christmas-themed fundraiser, let's have it outside. What's more festive than being here? Outside, all the decorations, people mingle over hot drinks to keep warm, that sort of thing."

He smirked as she took a bite of the chicken salad croissant. Had he heard anything she just said?

"What?" she asked.

"Nothing."

"Out with it."

"It's just, that's quite a spread you got yourself there."

She chuckled. "This is what happens when my local guru doesn't guide me to the best option. I had to get a bit of everything." She held up a hand and pointed at him. "Which is what will happen if you don't recommend a venue. I'll just have you drive me in all directions to see every single one of them."

He held up both hands in defense. "No, no. Not necessary. You said outside, good place to drink and mingle. I think I have the perfect place for that."

"Oh?" She raised her eyebrows at his confidence. And the fact he had listened to what she said. "All right then. You lead the way."

"I will." He smirked again. "As soon as you finish your sandwich buffet."

Laura scoffed. "Very funny." She signaled the woman behind the counter as to what to do with the tray.

"Just leave it there, honey. Have a good one."

"You too."

Steve awaited at the front door.

Laura slipped her jacket back on and stopped in front of Steve. "All right, Mr. Know-It-All. Let's see how well you know Waverly Lake."

Chapter Six

Laura cradled the handle of the BMW's passenger side door, keeping her eyes on the road while Steve drove.

He couldn't bring himself to tell her to keep her fingers off the leather. Based on their first encounter, she probably assumed he was prudish about his car. Did he know guys that went overboard with the care and attention to their cars? Sure. Was he one of those guys?

He shook his head. Just because he didn't want fingerprints didn't mean he was one of *those* guys. Those guys lived for their cars. Those guys were so obsessive they put their car first, above anything and everyone. He wasn't one of those guys. He just worked hard and saved his money to buy nicer things. Was it so wrong to want to keep those things nice?

"So...you're from Charlotte?" He took a stab at conversation. His satellite radio subscription had expired a few weeks back, and he'd been meaning to renew. Just never got around to it. That meant regular radio, which meant a country station that fizzled in and out.

"Currently, yes. Technically, I'm from Lake Norman, but live downtown now. It's where the homebase is of TLC."

"There are other offices?"

"A few. We have a branch in Raleigh and just opened one up in Wilmington this past summer."

"And you know the Bennetts?"

"I met them briefly once. I met Hannah and her father Danny at one of our events in Charlotte. Such a sweet girl, and Danny seems like a fantastic dad."

"Yeah," he nodded. "I've known Danny since grade school. I mean, we weren't in the same social circles, but as adults, I've gotten to know him. I actually helped him with the divorce." He suddenly felt exposed, as if he had said too much about Danny, or himself. She was a stranger to Waverly Lake and to most of its people. It was unlike him to be such a gossip. "He's been nothing but an advocate for Hannah." *Yes, stick to the safe topic.*

"That's great to hear."

They drove past the wharf and old-timey gas station building, the roadway of buildings turning into a roadway of scattered homes and flat meadows.

"I guess that was the end of town?"

"The official end of downtown, yes. Once you pass Bingham Station, you're in the suburbs." He chuckled. "If you can call it that."

She looked past his statuesque silhouette through the window at the lake, more visible with fewer obstructions. "Does it ever freeze over? I mean, I know Lake Norman doesn't. Too big and not cold enough."

"Same here."

"I wasn't sure just how cold it got here."

"It gets cold. During storms it can drop in the single digits at night. Supposed to get another here shortly." *Yet another reason we need to be done with this.* "The snow is frequent enough to have a winter tubing site on the west side, yet infrequent enough to get tired of it." He never really thought about it that way. Although he longed for the heat of the Florida sun, he never analyzed how he felt about the weather here. He did enjoy the occasional snowfall, the blanket of white, the town quieting.

"Can I ask you something?" he said.

Laura turned her gaze from the road to his eyes, her eyes a striking light brown, almost golden that brought out the color in her cheeks.

He choked on his words before getting them out. "This morning, you said to me, you know my type. What did you mean by that?"

She opened her mouth, surprised at his candidness.

"I mean, I got the feeling it was a negative connotation. I just wanted to know what exactly the type was?"

"We don't really have to—"

"No, I want to know." Heaven knew how much he had been looking for the right person to spend his life with. He was a veteran of first dates. Maybe he gave off the wrong kind of vibe. Maybe women assumed things of him that weren't true, and now was his chance to find out.

Laura took in a deep breath and turned to him. "Okay. I saw the fancy watch out of the sleeve of your jacket. The expensive car. The impatience you had with an out-of-towner like me trying to find where I was going with you permeating my rearview mirror. Then on top of that, you said you were a lawyer."

"So? I admit, I was impatient."

She held up a hand. "All that painted a picture of a high-maintenance guy. Someone who likes things a certain way. It's all about appearances, as if you are trying too hard to compensate for some flaw or secret you're keeping."

He opened his mouth to interject, and she held off his words again. "But that was me projecting. I just got out of...let's just say I had a bad experience with someone who fit that profile. I projected that onto you when I shouldn't be judging you, a complete stranger. I was wrong to do that, and I apologize."

It was not what he expected to hear. Any of it. The explanation of what he looked like to other people, the sincere apology. His brain rifled through past relationships, past dates.

"I'm sorry if I offended you."

"No." His lips tightened. He drove on autopilot as he absorbed the judgement. "I guess I never thought people would see me in that way." He looked at her briefly, her sympathetic look too much to stare at for long. "I know lawyers get their own bad rap. But I work hard, and I like nicer things. I was scraping by in college, and never had anything new, so when I was able to have this career and pay off my loans...I guess this is the way I celebrate my achievements."

She smiled faintly. "Like I said, I projected a negative experience onto you."

He nodded as they headed northward along the eastern bank of the lake. The bare aspens made a haunted wintery forest on their right, the mountains nearing ahead. Although there was still a lot to process about what Laura said, all Steve could think about now was what had happened to her. How she said it, how her confidence cracked in her quivering voice, it must've been either a serious hurt or a fresh one. Or both.

He tried thinking of something else to ask her, but nothing popped in his head.

"Where is it that we're going?" Her voice almost startled him in the quiet.

"Just up here, to the top of the road." They ascended, the lake drawing farther away below them.

"I had no idea the lake here was so big."

"Probably not so big compared to Lake Norman."

"It is the largest of the lakes in the state. But this is pretty impressive too. Have you ever been to Lake Norman?"

"No, but I hear it's nice." He also heard it was full of traffic from commuters. Something he hoped never happened to Waverly Lake. He laughed at himself. Here he was itching to get out of town, yet hoping the place never changed.

They pulled past a sign with a tree, an apple dropping into a lake. Colored lights strung around it, lit but not very bright in the midday, even with the overcast sky. A fake snowman with an oversized mitten on the end of its arm stood frozen in mid-wave below the sign.

"Offshore Orchard," Laura read.

"Let me show you around. I think there's a lot of potential here for an event."

He parked the car in the dirt parking lot, the orchard fairly empty of visitors during a December Friday afternoon. He guessed they didn't have a whole lot of visitors this time of year, post-apple season. In the spring the trees flowered, and the owners held a May Day picnic. Maybe hosting an event here during the holidays could bring more visitors.

He led her through the front end of the orchard past the wooden fence, trees aligned in rows, cordoned off by ropes through eyelets on poles. Without their leaves, they came up out of the ground like gnarled hands, fingers reaching for something to touch every which way. The first two rows of trees held giant ornaments, burgundy and gold spheres, silver teardrops and emerald blocks in the shape of presents.

"There's a beauty to them," he said. "Especially after it snows."

"I can imagine." She smirked, folding her hands in her coat pockets.

"What?"

"Nothing."

He took a breath. He was proud of thinking of this place. It seemed perfect for anything outdoors or indoors. "I think it's a great venue for a social event. You have the orchard, which the public can access in certain spots.

"How far back does it go?" she asked. "Are there any flat areas?"

"It goes back well beyond the store. I think there are designated picnic areas that are flatter. You do have to climb the hill." Hopefully, that wasn't a deal breaker. "It's all a soft slope. Has to do with the irrigation."

She nodded, no sign of approval or disapproval on her face.

"You have the main building here." He pointed to the stone structure behind Laura. "It's really nice on the outside with the porch and has a bakery inside, if you want to serve snacks. You also have the barn. I say barn, but it's really another building like this one, only painted to look like a barn."

"Where's that?"

"At the back end of the property." He stepped closer to Laura, his breath visible in the cold. "What makes this place so great is that where we are standing is a dry county, and farther back it's not. You can serve alcohol if you were thinking, say, eggnog. It'd be more complicated in terms of permits if you wanted to serve closer to town. If you want to keep it dry, you can do that too." He checked his watch, more out of habit when awaiting a response than to see the time. Although he did want to get out of Waverly Lake before dark. The mountain roads could be tricky on a sunny day, with no guardrails in certain areas. Nighttime made it exponentially worse.

"So, what do you think? Is it what you had in mind?" A simple yes, and he could drive her back to the bed and breakfast. By the time he'd clear the state he'd hit Atlanta before the rush hour traffic, and the rest would be smooth driving to the Gulf Coast.

She scanned the area, her breath more visible than his own. "I think I'd like to see more of the place."

Steve held back the impulse to tip back his head in impatience. He had already been impatient with her once today, an incident he apologized for. Apologies have no meaning if the incidents continue to be repeated. "Yeah, sure. No problem." Never mind this was well beyond the duties of a local attorney. She had labeled him as some bigshot lawyer. What New York attorney would agree to taking a client around Manhattan, sightseeing? Not that Laura was a client. Nor he a bigshot New York City lawyer.

This was Waverly Lake, and he was hired by the Bennetts. That meant he needed to suck it up.

He stretched out his arm, inviting Laura to explore. "Take all the time you need," he mumbled.

Chapter Seven

IT HAD ONLY BEEN A FEW HOURS SINCE SHE'D ARRIVED in Waverly Lake, but Laura found the town, the lake, the mountains it nestled in neatly to be full of surprises. Although smaller than where she grew up, downtown Waverly Lake had charm, and the lake impressed with its expanse. Most surprising was the apple orchard she stood in now, a gem in and of itself along the northeast corner of the lake. It felt like they could've been in Vermont, or somewhere in Europe, with the sloping rows of trees tucked amidst a valley, separated from traffic, from the world.

She walked to what Steve had called the main building. At two stories high, its stone facade and chimney were reminiscent of a simpler time here in Appalachia country. Its front porch invited visitors to sit and rock, tell a good yarn, or break out the instruments for a folksy jam session.

Inside transported her back to the present. The interior held a golden hue, the acidic yet sweet smell of apples melded with blueberry and cinnamon. Steve followed her inside reluctantly. He didn't have to say he was annoyed with her taking her time. His body language said it all—he walked slowly, not soaking it in, his arms, chest, and jaw tense.

She turned around, taking off her coat in the welcome heat and holding onto it with both hands. "What is this place?"

"Remember I told you part of the orchard was in a dry county, the other not? On this side, they make their own cider."

She turned around and analyzed the large vats behind the glass wall.

"In the barn building they make and sell hard cider."

"I've never seen anything like this before."

His face lit up for a brief second. "Does that mean you'd like to have the fundraising event here?"

She wasn't about to let him off that easily. This was her vacation weekend, after all. Kim would actually believe she got to relax if Laura told her about a fancy apple orchard and cider tasting. It was the closest equivalent to Napa Valley she had seen in the state. "It smells wonderful."

"Most of that is from the bakery." He pointed behind him.

"Mmm." She followed the aroma, which grew more powerful as the treats in the glass displays grew clearer in her sights.

"You can't possibly want to eat anything." Steve shoved his hands in his pants pockets.

"You know, for someone who didn't want to be judged based on his appearance, you do an awful lot of judging based on my diet." She raised her eyebrows and caught a slight rolling of his eyes. "Now, do you want to tell me what's good here, or shall I get a bit of everything again?"

He sighed and leaned into the glass display. "At Christmastime, they have a gingerbread-spice donut that's really good." He pointed to a plate near the top. "But their blueberry donuts are what they're famous for, year-round."

Laura nodded, assessing whether he was saying something just to be done with it or if what he said held truth.

"He's right," the lady behind the counter said. "First visit?"

"Yes, ma'am." Laura responded with a smile.

"Listen to Steve," she said. "He knows his stuff." The woman winked at the attorney.

"All right, then." Laura couldn't help grinning at Steve, who shrugged his shoulders in boasting, as if saying *told you so*.

"If you're going to do it right, you have to eat them with a hot cider." He held up two fingers.

"On it." The woman behind the counter fixed the hot ciders and handed over two donuts in a bag. "On me."

"Thanks, Bonnie." Steve put a tip in the jar and handed Laura her drink.

They walked to one of the tall, round standing tables, setting down their drinks and divvying the donuts.

"I guess you come here frequently enough?" Although it indeed was an interesting place, she couldn't imagine what would bring Steve here so often he'd know the staff. "And thanks, by the way."

"Don't thank me, that was all Bonnie. I think it's safe to assume that, in this town, if someone knows me, it's because I either helped them with a legal matter or was on the other end of it."

"Does that mean half the town likes you and the other half doesn't?"

He chuckled. "I guess that's one way to see it."

She bit into the soft cake donut; giant, juicy blueberries mixed in with blended berries that turned the dough a light violet. "Oh my gosh, that's amazing." She couldn't hold back the reaction until after she swallowed, that's how delicious it was.

"I wasn't lying."

She chased the bite with a sip of the hot cider. A perfect combination. "See, was it that hard to recommend something?"

Steve cradled his cider cup. "Here, it's easy. Back at The Cake Zone..." He shook his head. "Honest, I haven't tried anything there I didn't like. Heck, didn't love."

She thought over the smorgasbord of sandwich bites she tasted. "I believe it." She wiped her mouth with a napkin and took another sip. "I don't get it. Where does all the talent come from? I mean, these could very easily make it big in Charlotte, and those sandwiches could be served at Biltmore Estate, they were so professionally made."

He shrugged. "It may be a small town. But it's got the lake, the mountains, the western North Carolina charm." He smiled faintly, as if the last bit applied to him. "Honestly, I don't know if I'd do the same if I had that kind of talent. I'd probably be like what you expect, wanting to go somewhere bigger."

"Flashier?" She elbowed him in jest, then instantly overanalyzed it. She was getting more comfortable with him, that was for sure. But they had an assignment, and she needed to take off the vacation hat and put on the work hat.

"Would you happen to know who I could talk to about hosting an event here?" She looked around the room, as if the desired person lingered, awaiting her need.

"Adam is over there. He's a tour guide and knows the ins and outs." He transferred his donut from his napkin back to the brown bag.

"Aren't you going to at least take a bite of that?"

"I'm going to eat the whole thing. As a snack, on the road, on my way out of here this afternoon."

Laura had almost forgotten Steve's plans. The condo in Florida.

"Adam." Steve waved to the young gentleman. He wore a gray fleece vest, just like the other employees.

"Hey, Steve. Are you here for a tour?"

"Not today. Adam, this is Laura. The Bennetts have hired her to organize an ASD fundraiser for the holidays, and she's looking for a venue."

"Ah, well, you've come to the right place." He smiled, his grin shining through a short but well-groomed beard, and shook Laura's hand. She guessed without it he'd look years younger. "We host events of all sorts. We can set up a tent outdoors just behind this building. In the winter we'd recommend patio heaters."

"I was thinking more along the lines of firepits, for roasting marshmallows, or chestnuts?"

"Hmm, that may be a problem. Unfortunately, we can't have open flames around our trees."

"Well, we haven't set firepits in stone yet, right?" Steve

encouraged Laura. The truth was she had nothing set in stone, which made for more flexibility. Too much flexibility. The thought of having nothing concrete about this endeavor got her heart ticking faster. It was time to wrap this up.

Alex held up a hand. "But we do have indoor accommodations as well. The front half of the barn can be rented out, and both buildings have private tasting rooms."

"It really is a gorgeous place," she said.

"Where can we sign?" Steve flashed a giant smile, patting Alex on the shoulder.

Laura cleared her throat. "However, I don't think it's the appropriate place for what we're envisioning. I'll definitely keep you in mind for the future. Thank you for your time."

Alex nodded. "No problem."

She headed to the front door and Steve touched her elbow, stopping her. "What was that? I thought this place was perfect. You've got the trees outside, the two buildings."

She inhaled deeply, preparing herself to let him down. "Yes, it does have trees, but they're not Christmas trees. No Douglas firs, or pines, or anything coniferous that resembles Christmas. If the theme were *A Charlie Brown Christmas,* then yes, this would be perfect."

"You don't even have a theme!" He threw his hands up and looked past her, through the front door, then back at her. "You saw the trees when we first got here. You knew it then. You decided it was a no for this place when we arrived, didn't you? This whole time spent here, you've been dragging this out."

"I'm not dragging it out, exactly." He was right. She knew when they first arrived that it wasn't the right feel, even though she didn't have a theme or solid idea of what she wanted. "I wanted to make sure my instinct was correct and give the place a fair chance." *Liar.*

"I don't believe you."

She threw up her arms. "Okay, fine. What do you want me to tell you? It's my first time in Waverly Lake, and I haven't had any sort of vacation or time off since I don't know when. Was it that wrong of me to want to enjoy myself for half an hour and explore the place, imbibe a famous hot cider while I mulled over what this last-minute, enormous undertaking should be about?"

Steve's eyes grew big. "Oh, I see. It's okay for you to relax and enjoy your vacation. But heaven forbid I want to get the job done, one in which, by the way, I'm volunteering for, to get out of here to start my own vacation."

His voice grew louder, and the few patrons visiting began to stare.

"You know what, I don't have time for this." He hurried past her to the entrance.

"Oh, I know. You're going to the beach. You've made your disdain for your hometown very clear."

He swiveled around. "It's not disdain. It's—"

"It's what?" She crossed her arms.

He fought the desire to explain. "You don't know me. I don't need to explain myself to you."

"You're right." Why was she being so harsh on him again? She was the one who'd pulled him along the last half an hour. Why was she upset? Because he was leaving her? Did she really need his help? "I don't know you. And I only know what little I've seen of Waverly Lake. But you said so yourself that people come here, fall in love with the town, the surroundings, that they stay here. Make a life for themselves, here of all places. So, it doesn't make sense to me why someone like you, who sees the world through their eyes, has turned sour on it."

She shook her head and held up a hand. "You know what, it doesn't matter. What matters here is that there's a young girl here in Waverly Lake with ASD. Most likely there are many other children and adults in this area, in this state, with it, who don't even know it, or do and have nowhere to look for support. The Bennetts are doing what they can to help with that. They've asked for my help, so I plan on doing just that. If you need to go, then I'll do it without you."

Steve tipped his head back and covered his face in his hands. He let out a groan and ruffled his hands through his hair. It disheveled his perfect coif, and if he weren't so stubborn, it would've made him more handsome. Laura often found imperfection more attractive than perfection.

"Fine."

"Fine?"

"Fine, I'll stay." He pointed a finger. "Just until we find a venue. And no more prolonging. The minute—no, the second you know a place isn't right, you tell me."

Laura smiled. "Deal."

Steve gestured to follow him. "Now I think these folks have had enough of us."

Laura turned around, and the onlookers scattered, pretending not to have watched the encounter.

Adam waved, and Steve waved back. "We're getting out of your hair."

He looked at Laura. "Come on. I have another idea."

Chapter Eight

THE BOLDNESS OF LAURA CRAWFORD WAS SOMETHING else. As an attorney, he had seen some confident, forward, bold people in the courtroom. That was to be expected. It took a level of audacity to excel in this profession, and even the clients showed backbone now and then—when fighting over property in contention during divorce, heck, even when fighting a traffic ticket. But an outreach planner for a charity?

Yet she had him fooled for a good while at the apple orchard. The perfect pick for a fundraising event, in his opinion. She had the nerve to discredit it to herself and keep him that much further away from leaving for Florida.

It didn't matter now. He couldn't get that time back. He also wouldn't let her take him for a fool again.

He drove her back into town, his foot a bit heavier on the gas than during the trip out to the orchard. She held onto the door handle for a few of the turns, and he caught her moving her right foot, as if she controlled the brakes, when they slowed moving into the main part of downtown on Dowager Street. He would've considered it a cute quirk, had it not been for the irritation lingering in his gut.

"How much longer?" She took a deep breath, her skin paler than before.

"Nearly there." Had he really been driving crazy enough to make her nauseous? Now *his* stomach knotted with guilt.

He turned left onto a side road, past the courthouse and field, then parked in front of a white building. The building resembled a colonial look, but with modern windows, and a clock tower jutting from the roof. Scaffolding blocked the left front of the house, remnants of the repainting that had started in the fall. It was a large job, one that couldn't be started in the heat and humidity of the summer, yet wasn't finished before Thanksgiving. Although the winters weren't considered particularly harsh by anyone north of here, it was too cold for the workers to continue painting. Steve suspected it also had something to do with the holidays.

"The library?" Laura asked.

They walked through the front door, another set of double doors a few steps ahead of them.

"It's another place where you could have something inside or outside." He nodded to a short, squat, balding man at the front desk. "I'll let you look around before we chat with anyone."

He followed her as she stepped through the space, wide-eyed, taking in the parallel shelves running to the back of the building. She marveled at the skylighted ceiling, an architectural feature that was a highlight for visitors.

"This place is beautiful."

He smiled briefly, nodding his head. "I've attended a Fair and Ware event here. They serve hors d'oeuvres while you rummage through the stacks of old books they sell in the summer. If it's an information-themed fundraiser, or you want to present more information about your organization, you can use their multimedia room."

"Hmm."

He sighed. "You promised if it wasn't the right venue, you'd let me know as soon as you knew."

"You said there's outdoor space too?"

"Yeah." He led her to the double doors in the rear of the building. When he turned around, she wasn't behind him.

Laura had stopped at a round table where an elderly woman and man put together a floral puzzle. "Good afternoon."

"Hello." The woman looked up from her work. "Do I know you?"

"Velma, that's Ferguson's daughter," the elderly man said.

"Put your glasses on, Lou." The woman grabbed his glasses and slipped them on his face.

"Oh, sorry. That's not her."

"My name is Laura. I'm from out of town, and I'm just checking out your library. I'm planning on hosting an event in Waverly Lake, and wondered, is this a common place for people to gather socially?"

Steve touched Laura's elbow, well aware of the looks he was getting from the librarian. "Laura, come on. We can talk outside."

She held up a finger urging him to wait. "I think it's nice that there are activities like this for people, in addition to the books."

Steve nodded. He brought her here to scope out the venue potential, not to rate the library on its amenities for Trip Advisor. "Okay, let's leave these folks alone."

"Why don't you sit down with us?" Lou said. "We can't seem to find the rest of this stem."

"That's because you haven't had your glasses on," Velma said.

Laura beamed and headed for a chair.

"Laura." Steve raised his eyebrows in disbelief. "The assignment?" He barely moved his jaw getting the words out.

She pouted and turned to the woman. "Maybe some other time. It was delightful to meet you."

"Same here, child. You can swing by any Wednesday or Friday. We're always here." Velma winked as Laura reluctantly left the pair.

Steve saved his emotion until they'd exited the set of double doors out the back. "You do know we're in a library, right? You can't just have a chat as if it's a coffee shop."

"I thought I saw a sign for coffee when we came in?"

He shook his head, the humor of it eating through his anger. "Okay. Yes, there is a little coffee shop. But it's in the far end of the east wing, and still, people tend to keep their voices down inside."

"I didn't think we were being too loud." She softened her defense. "Look, it's my job to get to know people. Do you think people tend to donate more money to a charity of strangers or folks they know? Ones they can feel confident in who will do the most good with their hard-earned money?"

"I suspect the latter."

"Okay. I know we're here on a mission to find a venue. But it doesn't hurt if I get to talking to a few of the locals at the same time. We're going to need people who want to go to this event and who will happily donate for the cause. The best way I know how is to get to know people."

"How about we focus on the venue? Once that is settled, we can go our separate ways, and you can do all the chatting you want to do."

He caught a slight roll of the eyes, her lips pressed together. "So, what is all this?" she asked.

They stood at the top of the steps, the stairs leading down to an open field walled off by trees.

"The library owns this bit of land. In the summer, they show old movies. They rent the field out with the building if that's what you're thinking you'd like."

She walked down the steps, into the grass, about one third of the way across the field. She placed her hands on her hips and scanned the space to each side of her. A bird squawked ahead, and she pressed her hand above her eyes to see what caused the commotion.

Steve checked his watch. At this rate, he'd be hitting Atlanta rush hour traffic.

He hurried down the stairs and met up with Laura in the field. "What do you think? Plenty of space for lots of people."

"That's very true."

He heard it in her voice. She had agreed, but the inflection said it all. There was a but.

"What is it this time?"

She looked at her black flats, her toes probably freezing, and bit her lip. "I promise I'm not trying to be difficult. You have picked two great spots for gatherings."

He massaged his neck, keeping his words to himself.

"But it's just a field, and I'd need to fill it up with trees to light up. Christmas trees, not what was at the orchard. This is a giant space, and we would need many trees to really get it looking festive."

"How about this? Rather than I show you around all corners of the town, you tell me what your vision is for this event. Because I have yet to hear a clear one."

"It's coming together for me, now that I've seen more of the town and spaces."

"Then, please," he said, "do enlighten me."

"I'd like to have it outdoors, with or without an indoor facility. I don't think the lack of an indoor facility is a deal-breaker. And it has to have at least some coniferous trees. I want to make sure we string some lights on trees to give Hannah a clear indication of her favorite holiday. I'm thinking a park. Yeah, a park would be perfect. Isn't there a park here that we passed?"

That wasn't going to work. "I'm not sure—"

Her mind whirred, and she spewed her thoughts out seemingly as quickly as they occurred. "I'm thinking stations or booths. You know, one for hot chocolate, gingerbread cookies, all the treats. And then have activities. Maybe we can have a decorate-your-own-cookie type of thing; provide the icing and toppings. Have games like snowman building with cotton balls, or ornament-making. It could be an assortment of activities and treats." Her smile grew and her eyes lit up with such passion they almost sparkled. "Can you picture what I mean? Am I making any sense?"

"Oh, you're making sense all right." He smiled, holding back the chuckle. If only she knew how well he pictured her ideas. It almost was sad he'd have to break her heart. Granted, finding a place was going to take more time, but the Florida-trip window was quickly closing. It may be too far along for him to squeeze out today.

Why not leave tomorrow instead? Saturday was filled with shoppers for the holidays, but at least he wouldn't be dealing with workday commuters. Yes, it was frustrating to have to change his plans. Not that they were such long-term plans. Heck, two months ago when he left his second-floor apartment for Lovetoberfest, he had no idea he'd be itching to leave for Florida to escape the holidays in Waverly Lake. But Laura didn't know that. For all she knew he had planned this trip for himself for half a year.

Which made it all the more infuriating she didn't seem to care about his plans.

He took a deep breath. Why was he attacking this woman? Outwardly, he controlled his outrage, but why such internal struggle? She was obviously smart, determined, and if it came down to admitting it or not, she was beautiful. Gorgeous even. If he had met her at Lovetoberfest he would've been thrilled to have been paired with her for a date. Perhaps it would be different if that were the case.

But he didn't meet her back in October. He met her on a brisk December day, when he was reminded how short and temperamental the people of Waverly Lake could be around Christmas. He met her when he'd already concluded the holidays would be better off spent elsewhere, away from the townsfolk for once. Away from the mountains closing in around him.

She anchored him here. That was why he struggled.

"What do you think about it? Is that something people here could get behind?"

Despite his frustration, there was a part of him that didn't want to tell her the truth. But she needed to know.

"Before I answer that, I think I'd better show you something."

Chapter Nine

A VISION FOR THE EVENT FINALLY PRESENTED ITSELF. Once she thought of different themed stations, she couldn't stop thinking of the possibilities. They could even change some of them up each night of the event, enticing people to come back for another night instead of a one-and-done.

The giddiness built up as she rode in Steve's car. She hadn't paid a whole lot of attention to the park on her way into town, but her gut told her it would be the perfect place to hold the event. It now seemed silly she hadn't thought of it first as a venue.

Steve turned after the Lakeshore Park sign, easily finding a parking spot. A row of vehicles took up the farthest edge of the lot, like a row of employee cars at a supermarket far from the closest parking.

Must be a gathering here today. If that was the case, even better. She could chat with more of the locals, maybe even recruit some volunteers to help make her vision a reality.

"Here we are." His apprehensive look confused her. On the one hand, he'd made it very clear how eager he was to find a venue and finish this job. On the other, there was something about his slight sneer, mixed with a worry in his eyebrows. Was he afraid she wouldn't like it?

She closed the car door and sucked in the cold air. To her right was a building, a clubhouse with a big raised deck. A handful of picnic shelters dotted the sprawling lawn out to the lakefront. The grass looked more the color of hay in its winter dormancy, and a few snow piles left from plowing the parking lot during the past snowfall remained.

"Mind if I walk to the lake?" she asked.

He shook his head. "Not at all." He gestured to her to lead, and they walked along a path around the decked building, then cut through the grass over a soft hill and downward to the water. She had stopped feeling her toes some time ago, noting to change out of the thin flats at the next chance.

The mountains looked larger from this vantage point than when she stood amidst them in the orchard. It was a breathtaking view. While the water held a fine chop, speckling the surface with murky grayness and white foam, she could picture the scene on a calm summer day—bugs chirping in unison, the mountains reflecting off the glass surface of the lake, the cold water an enticing treat to shake off the humidity.

"I thought the view from the top of the orchard was beautiful. But this...this is even better." She folded her arms over her chest to keep warm but didn't mind the chilly lakeside breeze. "This really is a hidden gem. Of course, I've heard of Waverly Lake, and someone I'd meet would talk about it here and there. But I had no idea it was like this."

Steve had his eyes closed, and he opened them, his long exhale visible in a smoky swirl. "It is beautiful."

"I can see why someone who was born here would never leave."

He nodded slowly, then stared at his feet. "You know, no matter where you are, when you get into the grind of daily life and are immersed in your work day in and day out, you sometimes forget to appreciate what's around you."

It was poignant, coming from this acquaintance. They'd spent half the day together and he kept surprising her. With his knowledge, his perception. His ties to home, even if he was eager for a respite.

"I get it." She nodded in agreement. "It's like that even in the city. I mean, how many people want to live in the heart of a city to be close to everything? In Charlotte you have the restaurants, nightlife, theater, and arts. You think it will be this grand time living amidst this cultural hub. But you get into your routine. Like you said, you focus on work and eventually forget about all those extra things that drew you there in the first place."

She hadn't reflected on her time in Charlotte in such a way before. It wasn't long living on her own after school that she'd met Logan and he became the focus of her world. Not the culture of the city that had lured her there. Sure, they wined and dined, but Logan liked his tried-and-true places, and eventually they rotated through the same three restaurants and a handful of bars for afterwork drinks. Then he was out of the picture, and she focused on her job. It didn't take long for Charlotte and its enticing happenings to become background noise in her daily life.

She turned around and scanned the park. A handful of visitors dotted the place, except for one corner where a crowd gathered with the noise of hammers and electrical saws. She had blocked it out when her eyes caught the Appalachians and lake. Now she wondered if these were the owners of the parked cars.

"What's going on there?"

Steve sighed. "That's what I had to show you."

"Okay..." A knot of worry formed in her stomach.

"Come on."

He led her back over the hill, and she noticed a plot of Christmas trees roped off. She shook her head as they walked, baffled she hadn't noticed any of this when they first arrived. Overwhelmingly hypnotized among the beauty here, her mind shunned the ordinary noises of everything else.

"Is this a Christmas tree lot?" She analyzed the roped off Fraser firs and blue spruces. "Are you worried that will cut into the space or donation pool for our event?" Her mind whirred at how she could incorporate the tree lot into the whole vision of the event. Perhaps they could donate a certain percentage to the organization's proceeds.

"That's not the main thing, although it's a side effect." He led her closer to the workers, sawdust flying in the air near a goggled man, while two women painted a large slab of particle board, putting finishing touches on the sparkly silver paint over the blue background.

"What is all this?" A lump formed in her throat to accompany the stomach knot.

"You know how you were talking about booths, and having different stations for food and activities, games and such?"

"Yeah. Are you thinking it's a bad idea?"

"No, not at all." He bit his bottom lip. It was almost cute how hesitant and flustered he was, were it not for the anticipation of the bad news he was about to drop.

"It's a great idea. So great in fact, that we kinda already have that going on."

"What?"

"Yeah, right here in Lakeshore Park. This crew will be finishing up this afternoon for the opening night of Winterfest."

Her knotted stomach made its way to her feet. "Winterfest?"

"Each year, around this time, the Waverly Lake school district hosts Winterfest. It's like a winter carnival of sorts. They have games, food, arts, and crafts. Horse and carriage rides, whether or not we have snow. Many of the teachers and staff, even students volunteer their time to raise money. Half goes to the school and the other half to the city. The funds help put on our own summer festival and regatta."

Her knees felt weak. She walked to the nearest picnic table and sat on the bench.

He made his way over to her. "This is where they have rows of tables and booths, and guests can buy a Christmas tree there while they're at it."

The more he spoke the worse it became.

"So, if I get this right, you're telling me that the event I had envisioned already exists."

"Yes."

She swallowed hard. "Not only that, but it's also a fundraiser. A fundraiser that benefits the town and the schools here."

"That's correct."

She rubbed her forehead, her icy fingers the only thing feeling good now. She tallied the bad news on her fingers. "For one, we have to figure out another event. Two, we still have yet to find a location for an event I have no vision for." She pursed her lips. "Three, we now have a competing fundraiser to contend with."

Steve shrugged. "I wouldn't look at it as competition so much—"

She held up a hand. "I'm not saying we need the money that goes here to go to our event. But, having another fundraising event, a well-established one that also goes to great causes, makes it that much harder for people to open their pockets for the new, less-established event that currently has no theme or location."

"When you put it that way." He shoved his hands in his coat pockets and sat next to her. "Just minor details." He smiled. There was no maliciousness in breaking her hopes. In fact, she read a hint of optimism.

Or maybe in her wallowing, she lacked the proper judgement of this man's angle.

"I'm sorry," he said. "I thought if I only told you what was happening here, you might not believe me. Or want to see it for yourself. Like I was just saying it all to be difficult, but I promise that's not the case."

He was right. It was better to have brought her here to see it for herself because she would've thought he was being difficult. Which made her disappointed in herself once again for judging this man upon barely knowing him. Plus, she'd want to know what all they had going on for Winterfest—the space, the setup, the activities.

"You're right, I do want to see it for myself."

He nodded. "Well, here it is. I know it's hard to come up with an idea you're excited about only to see it's not possible. But we are running out of time here. Anything else spark your creativity? Any other ideas you may have? If I'm being honest, I'm running out of places to hold this thing, whatever it ends up being."

"No." She shook her head and stared him square in the face. "I don't have any ideas, because I want to see this for myself."

He raised an eyebrow and leaned back. "What do you mean? We're here."

"I mean for real. You said the first night of Winterfest is tonight?"

"Yeah, but—"

"Then we go to Winterfest."

He scoffed and took his hands out of his pockets, folding them together in either frustration or prayer. Or both. "I'm not sure if you recall, but I do have other plans which involve getting out of here."

"And the sooner we come up with another fundraising idea and venue, the better."

"Right. Which is why we should maybe drive around more before it gets dark. Who knows, the drive might get us thinking of something. I don't see how going to Winterfest is in the best interest of our time."

"I don't see how driving around aimlessly is at this point." It came out sharp and she exhaled, relaxing her shoulders and attitude. "Look, I need to know exactly what Winterfest is like in order to make our event different enough. Not just different enough, but something that people would happily pay money for, after they already spent some at Winterfest. There is only one way to have that information."

He closed his eyes for what seemed like an hour before opening them again. She could imagine the internal battle happening between his desire to get this favor done for the Bennetts and the need to head south. If he were being honest with himself, though, he'd know she was right. The best way to know what they should or shouldn't do was to experience Winterfest tonight.

He slapped his hands on his thighs before standing up. She remained silent, not wanting to get in between his logic and his fancy.

"Pick you up at eight, then?"

Chapter Ten

By seven the night sky was black, save for the soft glow of nightlife in downtown Waverly Lake. A few years back, people in the county petitioned to not end daylight savings, wanting to hold onto the evening light for longer. Steve didn't mind the change. He enjoyed having a full four seasons in Waverly Lake. Plus, there was something about the early darkness that added to the spirit of Christmas. There was more opportunity to enjoy the full effect of the golden lights strewn up the lampposts and Christmas displays in the windows.

He walked through the entrance of Waverly Lake Bed and Breakfast. Three people sat near the decorated tree by the fireplace, drinks in hand, and chatting away. He decided to stand in the lobby, awaiting Laura's arrival. He couldn't believe she'd talked him into staying another night in Waverly Lake, let alone attending Winterfest. The first night drew the largest crowd of the event.

What worried him most was that they were no closer to finding a venue or materializing an idea for the Bennetts holiday fundraiser. He considered calling them, pleading with them to delay it until after Christmas, or even until next holiday season. But he knew Beverly well enough to know she wouldn't have any of that. Plus, he'd feel a bit of a failure for having given up after one day. Even if it did eat away at his plans.

"That's what we're going to do right now." Laura appeared from the stairwell, wearing a long-fitted jacket nearly reaching her knees and tall dark brown boots, the same color as the jacket's buttons. She held her phone to her ear, the other hand signaling for Steve to hold on one second as she smiled briefly in greeting.

"I'm not going to talk about that right now." It was in whisper-speak, and she looked back at Steve before continuing. "Probably... I'll find something, then. Don't worry yourself over it. I can manage on my own...all right, I will." She hung up and slipped the phone in the handbag dangling from her elbow.

"Sorry about that. My boss keeping tabs on me."

"No problem." What were a few extra minutes when his whole evening was hijacked? "Are you ready now?"

"Yes, let's go." She examined him head to toe, long enough to feel self-conscious about his choice in jeans and the maroon sweater underneath his unzipped coat. Suddenly, the lobby felt like a sauna.

"You look...different." She caught his eyes and shook her head. "I mean, a good different. You look nice."

He cleared his throat his collar choking him. "Thanks. Decided to ditch the suit."

"You should ditch it more often." She bit her lip, her cheeks flushing. "I'm sorry. I don't mean to say you look bad in a suit. You looked great today." She blew air up her face, waving the shorter tresses framing her face. "You just look more relaxed, that's all. Can we go now?"

He smirked. Truth was she looked pretty amazing. But if he had said it out loud, he would've floundered worse than she had. As a lawyer, there was a time to admit how you felt, and sometimes it wasn't until the case was settled. Or never.

They walked down the front porch stairs to the parking lot.

"I thought you might be open to walking there. It's just down the street, plus with parking we may end up just as far away."

"Sure, we can walk."

She followed him as he crisscrossed through a worn-down pathway between the line of trees on the north side of the parking lot. It led to the back alley of shops, and they walked until swinging around Nichols and Dimes onto Dowager Street.

"It's nice how they decorated the main road here." Laura scanned the lights and window facades. "Judging by the bookings at the B and B, Waverly Lake gets quite a crowd this time of year?"

"Oh yeah. We have two popular seasons. Summer, we have the lake trotters, people who bring their boats and swim. Plus, we have the regatta and fair close by. And our other peak season is now, starting up right after Thanksgiving."

"Holiday shoppers?"

"We get those, yes, but with the mountains we have all the winter sports. There's the tubing hill west of here, and skiing within a thirty-five-minute drive. You can stay at the ski resort, but Waverly Lake offers more amenities." His body warmed as they walked east along Dowager, past Bingham Station. "Whether it's good news for us or not, Winterfest does bring in the visitors too."

Laura took a deep breath, staring ahead at the gathering of parked vehicles in Lakeshore Park's lot. Parallel-parked cars crept farther down the street in the overflow. "I'll try to think of it as a positive. If we can set our fundraiser up while the visitors are already here, maybe it's a good thing."

He nodded, more to encourage her positivity than in agreement. He wasn't sure with the gift buying, charity event, and general added expenses over the holidays if people would be willing to give to another event. But his job was the legal stuff. It was Laura's job to worry about the fundraising.

As they weaved through the parked cars, the music of Bing Crosby's *Santa Claus is Coming to Town* grew louder. Cheers of the crowd sounded off from different booths, and the smell of chocolate and toasted marshmallows permeated the air.

"It's pretty booming." Laura scanned the crowd as they waited to pay admission.

"I told you it's a big deal here. Which is why I'm surprised the Bennetts didn't consider what position that puts us in."

Laura raised her eyebrows and grinned. "Or maybe they did but assumed you and I would figure it out."

They both talked as if they were a team on this project. That was not what he'd signed up for—not that he had asked for any role in it—but he let go of the semantics as the holiday cheer swept through the festival as strongly as the smell of roasted chestnuts.

"Here you go." A teenager gave them armbands. "Make sure you wear those. They'll get you some freebies scattered around the festival."

Laura wrapped hers around her dainty wrist. Steve struggled with his, holding one end down while trying to flip the other end around his arm to meet it.

"Let me." Laura's fingers grazed his wrist as she secured the armband in place. Her soft fingertips sent chills up his forearm.

"Thanks." It came out faint, as if his body said it before he could think. He let out a cough, expelling the weakness in his voice. "I always have trouble with those things."

"No problem."

They strolled down an aisleway formed by rows of booths. Two women in overly decorative Christmas sweaters sold personalized stockings. The next table displayed handmade ornaments, and it continued down the line with homemade crafts from local artists.

"Hey there, Steve." A blond woman stood beside colorful hair bows adorned with tinsel and mini jingling bells.

He nodded once at her. "Mrs. Fletcher."

"Who do I have to sue to get you to call me Carly?"

He grinned but continued walking as she greeted a customer.

"Who was that?" Laura asked.

"Carly Fletcher. She owns a salon in town."

"That explains the merchandise."

"We can go back if you wanted to check it out." He nodded to the booth behind them. "Problem is, she'd explain the merchandise, along with anyone and everyone's business in town."

Laura shook her head. "Well, it wouldn't be a small town without at least one gossip, now would it?"

He broke a smile. "No, I guess it wouldn't."

Steve approached an elderly man leaning on a walking cane in front of a table, his free hand reaching for his back pocket.

"I got this," Steve said.

The man stared at him with his deep-set eyes, as beautifully dark as his aged skin. "Now you know I can't let you do that, Mr. Albertson."

Steve waved a hand in protest. "Mr. Bingham, you helped me out finding the right tire when I got that flat. It's the least I could do."

Steve purchased the bag of gingersnaps, wrapped neatly in plastic and tied with a red bow. "There you go. What do you say, are we even?"

Mr. Bingham chuckled. "We were even before. But thank you." He patted Steve on the shoulder before moving down the line of tables.

Laura pursed her lips, strolling by his side.

"What?"

She shrugged. "I can't say I know many lawyers. Is it common for them to be so friendly?"

His chuckle was heartfelt, but nowhere near the impact of Mr. Bingham's. "When you're in a small town like this, everybody knows you. Put on top of that, being one of the few attorneys in town, I'm the most known guy out here."

"Surely there aren't a whole lot of huge legal matters you have to deal with here."

He walked by another booth, briefly saying hello to George, the owner of the flower shop, selling poinsettias.

"They're not huge legal matters, but they do exist. You wouldn't believe what happens when people really do know everyone in town. It makes it harder to resolve anything when you're worried about hurting feelings, or half the town is siding with you, and the other half sides with the other person. That's when I come in. And believe me, it's all the time. Especially this time of year."

"That's kind of sad to think that. These friendly neighbors bickering over petty issues."

"It is. Why do you think I was planning on getting out of here for the holidays? I needed a break from it all."

Laura stopped walking. "But what about your friends? And family? You have family in town? Won't they miss you over Christmas?"

He sighed, staring at his shoes before answering. "My parents are here, but I can see them any time of the year. And as far as friends...I might be the most well-known guy in town, but I'm also the most friendless."

"What do you mean?" Her eyebrows scrunched in a line. The second of cuteness pulled him to touch her shoulder or cheek, even hold her hand. The desire surprised him, and he threw it back where it belonged, hidden and locked away.

"No one wants to be friends with a lawyer. Acquaintances, sure. But genuine friends? The problem is if they were my friends, I'd know them too well. I'd know their secrets, and they'd be scared I'd use something against them if there ever was a feud in the future they find themselves on the wrong end of."

She bit her lip. "I guess I never thought of that. It almost seems like being a lawyer in a place like this is in itself a conflict of interest."

He laughed, and she smiled. A warm smile that shot to his heart.

"That's sad to imagine, though. Friendless."

They continued walking, and she stopped at a booth. She picked up a white plastic ball and tossed it lightly in the air, then caught it. "I'll be your friend." She held up one finger, and the attendant gave her a bucket of balls. She threw the first one at a stack of bottles painted like snowmen. She knocked down two.

"That's either sweet of you or incredibly pitiful."

She laughed again. "I know the start of our day wasn't how either of us wanted it to go. Words were said, judgements were made. But I can fess up to when I'm wrong about something. Or someone." She threw the second ball, knocking down one more snowman. "Seeing you out here, knowing these people; what you did for that man back there in thanks." She shrugged. "Maybe I was wrong about you. Being your friend wouldn't be such a bad thing, would it?"

It was touching. And frightening. He was warming up to her after the drama of today. She was relaxed and carefree—hadn't even mentioned the fundraiser since they'd reached Winterfest. But that was it, wasn't it? She was here for the fundraiser, and he was only here to help in giving it a home.

She used the remaining balls to knock down two of the last snowmen, leaving one standing.

"Oh, I don't know." He pointed to the remaining snowman bottle. "I'm not sure I can be friends with someone who can't throw."

Her jaw dropped, humor dancing in her light brown eyes. "You think you can do better?"

He sighed. "I don't want to embarrass you."

"Oh, it's on now." She waved down the attendant for another bucket and placed it in front of him.

"Let's see what you got, Mr. Albertson."

Chapter Eleven

LAURA HELD HER BREATH AS STEVE PITCHED THE LAST snowball at the snowmen. Three fell, leaving one standing.

"No!" Steve waved fists in the air in mock defeat. "So, it's a tie."

"I believe you thought you could do better, though." Laura shook her head and made a *tsk* with her tongue. She patted his back. "Maybe next time."

The attendant gave them both keychains as a consolation prize. Laura examined the photo of a black and white squat lighthouse on one side, words on the other. "Cavidge's Souvenirs."

Steve stuffed his in his jacket pocket. "It's a souvenir shop downtown."

"Is this actually a lighthouse somewhere on the lake?"

"No." Steve chuckled. "Who knows where that is. But according to Mr. Erol Cavidge, being on the lake means you can sell anything related to a body of water, whether Waverly Lake has it or not. Lighthouses, bays, seagulls."

"Whales and dolphins?"

"Of course."

"And people buy these?"

"I'm guessing there's a reason they're a prize at a festival."

She chuckled and they walked up to a crowd gathered around

an open section in a row of tables. Laura stood on her tiptoes, trying to catch a glimpse of the commotion in front. A middle-aged man in a wetsuit sat on a platform.

"Ah, we've come to one of the more popular events of the festival." Steve pointed at a teenager, who grinned while staring down the suited man. "It's the Polar Dunk."

"You mean, a dunking booth? In this weather?"

Steve nodded. "Hence the polar."

"Who would volunteer for such a thing?"

"The teachers. The kids get a real kick out of it and are willing to pay top dollar."

The teenager threw the ball, hitting the target and the teacher splashed down with a yelp.

He resurfaced, mouth agape. "Cheese and rice!"

The student laughed, then approached the booth and shook the teacher's hand. "No hard feelings, Mr. Yearwood."

The man accepted the shake. "We'll see come exam time," he chuckled.

"It gives me chills just looking at him." Laura tightened the closure of her coat, a flurry of goosebumps running over her skin.

"Come on. I've got a cure for that."

She raised an eyebrow, leery of whatever Steve may be leading her into.

"My treat. It's the least I can do for joking about your throwing skills only to fall flat on my face."

She chuckled. "It wasn't flat on your face." They walked a few paces towards a food truck set up at the end of the aisle. "Although, it was a little embarrassing. For you."

He closed his eyes and shrugged.

This night wasn't anything how she imagined. Rather, Steve Albertson wasn't anything like she had imagined at the start of the day. She thought she had his personality down within five minutes of meeting him. He was another Logan, worried about success and appearances. But this afternoon, and here at the festival, he was sociable and fun. A sensible guy.

Steve handed her a cup, steam escaping from the tiny hole in the cover. "Give it a minute to cool."

"Hot cocoa?"

"Even better."

"What's better than hot cocoa on a night like this?"

"Hot cider. Fresh from Offshore Orchard."

"You mean where we went today?" She cradled the cup, enjoying the warmth on her fingers. Thoughtful came to mind to add to her list of Steve's qualities. The fun of the moment subsided as the memory of their task emerged.

"This has been fun. Thank you for agreeing to take me."

He sipped from his cup and nodded.

She waited for words, which seemed unable to come out of his mouth for an eternity. "I had almost forgotten the reason why we're here," she said.

"Which is?" His eyes turned serious. This must be what it felt like to undergo his questioning on the witness stand.

Laura swallowed; her throat dry despite the warm apple goodness making its way down. Did he think her crazy for proposing this? Was it that unreasonable to check out the competition? "I—we—"

"If you wanted to go on a date, all you had to do was ask." He broke a smile, and Laura's nerves eased.

She tapped him on the sleeve. "No, that is not why we're here." She shook her head, taking in the crowd, the lights reflecting off the water, the dark mountain in the background. A date was not something on her radar in visiting Waverly Lake. It wasn't on her radar in any town. Steve was handsome and all, but...

"Wait. Do you mean to say that if I had asked you out, you would've accepted?"

Steve lifted one shoulder in a half shrug. "If I didn't already have plans to go to Florida, and you weren't leaving town so soon, I would've considered." He looked at her soft expression, his eyes as hazel as the cider. "But now that I've seen you throw..."

Her jaw dropped. He had gotten serious for a split second there.

She had almost believed he found her attractive. "I see how it is. Can't stand when a woman is your equal in anything."

"That is not true. I would love to find someone who was my equal."

"It's just that the bar is so high, right?" She smirked.

"You said it, not me."

Maybe it was because she had been with Logan for so long or hadn't had the freedom of singledom even longer. Or maybe it was because the hot cider was comforting, the holiday spirit around them intoxicating. But the banter with Steve weaved over the line into flirting.

And it felt good.

It felt good to even think this guy she'd met today liked her, even if it was in jest. Even if she will be leaving as soon as they get the fundraiser planned.

The fundraiser.

"Uh oh, what was that look for? Cider not settling well?"

"No. It's great, really. I was just thinking of what I have ahead of me. We spent so much time today, and I feel like we got nowhere."

"We're here at Winterfest, aren't we?"

She nodded, not feeling reassured.

"You came up with a great idea for the Bennetts. But now we know it already exists with all of this." He spread out his hands, the laughter and din of the people delightful and nerve-wracking at the same time. "What is it you wanted to do tonight? Why are we here?"

"I wanted to see this for myself."

"You didn't believe me?"

"No, I believed you." She caught a hint of frustration in his stare. "I needed to see it. This is what people are paying for already. Which means I have to come up with something completely different. No hot cider, no dunk tank, no arts and crafts and games. They're getting that here. I have to come up with something unique, something even better." She sighed. "Honestly, I've got nothing."

"Hmm." He put his free hand in his pocket. "I see what's going on."

She tilted her head, not able to read his thoughts. "What do you mean?"

"I think you're so focused on having a big idea, you're not opening your eyes for inspiration."

"I'm still not following."

He shifted his weight from one leg to another. "Sometimes, when I have, say, a complex divorce case, I get fixated on getting my client as much as I can. I start looking at the tiniest of things, picking at them, and being hard on myself if I can't find a way to get at it. I lose sight of the big picture, the overall achievements I have made or would be making for my client. I lose perspective."

"You're saying I need to take a break from thinking about it?" Being here with him did give her a break, at least for a while. It was amazing enough it happened for as long as it did.

"I'm saying you need to regain perspective. It's going to be a Christmas fundraiser. So do something that gives you the Christmas spirit."

"We're here at the festival."

"I know, but—" He held up a hand. "I've got it."

"You do?"

"Yes. Follow me." He waved her along, and she followed him, Steve walking briskly through the crowd. Two more folks offered a hello as they brushed by. She nearly walked into him when he stopped.

Laura looked ahead. "The Christmas tree lot?"

"What better way to gain a little Christmas spirit?"

"But I'm staying at a bed and breakfast. I can't bring a tree in there." Plus, she hadn't fulfilled her task today, which meant she most likely had to stay another night in Waverly Lake. Which meant she had to find an available room somewhere else.

The stress pulled at her, away from the unexpectedly excited Steve.

"Ah. But you haven't been to *this* lot."

What did it matter at this point? She wasn't going to accomplish anything productive the rest of the night. Besides, Kim sent her here in part to get away from the Logan drama and have some fun. It was practically her job to partake in this.

She followed him through the entrance into the roped-off square of trees.

"All right. I admit, I'm intrigued," she said. "What makes this lot so special? Different species? Do they come decorated already?"

"That wouldn't be very fun now, would it?" He smiled, handsome in the spotlight casting shadows across the lot. "Because Winterfest gets so many out-of-town visitors, Mr. Crassus came up with an idea. A product for tourists that they can bring home but giving them the same—a unique—experience even, while still raising money for charity."

She followed him as he weaved past the tall Fraser firs. No artificial candle could rival their fresh clean smell. He led her to an opening, where he stopped. Rows of tiny trees stood at their feet, small saplings with roots tied in burlap.

"Oh, my goodness."

"See. This way you can have a Christmas tree while visiting. And Mr. Crassus has a working relationship with tree farms across the state, so that after Christmas, you can bring the sapling to the farm where they'll plant it to grow to a full-size tree. Some people even plant them in their backyard."

"What a great idea." She crouched low, feeling the soft bristles of the trees.

"What do you think? Maybe having one in your room might spark inspiration?"

She smiled. "Sure. I'll take one. I think I can manage to fit it in my car." She winked.

She took another five minutes to make her selection, chatting with the owner over what a great idea he'd had. He gave her a box to set the tree in, making it easier to carry. She walked out of the lot with Steve, no closer to a fundraiser solution, yet a little bit happier overall.

"Thanks for that," she said.

"No problem. 'When in Waverly Lake at Christmas time' kind of thing. Couldn't let you leave without at least seeing them."

"There's only one problem with these, though."

"What's that?"

"How do I decorate it? I guess I could still use popcorn strings, but the usual ornaments I think would be too heavy and overwhelm these branches."

"That's why Ms. Velma is here at Winterfest. You know, the woman you were chatting with at the library?"

"Doing the puzzle?"

"That's her. If I'm not mistaken, she'll have a table over by the crafts." He started walking that way and took the box from Laura's hands.

"I can carry it," she said.

"I know." He smiled, and she didn't argue.

"Ms. Velma is retired, but throughout the year she makes accessories for this purpose." He nodded at the box. "She handcrafts tiny ornaments for these trees. Little balls, stars, candy canes. Makes them out of anything and everything you can think of—cotton balls, toothpicks, crystallized gumdrops, recycled newspaper. I think a set of her ornaments should get you started."

She stopped walking and placed her hands on her hips.

Steve paused in confusion. "What?"

"I have no venue, no idea for a theme or event. Heck, I have no place to stay for tomorrow night. Which, with the way things are going, I'm going to need. And somehow you managed to help me not care about any of that, even if for a moment."

He grinned. "I'm glad I could entertain you. If even for a moment."

She met up with him, standing by his side. "Me too."

Chapter Twelve

Saturday, December 17

"Coffee, black." Steve rifled through his wallet for his credit card. While yesterday was exhausting, he'd had a tough time falling asleep last night. For now, at least as far as he knew, Margaret figured he was hundreds of miles away in Florida. Unless her aunt shared that he'd never checked in. Or word spread around town and reached her desk. The latter was more likely.

"Morning, Steve."

Steve stepped aside from the ordering counter at The Cake Zone, shifting to the pickup counter. "Morning, George." The flower shop owner definitely had more pep in his step than Steve this morning.

George happily ordered a muffin and coffee. "I heard some business about you working for Beverly and James?"

Yep. Margaret had to know.

"I'm helping them out with a charity fundraiser." He received his coffee and held it, too scorching to consume. "I was scoping out venues with the rep from the ASD organization."

"I see."

"Very sweet lady." Jessica, the owner, smiled behind the counter. "Had a bit of everything, didn't she?"

"Yeah." Steve chuckled, remembering Laura's lunch smorgasbord. He wiped away the lingering thoughts and returned to George. "Anyway, with finding a venue—it's a bit hard on such short notice. Any advice, being on town council and all?" Steve hadn't attended all the town council meetings. He could probably count on one hand the number of meetings he had attended in the last five years, and those were because the topic related to a client's property or rights. But he knew the folks in town enough to know who was currently on the council.

"What's the timeline?"

"Anywhere from yesterday to Christmas Eve." The time crunch was so severe it hurt to say it out loud.

"I'd say that is short notice." George received his muffin in a bag and held onto his coffee.

They moved away from the pick-up counter, Steve dying for a sip of the coffee yet not willing to sacrifice his tongue. If that first sip burned, it ruined the experience of the rest of the cup.

"Will it be a fundraiser on site? As in, collecting donations as people enter or do whatever it is they're doing."

"I'm gonna go ahead and say yes." Honestly, he had no idea if they would be selling admission beforehand or have bins to collect money at the event. There was that word again. *They.* He had agreed —reluctantly—to help with a location and nothing more. Yet it felt like it was a Laura and Steve effort. Putting their names together tickled his throat, and he went for the coffee. *Still too hot.*

"I don't know if you're aware, but if you have it outdoors within town limits, and you will be raising money at the event, you're going to need a permit."

That was something he should've known, or looked into, seeing as he had the legal experience of the pair. "How long will that take? Should I go ahead and put in a request now?"

"I'm going to be honest with you. Getting a permit approved

takes several weeks. I know of permits submitted weeks ago for events in January."

His desire for the coffee turned sour. "Any way to expedite it?"

George shook his head. "I can put in a word, but you know how it is with the holidays. People are in and out of town, have family visiting. It's not regular working hours, plus the official holidays on top of that."

"What about indoors? No permit needed?"

"Private property, no. Unless you'd be selling alcohol, and that's a whole different ball game."

Maybe he could convince Laura to keep it indoors. He got the feeling that wasn't her preference, but on such short notice, she'd accept it. But where could they have a big enough space?

The thing to do, if they really wanted to do this thing right, was to convince Beverly Bennett to hold off until next year. He might as well say they were going to have a tea party at the bottom of the lake. That was more likely than Beverly changing her mind.

"Sorry I can't be of more help. I can keep an eye out for places for you, though."

"Thanks, George."

"Hey, didn't I see you at Winterfest last night?"

He could've asked anyone in town and the answer would more likely be yes than no.

"Yes, I was there. I think I walked by your table but didn't get the chance to stop."

"Oh no. No big deal. I had my hands full selling poinsettias and keeping Sebastian's spending under control. The past three Christmases we set a budget for Winterfest, and every year, he ends up ignoring it."

It made Steve think if there was truth to Laura's worry. Locals and visitors alike did spend quite a bit at the event and planned for it. What would happen having another event after it? Would they come out in droves like they did for Winterfest? Would they be as willing to spend money for charity?

"It did look like you were having a good time with a lovely lady."

He grinned, flirting with the line from cordial conversation to gossip.

"That's Laura, the one who works for the charity organization. I told her about Winterfest, and how it goes to a good cause." Laura was a lovely lady on the outside, and the more time they spent together, the more obvious she was on the inside.

"She wanted to see what the event was like. What activities were there, what got people excited about it. I thought I'd bring her so she wouldn't have to go it alone." He had let his guard down last night, forgetting their goal and just rolling with the evening. Yes, it had been fun, and it felt good to make Laura smile. His idea about the mini-Christmas tree brought an especially beautiful joy to her face, her whole aura.

But he had no time for any more of that, and dwelling on the evening didn't get him anywhere.

"I'd better get going. Thanks for the information about permits. I think we'll have to limit whatever we end up doing to the indoors."

"No problem. Let me know if you need anything else on the city side of things."

Steve gave a nod and walked out of The Cake Zone. He was no further in finding a location than he had been twenty-four hours ago. Except maybe for knowing outside was not a viable option.

He checked his watch. 9:17. He had wanted to meet Laura at the bed and breakfast by nine, but his darn insomnia last night messed that all up. He fell asleep so late, by the time his phone alarm went off, he had to hit snooze three times.

He walked to his car, parked two stores down on Dowager, and made the short drive to Waverly Lake Bed and Breakfast. With Laura in his car yesterday, he had felt something for the first time since purchasing it. Embarrassment.

Which was silly. He worked hard for it, and shouldn't be embarrassed for wanting something reliable, with great service and a luxurious interior. He often had to make trips to the county courthouse, and the BMW took the curves through the mountainous roads like a dream.

But Laura had him questioning his choice. Why did he care what she thought of his car? She'd misjudged his character from the start—even apologized for it. Just because he drove this car didn't mean he was a certain type of person.

Yet he'd had several women in the car, throughout his dating history. They didn't seem to care, or the opposite—loved his car. Their stance on his car though had no discernible effect on whether or not they continued dating. Why labor over Laura's stance, when he wasn't even trying to date her?

The languishing thoughts grew into a hint of anger. *Focus, Steve.* They needed to sort out this fundraiser so he could spend the better part of the holidays at the beach. In solitude.

He walked up the stairs of Waverly Lake Bed and Breakfast, through the front door. The air felt warm, with a buttery smell of waffles and pancakes cut with the distinct aroma of sizzling bacon. His stomach grumbled, defying his choice of mere coffee for breakfast.

That was okay. Tell Laura the news, finalize a place, and he could stop on the road somewhere for food.

He waited for her near the Christmas tree. He had told her last night he'd be there by nine, but maybe she had slept in. Heck, if he could've, he would've slept longer than the three rounds of extra minutes.

He examined the ornaments on the Christmas tree by the fireplace, an assortment of teals and silver, with peacock feathers, shiny baubles, and tinsel. After anxiously waiting for five minutes, he approached the front desk.

"Good morning. Could you phone up to Ms. Crawford in Room 6?"

The attendant nodded and picked up the receiver, then placed it on his chest. "Laura?"

"Yes, Laura Crawford."

"Are you"—he checked scribble on a piece of paper—"Steve Albertson?"

"That's me."

"She checked out this morning. We tried working out a room for her, but we're completely booked. She wanted me to let you know that she was checking into Woodsman's Lodge."

"Woodsman's Lodge? But that's on the other side of the lake."

"Unfortunately—and I say that from a visitor's perspective—lodging gets pretty tight here at Christmastime."

Steve barely processed the words from the desk clerk, thinking over Laura's quick move across the lake. It was surprising to hear Woodsman's Lodge wasn't fully booked.

He snapped his fingers. *Tracy Bennett.* It was definitely Tracy's doing. She had mentioned Woodsman's Lodge in yesterday's meeting, hadn't she?

"Okay, thank you." He turned around, then backtracked. "Did she leave a number?"

"No, sir. Sorry."

He cursed not having exchanged numbers with Laura. She could've texted him and saved him the trip this morning. And the next trip.

The last place he wanted to visit was Woodsman's Lodge.

In a moment of weakness, or just out of blind optimism, he had signed up for Lovetoberfest at Woodsman's Lodge. It was Tracy's great-aunt's experimental new event, pairing ten strangers together on a variety of blind dates.

Who knew why he did it. Something about fall in Waverly Lake, knowing that summer had died down and the holidays were coming up…Was it so wrong to not want to be alone? To try to find love?

If only he hadn't participated. It was embarrassing enough that people in town knew that he, the most popular lawyer, was desperate enough for love that he willingly signed up for the crazy experiment. Then to find someone he clicked with, someone he felt he had a connection with, only for her to break it off shortly after.

He felt like a failure.

The sight of that place, the *Wizard of Oz* mural, the hillside grounds, heck, the entire northern shore of Waverly Lake, was a staunch reminder of that failure.

He went back to his car and sat in it, eyes closed. As if wishing it away would make it go away. But nope. He had to see Laura to be done with all of this.

He drove the half mile down to Pearson's Wharf. He could drive around the lake, but it would take longer than boating across on *No Objection*. Fortunately, his childhood dream of becoming a lawyer had played out, else his parents' campy naming of their sailboat would've looked foolish.

Luckily for him, his parents didn't bother winterizing *No Objection*. Something about not using a boat for a long period of time made them think it would deteriorate and not work. Like a car that sat in a driveway. It was best to get the motor running, let the parts move every now and then.

He called Mom since Dad never answered his phone, regardless of who called. It was a wonder he had a cell phone at all. Mom's line went to voicemail. "Hey, Mom. I just wanted to let you know I'm going to take *No Objection* out this morning, on an errand. I'll call you again later."

Great. Not only did he have to go to Woodsman's Lodge, he had to talk to Mom later today. Yes, he loved his mother. And it was nice to share a boat with the family and enter the regatta at Waverly Lake as a team each year. But Mom tended to drag out a five-minute conversation into thirty, and Dad let it happen. That was time Steve didn't have to spare this morning—or any other time of the day.

He'd save the conversation for the drive down to Florida.

Right now, he had to set sail northward, to Woodsman's Lodge.

Chapter Thirteen

THE WIND WHIPPED TRACY BENNETT'S HAIR EVERY which way, the curls slapping her face and bouncing with each bob of the boat. "You all right?"

Laura snapped out of the hair envy. She could never get her wavy tresses into full-blown curls, and it required herculean effort to fully straighten them.

"Yeah." Laura's arms locked around her torso. The winter air had been cold during her visit, but nothing unmanageable. The journey on the small motorboat across the lake was a different story. Her eyes watered and ears stung, her shoulders high to protect her neck. "Just cold, that's all."

Tracy pulled back on the throttle. "I can slow it down." The decreased noise of the motor was a relief.

Laura wiped the tears from her eyes. "I guess I should've dressed better."

Tracy smiled. "It's okay, we can go slower. I wasn't even thinking about it, honestly." She sat in the captain's chair as the boat leisurely lobbed northward. "This way you can actually enjoy the scenery without being a popsicle."

"Thank you. For slowing down, and for taking me out here, finding a room. I owe you."

"It's no problem. Aunt Dee owns Woodsman's Lodge. It's pretty booked up through Christmas time, between Winterfest, the hot springs and tubing area. Even skiers stay out this way, seeing it's only a half hour on a clear day to get to the resort. But a guest checked out suddenly yesterday, a few days earlier than planned. Some sort of emergency at home."

"I hope it wasn't something serious." It was only natural to feel a little guilty gaining an advantage off someone else's misfortune.

Tracy waved her hand. "I wouldn't work yourself up over it. Could've been anything. Anyways, you were in a bind and now you have a room."

The boat puttered past an island, an arbored patch of land larger than the others sprinkling the lake. It looked big enough to have a few houses on it, although if this were an Italian lake it would fit one estate and go for a fine price.

"Is this the only way to get to the lodge?" She imagined a small cabin tucked away on an island or jetty. If boat transport was the only way, it seemed like there would've been a ferry service or boat cab, something to bring guests to and from the place.

"No, you can drive there. But it does take longer. Plus, my brother Danny works for Pearson. Some owners don't winterize their boats. Instead, they pay Danny to inspect them, run them every so often, especially when a storm has passed through. We're kind of in that shady area of climate—far enough south the lake doesn't freeze, but far enough north to get snow and a few freeze spells that can cause icing on the vessels. Anyway, we're helping Danny out with one less boat to worry about.

Laura was grateful if the ride indeed saved time. Today was a fresh start on the fundraiser event, and she needed as much time as possible to make it happen. Hopefully, Steve got the message on her whereabouts. Although if he truly had run out of location ideas, then the point of him coming along all but vanished. Maybe she should look into the hot springs or tubing place Tracy mentioned, even if they were a bit of a drive from town.

"Just sit tight until we're secure." Tracy slowed the boat, letting the momentum propel them toward a wooden dock running parallel to the shoreline. Her movements were agile, hopping off onto the dock, guiding the boat's stop and securing the line on a cleat.

Laura acquired boating experience growing up on Lake Norman but kept quiet during the ride. She wanted to take in the sights, once her eyes stopped watering, and enjoyed the authority and grace Tracy had over the vessel. It was a different type of familiarity with boating—more mechanical and physical, while Laura learned how to read the water and catch the wind on her parents' sailboat.

Tracy stretched out a hand and Laura handed over her luggage, cradling her Christmas sapling, then stepped over the starboard gunwale onto the dock. They walked up a flight of stony steps and crossed a level parking lot before reaching the front porch stairs to the lodge.

Laura had been right in that it was a wooden building. But it was larger than she imagined, a wider building of two stories with dormer windows commanding attention over the lake amongst the trees.

She plopped her tree and bag down at the check-in desk, just inside and to the right of the front door.

"You just can't get enough of this place, can you?" The silver-haired woman smiled at Tracy. Although her wrinkles gave her age away, she was physically fit and held an energetic aura about her.

Tracy walked around the desk and hugged her. "I think October gave me my fill."

"That was nice of you to bring this guest."

Tracy gestured to Laura. "This is Laura, the visitor I told you about."

"Aunt Dee." The owner extended a hand, and Laura shook it. "Nice to have you here."

"Thankful you could squeeze me in."

Aunt Dee put an arm around Tracy's shoulder. "Anything for my great-niece."

"You sort of owe me anyways, for all the extras you had me do this fall."

Aunt Dee rolled her eyes. "Did she charge you for the ride over? Because I wouldn't be surprised."

Tracy scoffed.

"I paid Tracy rewardingly, and don't let her convince you otherwise," Aunt Dee said. "Not to mention I had something to do with finding the love of her life." She winked.

Taken aback, Laura analyzed Tracy. "Is that so?"

"Some other time," Tracy said.

"I held a little event called Lovetoberfest."

Tracy closed her eyes, shaking her head. "I didn't meet Ben at Lovetoberfest."

"I know, but you worked on it together." Aunt Dee leaned over the counter, too giddy to mind the papers beneath her elbows. "It's something I started last October, pairing guests up on blind dates— willingly and voluntarily of course. Ben and Tracy were both working for me at the time, so I had them scope out the dating events and help choose which ones were the best experiences. They ended up falling for each other."

"Speaking of Ben, I'd better head on back to the community center." Tracy made her way to the front door. "Plus, I have to return that boat."

"Thanks again," Laura said.

"Don't be a stranger," Aunt Dee said.

"Am I ever?" Tracy grinned and stepped outside.

"I don't think she wants me to honestly answer that." Aunt Dee chuckled. "Now, let's get you settled into your room. As I told Tracy, I had a guest leave early yesterday, so your room should be ready for you."

Laura smiled. "I really am grateful. I called probably half a dozen places—"

"There's your problem right there. From now on you call me first." Aunt Dee retrieved a key. "Your room is upstairs, second on the right. Breakfast is served down here, just have a seat at any of these tables between six and nine a.m."

Laura examined the table and chairs in the back corner of the room, set up in front of a mural of a forest and yellow brick road. A fireplace warmed up the room along the eastern wall, and cozy chairs were arranged by bookshelves beyond the front desk.

"What a great place you have here."

"Thank you." Aunt Dee scanned the interior as if lost in memories. "It has a lot of history. If you're interested, I have a few books on the shelf back there."

"I'll have to take a look." Laura looked behind her, spotting the kitchen and the stairs up to her room. "How big was Lovefest, if I may ask?"

"Lovetoberfest. I know it doesn't really roll off the tongue. We paired up ten guests. Not a bad turnout for the first time."

"Have you hosted other events here, larger ones?"

Aunt Dee furled an eyebrow.

"I don't know how much Tracy has told you. I've been hired by the Bennetts to host a fundraiser event this Christmas, and I think this would be a great venue. You've got a kitchen right here, nice indoor space, and a flat parking lot we could use for an outdoor tent."

"Well, I'm flattered you think of Woodsman's Lodge in that way. I just don't think I could accommodate a large crowd like that —block off parking, use up the kitchen—while having a full booking of guests."

Laura's hopes were dashed as quickly as they had risen. "I understand. It is very short notice. It's also a bit of a ways from downtown. I think the Bennetts were looking for something more accessible from town. It would be quite a feat getting people out here."

"Oh, now that wouldn't be such a problem. If we had more time to do it here, that is."

"Really?"

"Sure. You can hire a water taxi service. There's a guy out of

Asheville, Harjeet Barsar, who runs such a business. There wouldn't be enough business to keep him here all year, but the town hires him for special events like Regatta Week. Maybe even a few locals wouldn't mind doing it. But this season?" She shook her head. "We could talk about your ideas for next Christmas, if that's something you'd like to do."

It was the same answer every other owner had given them. Why hadn't the Bennetts approached them sooner? Why such a push to get fit it in this year? And hadn't they known about Winterfest?

Bottom line was the answers to those questions didn't matter. It didn't change the assignment she had to complete. She and Steve had looked, as far as she could tell, everywhere around the lake with a close enough proximity to town—south at the library, in town at the park, northeast at the orchard. Here she was north, and the answer was no. Would going around to the western shores prove any better? There was only so much lake to go around—

Laura perked up, the ride over replaying in her head. "Aunt Dee, what can you tell me about that island I passed on the way in?"

"You mean Moonlight Island?"

"It looks like the largest on the lake. What's over there? Anything on it?"

She shrugged. "A bunch of trees. It has a short shoreline where kids hang out in the summer. You know that island almost has as much history as this lodge. Why do you ask?"

"Maybe I was thinking about it all wrong."

"About what all wrong?" Aunt Dee's confusion was understandable.

"I've been looking for a place to hold this fundraiser, an event which we don't even know what it entails. The whole time we've been looking *around* the lake, but what about having an event *in* the lake? As in, the middle of the lake, on that island."

Laura's ideas formed and branched like cracks in a frozen lake. The travel experience alone would be novel enough for visitors. How many tourists had the opportunity to go to that island, and see the mountains, the town, from that vantage point? They'd probably pay for the boat ride out there, without some grand event on the island.

But what could they do on it? If she was able to host something there, what would it be?

The front door opened, and a man walked in. He took off his hood, and she recognized Steve, who rifled his hand through his hair. "Freezing out there."

"Hi." It was what Laura could get out in her excitement. She took in a few breaths. "I take it you got my message."

"I did. Which reminds me." He rummaged through his pockets and located his cell phone. "We really need to exchange numbers."

"I'm telling you. Something about this lodge brings out the romance between people." Aunt Dee stared at the two of them with mischievous eyes.

Steve fumbled with his words before getting them out clearly. "I didn't have a way to reach her other than coming here."

"So nice to have you back," Aunt Dee said. "Sorry to hear Lovetoberfest—"

Steve held up a hand. "Don't worry about it. Wasn't your doing." He gave Laura his cell, screen open to her name typed into the new contact form. "Hello, by the way."

Laura wasn't sure if he meant it for her or Aunt Dee. She replied with a smile while she entered her number. She'd have to ask him later what that conversation was about. It seemed like one to ask outside of Aunt Dee's presence.

Not that she wanted to pry into his life. Perhaps it was none of her business.

Better to see it that way now that she had a great idea for the fundraiser.

Chapter Fourteen

STEVE POCKETED HIS PHONE. HOPEFULLY, HE WOULDN'T have the need to call Laura much longer. At least not about the fundraiser. He did get a little jolt of giddiness knowing it was in his phone. *Ridiculous.* She's someone he had to work with for another day, who happened to be attractive. *Get over it, Steve.*

"I need to tell you what I found out this morning." He unbuttoned his coat, the warmth of the lodge thawing the remnants of the brisk journey across the water. "I happened to see my acquaintance George at The Cake Zone, who is on the city council."

"City council!" Laura threw her hands up in the air. "Why didn't we think of contacting them for ideas?"

"He didn't have any ideas per say, but he did inform me that if we were to have this thing outdoors in Waverly Lake, we'd need a permit." Steve shook his head and closed his eyes. "I know what you're thinking, and I asked him about filling one out ASAP. But he says—he downright assured me—that we wouldn't be granted one in time for an outdoor event this Christmas season."

Laura seemed unfazed by the setback.

"At least we can narrow it down to indoor venues." Perhaps she thought the same thing, hence lack of negative reaction. Granted narrowing it down wasn't that much of a positive.

"So, on my way here, I had an idea," he said. "What if we could convince business owners along Dowager Street to open their doors for the evening, or evenings, of the fundraiser?" It blew his mind they didn't even have a timeline for when this thing would be held and for how long. He had only assumed evenings. "People could see what makes Waverly Lake so quaint and unique. See the shops, grab a beverage or pastry from The Cake Zone, like a walking tour. They'd see all the Christmas decorations, and we may get by saying the event is indoors, if it is technically taking place inside the shops." The lack of response was killing him. "Have you heard anything I've said?"

Once again, he thought he had a clever idea, one that ticked off the boxes and gave the guests a new experience. Whether they'd pay for it, who knew.

"Yes, every word." Laura eyed Aunt Dee, then turned her gaze back to him. Those dark golden eyes certainly had a way of sending tingles up his spine. "I was thinking of something a little more...unique."

He stifled a groan and stepped back. With one idea after another being shot down, with no time to spare, he was ready to throw in the towel. He'd have to disappoint Beverly Bennett this time. She'd forgive him.

Eventually.

Laura bit her lip, nearly squealing. "What if we had it on Moonlight Island?"

"Moonlight Island? Out in the middle of the lake?"

"Would we still have to get a permit for that location?"

"I—" His thoughts crashed in a traffic jam, too many to come out of his mouth single file. He took a second to filter through them. "From what I know, there's some discrepancy about who the island belongs to. Whether it's the town or the county." Lakes in general were in shady territory when it came to ownership, and islands in them even more so. "I'd have to look some things up, including ordinances." It could take hours, perhaps days of fielding phone calls and finding legal documentation. Was he really entertaining this idea? Beyond what was permissible, the logistics of hosting an event on that island were darn near insurmountable. "Even if there weren't legal restrictions, how would we get people out there?"

He had a longer list, but Laura held up a hand.

"Aunt Dee seems to think we could hire the same water taxi company the town hires sometimes to boat people out there."

It was his turn to stop her. It was an answer, but whether it sufficed remained to be seen. Who was to say that would work?

"What about power? If you want lit Christmas trees, or any kind of refreshments available you're going to need power. That's something I don't foresee being able to finagle, even for *next* Christmas."

"What about generators?" she asked. "That's something we could look into? Have a few for the things we need."

"You'd have to refuel them daily, plus how would you cover up the noise? Generators are loud and heavy." This conversation was absurd, and him entertaining it passed into laughable.

"Power may come easier than you think." Aunt Dee grinned, more than delighted to be a part of this. Probably happy to side with Laura.

"How so?"

Steve leaned toward Laura. "This oughta be good." Especially knowing Aunt Dee and her wild ideas.

Aunt Dee walked around the desk, in between the armchairs, to the bookshelf. She browsed through a book and brought it over to the counter. "What do you think of when you hear the word moonshiner?"

Laura shrugged. "People back in the early 1900s making their own liquor."

"Yeah," Steve said. "By the light of the moon. Hence the name."

"I don't know why, but folks in your generation think things happened way back further than reality." Aunt Dee pointed to a black-and-white photograph on the page. The man wore a beat-up bowling shirt and held a glass of clear liquid, face beaming with his smile. "This was just one of the moonshiners around the area, back in the 1950s. Men made shine all over these hills. In dark valleys, or high up away from roads. Even some of the caves were used, which brought on a whole slew of problems in addition to shining. Anyway, as more were caught in the mountains and areas closer to town, shiners were scrambling to find new secret places they could brew without being seen or heard."

"They made it on that island, didn't they?" Laura asked. "And that's where it got its name. They made it by moonlight."

"Yes and no." Aunt Dee looked up from the book. "You have to remember back then the town had fewer people, meaning fewer boats on the water, especially in the evening. We also didn't light up the shoreline with our houses and businesses. The lake at night was a black abyss, and the moon did little to alleviate that. But yes, locals had called the island many things before then, but Moonlight Island stuck."

"I don't see how this helps us in getting power to that island." Steve never backed down from a good history lesson, and indeed Aunt Dee grabbed his interest. But this was merely an entertaining distraction.

"Now hold on." Aunt Dee held up a hand. "You're right, in that shiners don't need electricity to actually make the shine. However, as the authorities were cracking down on illegal alcohol sellers and makers, it was becoming more dangerous to leave the stash and supplies unguarded. One of the men, by the name of Lawrence Laraby stayed behind on the island, day, and night, for weeks. His buddies would bring him fresh water and food. But eventually, he had an electrical line put out there."

"Okay, even if we were to entertain the idea of this tall tale being true..."

"Oh, it's true," Aunt Dee said. "Just because you don't believe it doesn't make it false."

"Fine." Steve kept his composure. "If there's still a line out there, that means it has to be underwater. As in, an underwater cable. How on Earth did he manage to get a cable out there, without being discovered?"

Aunt Dee smiled. "Think of it this way. If you're already performing an illegal activity, why go about the legal route for other things?" She waved her hand in dismissal. "He had a friend or two at the power company, profiting off the sale of shine. And if he needed someone else's expertise or help, he'd find a way to either make them a partner or provide them with shine free of charge."

"The town had to have seen the cable go down." Steve shook his head. Why was he even entertaining the idea this was reality? "I don't buy it. My Uncle Wes lives in one of a dozen houses on a lake island in Wisconsin. They petitioned for the county to supply electricity out there, but even with the offer of the owners to provide one-third of the cost, it'd be in the tens of thousands to lay down a cable. The county just won't do it."

"Well, I'm sure it's not the kind of cables they have today. Heck, maybe it's not even functional anymore. But I promise you, a cable went down. As a kid, I remember seeing a line of boats off that island, and ordinary citizens—in on it, of course—formed a sort of patrol unit, telling people who inquired that they were performing some study about dredging. I think another told my daddy it had to do with a sunken boat from years before. They all lied to make it happen."

"What happened to Mr. Laraby?" Laura leaned in close, pulled into Aunt Dee's story.

"He built a shack on the island and stayed there. Eventually, the demand for shine declined, so the money to keep people quiet eventually ran short. The risk outweighed the reward, I suspect. Lawrence and his crew up and left one day, never to be seen again."

Steve chuckled. He wiped his hand through his hair and stepped back from the counter. "If what you're saying is true, there'd be a transformer on that island. Don't you think someone would've discovered it since then?"

"Well yes. Which is why the transformer looks like it does."

"This is ridiculous," Steve said.

"South side. Post. Looks like a bird feeder on top." She smirked. "Funny how people never questioned a bird feeder on an empty island. One of the things teenagers don't pay any mind to, if they ever cared to venture past the eastern shore where they hang out."

Laura got out her phone and dialed, putting it up to her ear.

"What are you doing?" Steve asked.

"I have to check it out. Maybe Tracy can borrow a boat from Pearson's again and take me out to the island."

"Oh no you don't." Steve stole the phone and pushed the red button just as Tracy said hello.

"Excuse me, that's my property." Laura snatched the phone back. "And Tracy is my way of getting to that island."

"I'm taking you there." Steve planted both feet on the ground, as if the stance firmly rooted the decision.

Laura leaned back, mouth ajar. Surprised.

"I can't have you doing anything to jeopardize the legal standing of this fundraiser. Plus, the last thing we need is for the people of Waverly Lake to see Tracy Bennett and an out-of-towner poking around on Moonlight Island." If there really was a power source to the island, what would that mean for the town? How would people react? It would be chaos. Someone would want to tear down the trees and build a house there, or worse.

But the real reason he wanted to take Laura was that he was just as curious, if not more so, about the island and its history. If the transformer still existed, what about the shack? Or tools they used? If any historical artifacts remained, could he help turn Moonlight Island into a historical landmark, or site? What was required to do that?

For the first time in—a year, three years?—he was excited about what he could accomplish as a lawyer.

If any part of Aunt Dee's story was true.

The more he thought about it, the more likely they'd find Jimmy Hoffa or stairs leading down to Atlantis than a transformer or any sign of moonshiners.

"I don't know what's going on in that head of yours." Laura waved her hand. "But you need to remember we have a job to do. And if there's power on that island, then we have a venue. But if not…" She spread out her arms and shrugged.

She was right. If they couldn't use the island for the fundraiser, then, according to George, they had to find an indoor venue. Which meant spending the rest of the day, or who knew how many days, looking for a place. Heck, he'd volunteer his law office if it meant he'd be able to move on from the fundraiser task.

No way Laura would concede to that, though.

"How about this?" he said. "I'll take you out there. If there's power, I'll do what I can to have it on that island."

"And if not?"

"If not, then you promise to go with my idea."

"The tour of the town?" Laura scowled at Steve, who failed to hide his smirk.

"What's so funny?"

"I didn't think you were listening."

"I've listened to everything you've said. Doesn't mean I have to like it, though." She grinned.

He nodded with a smile. "Fair enough. Do we have a deal?"

Laura nodded. "Deal."

Chapter Fifteen

LAURA FOLLOWED STEVE THROUGH THE PARKING LOT, down the hillside to the dock. A white fiberglass sloop awaited them in place of the boat Tracy had brought her on, both sails raised.

"This is the boat you came on?" Laura guessed it was around twenty feet long. It looked well kept, with a clean hull and unstained sails.

Steve held out a hand to help her aboard. "Belongs to the family."

She stepped in, then watched him untie the line. "I can use the motor the whole way if you're not comfortable sailing."

"I'll be fine."

"Okay. I just know people prone to motion sickness fare worse sailing."

"You want me on trimming duty?"

Steve stood upright, hands frozen holding the line. "You sail?"

"Surprised?" She smirked. She was just as surprised he knew how. They were in a lake town, so it shouldn't have been that surprising. "Push us off here, and let's see how she does."

Steve gave a push and hopped in. "I can run the motor to head us in the right direction."

Laura grimaced with her stare. "So you're *that* kind of sailor."

"Very well." He manned the wheel, taking rudder duty. "Let's see what you got."

She hadn't sailed much in winter. In fact, her parents usually lifted their boat out of the water for the winter. But if she read the wind correctly, and managed to keep the feeling in her fingers, it shouldn't be any different than sailing in the summer.

They started out facing west. As Steve turned the tiller, Laura trimmed the mainsail and eased the jib slightly, shifting her bodyweight portside. The boat veered away from the shore, out into the open lake. As they aimed directly into the easterly wind, the sails flapped for a second before she moved starboard and regained control, the mainsail taking on the brunt of the force.

"Not too bad." Steve stood at the helm, a smile partially concealed by the popped collar of his jacket.

"Is this when you tell me you could do better, only to match me at best?" Talking warmed her chest but chilled her lips.

"No." Steve shook his head, jacket collar brushing his ears. "I tried that last night with a friend, and it didn't turn out so well." He grinned.

"You could've shouted commands. You're the captain, after all."

"I wanted to see how you read the wind." He dabbed his eyes. Tears welled in hers too, the wind soft yet powerful enough to get them across the lake. "Besides, would you have listened?"

"I told you back there. I always listen to what you have to say." She stood as the island neared. "Doesn't mean I'll like it."

He chuckled. "Where did you learn to sail, anyway?"

"My parents. It helped that we lived on Lake Norman."

He nodded. "Same here with Waverly Lake. Ever been to the regatta?"

She shook her head.

"I did it with my mother this summer. It's kind of a tradition."

"And your dad?"

"Dad enjoys being a passenger but never really had interest in learning. Anyway, we head out knowing we have no chance to win.

It's enjoyable just being a part of it, seeing all the other boats and sailors. You should come out for it sometime."

"Maybe I should."

He pointed to the island. "I'm gonna go ahead and start the motor for this bit. It's best to maneuver around the shallows and get up on the east shore. It's sandier and that way we won't have to get our feet as wet."

She nodded, bringing in the sails and letting Steve control the boat. Although she didn't get to see him sailing, his movements were fluid, reading the water, coastline, and wind like a pro. The bow caught on the bank of shelly sand and Laura hopped over, catching the line Steve threw out, and bringing the stern in toward shore.

Laura waited for Steve to step onto land. "Is this the best way onto the island?"

"It's the only way I've come here. It's where the teenagers come in the summer."

"Hmm." She marched away from the shore, into the trees.

"What are you thinking?"

She shrugged. "If we plan on bringing people over here, it might be worth building a temporary dock. Nothing fancy. Something to make it easier to disembark and board."

"How about we find out if the power source is real first?"

The island wasn't as lush as Laura had expected. The brush was low to minimal at ground level, the mini forest filled with pines and sporadic bare maples and oak trees. "It's actually quite easy to walk the place." She stopped, hands on her hips, staring up at the canopy. The December sky was a murky gray, a few shades lighter than the water.

She looked at Steve, who seemed to study her with the confused look of an art major taking Physical Organic Chemistry.

"I think we could easily make a walking path." She moved ahead, stepping along the pine needles covering the forest floor. "Yes. It's perfect."

"Perfect for what?"

"A Christmas wonderland." She spread out her hands. "Imagine if we cleared a walking path, a loop around the island. Twisting through these trees. They could all be decorated in a different theme, or groups of them following a theme. Yes." Her delight grew as she clearly pictured the possibilities. "It would be gorgeous. They can have a boat ride out here, receive hot chocolate when they arrive, and stay warm as they wander through the Christmas forest."

"Christmas Island."

"Yes!" Her heart raced with the vision. "Christmas Island."

"Just one problem."

She stared down Steve for breaking her euphoria.

"Well, more than one, but let's address the major issue —electricity."

She inhaled and let out the breath in a big sigh. "Aunt Dee said the transformer was on the south shore?"

"That's what she claims."

"Come on then."

They turned south, clearing the trees after fifty yards or so. The southern shore had less of a slope and rockier terrain. Almost as if she would be engulfed by the lake if she stepped off the farthest rock out.

"My bet is that it's farther west. Otherwise, you'd have sixteen-year-olds plugging in speakers for music."

"So, you do think it's a possibility there's a transformer here." She grinned. He put on a show of skepticism, but she could tell he was excited to come out here. He hadn't been so enthusiastic about scouting any place yesterday.

"I'm saying if there was..." He stopped, Laura nearly walking into him. "It can't be."

Ahead ten yards was a red bird feeder, held up by a thick, rusty silver post. The red paint had chipped, leaving raw wood exposed, while the roof was all but bare wood, a few flecks of green paint around the trim.

"Look." Laura pointed to the right, north of the bird feeder.

Weeds and pine needles adorned a rough rectangle of stones. "You think that's where the shack was?"

Steve didn't answer. Whether it was in awe of the truth or embarrassment for not believing Aunt Dee, she didn't know. He grabbed the bird feeder, shaking it, lifting it, bending over, and looking under it.

He gripped his fingers beneath one of the walls and pulled hard.

"Careful not to break it."

The wood snapped, flinging into pieces. She lifted her hands in the air. "You're hopeless."

"I wanted to break it. Look." He guided her closer. "Whoever put this out here built the bird feeder around metal." He wriggled the rest of the house off the metal top of the pole. The underside of the box was as rusted as the pole it sat atop of, but the rest of it, including the hinge atop, were in good condition.

Steve flipped the metal cover up. "I can't believe this." He stood up.

"What is it?"

"Looks like an old transformer and drop box. Do you have anything to plug in? See if this works?"

She rifled through her cross bag.

He sighed. "If all else fails I guess we can try to find some piece of metal and stick it up there."

She momentarily paused her search, giving him the I-can't-believe-you eye.

"I'm just kidding. It's a miracle this exists. The last thing I want to do is blow out the whole system."

She grasped her phone charger at the bottom of the bag. "Here."

He plugged it in, and she connected the other end to her phone. "Here's to hoping we don't fry my phone."

"That'd be a shame." He smiled at her. "I just got your number."

She wanted to slap him playfully but couldn't take her eyes off the battery icon on her phone. "It's working. It's charging. It works!"

Steve grabbed her phone and investigated the screen.

"You have a bad habit of doing that," Laura said.

"I—I can't believe it."

"We have power."

"We?" Steve handed the phone back.

"Yes, we. You said if there was power here, you'd do what you can to help me have the fundraiser on this island."

Steve sighed. "I did say that." He rubbed his bare chin, a strong square one but not overly so.

"Are you regretting promising that now?" If he didn't want to stick around, she'd rather him not be there. Nothing was worse than working on a project with someone who didn't want to be there, who constantly looked for ways out or didn't pick up the slack. Not that she would be slacking.

"No, I meant what I said."

"Then what is it?"

He walked over to a stump and took a seat. "I guess, I'm almost disappointed that this exists. Yeah, it's great for the fundraiser. But what happens to the place after that? I mean, look at this place. That, most likely, is the foundation of Lawrence Laraby's shack, from nearly three-quarters of a century ago. I can think of some people who'd exploit this place for business, for their own personal gain, rather than preserve it as a historical site, or city or county park."

He stared at the remnants of the shack. "Just imagine someone putting a restaurant out here. The kids would be all over that in the summer. Or setting up a bed and breakfast, or a tacky souvenir shop. All I see are visitors flocking here, boats cluttering the lake twenty-four-seven. I don't want this to turn into another Lake Norman." He looked up, wincing. "No offense. I didn't mean—"

She held up her hand. "I get it." She approached, crouching to the ground. He stood and offered the stump, but she continued to take a seat on the ground.

"The lake had been so quiet as a child," she said. "Who knows, maybe some would say it was busy even then. But I do know what neighbors and friends say about it before my time, and they all say the same thing. It was desolate and serene. A place to escape the city. Now it's highly trafficked, full of cars and boats."

Maybe that was what had pulled her to Waverly Lake. A sense of nostalgia, a bygone time of her youth when things were less hectic, less crowded. A slower way of life. It showed her what a gorgeous place like this could be. Serene and beautiful.

Steve had a point. If Waverly Lake meant to stay that way, progress had to be questioned and scrutinized, or else it was at risk of losing the pieces that made it magical.

The grief of having to leave the town struck her. She had only been here a meager twenty-four hours, yet she felt connected to the place. On the other hand, that was another twenty-four hours of not having a fundraiser planned.

She worked her way up off the ground. "I don't know what to tell you about after the fundraiser. I can't guarantee things won't change or even that they will. But I do think this is the perfect place to raise money for ASD, like Beverly Bennett has commissioned us to do. The best I can offer you for now is that we will do our best in keeping the integrity of the island."

Steve took a deep breath before nodding. "I know." He stood from the stump. "It's not your responsibility or concern what happens here after. You'll be back in Charlotte, celebrating Christmas and helping all the kids you help out." He smiled briefly.

She nodded. His words left her in confusion. He was right, she'd be back there, doing her job. But the idea also left her with a sense of sadness.

She couldn't shake the feeling he felt the same.

Chapter Sixteen

Sunday, December 18

THE LAST THING STEVE NEEDED TO START OFF THE morning was a visit from Mom. But there she was in her staple look of jeans, turtleneck, and sweater, standing in front of his desk.

"What brings you in today?"

"What brings me in? Are you forgetting that you borrowed *No Objection* and then promised to call me?"

Shoot. He did forget. After discovering Moonlight Island was powered, he had to figure out whose jurisdiction it was, whether they needed a permit to hold a fundraising event there, and call the power company to sort out an account for usage. The latter was a major ordeal because for decades the line hadn't been in use, nor had it been shut off, causing some friction in upper management. Turns out in the eighties the state tried to protect all the lake's islands under the state park system. An agreement was made to keep the power on for a possible ranger's station. Even though the park designation never happened, the contract remained in effect for decades.

Luckily, the history worked in their favor in that they didn't need a permit when neither the county or town could definitively claim it as their property. They both initially wanted to, until they realized the red tape they'd have to go through to formalize ownership. No one wanted to do that over the holidays, and neither minded the temporary use for charity.

"I could say the same for you, being here on a Sunday morning. Not only that, but making Margaret come in too?"

"I didn't make her come in. She offered."

Mom gave him the same look she had given him as a kid whenever he'd try to argue his way out of being grounded.

"There's a lot going on that needs to be immediately addressed, and all I'm going to tell you about it is that it's for charity, and we're on a tight deadline. Margaret asked if she could help, and I accepted."

Mom set her purse, which could be classified as a large duffel bag, on a client chair. Her short brunette hair thinned by the day while she permed and fluffed it to seem fuller. He had one of the oldest sets of parents compared to his peers. Elaine and Thomas Albertson had him at forty-one and forty-four, respectively. Both made it a point to be active and participate in everything they could while he was growing up and even now, with the tradition of sailing in the annual regatta.

"I heard you took the boat out to Moonlight Island."

"I did, among other places." Woodsman's Lodge was the only other place, but no need to tell her that.

"With a girl." Her green eyes grew big. "The same one people saw you with at Winterfest Friday night."

"Do you have spies following me? Because I wouldn't be surprised."

She chuckled and brushed him off with a wave of her hand. "In this town, everyone is a spy. So, tell me, is she another one of your dates? Or is this more serious?"

Unfortunately, Mom knew too much of his dating life. Like the rest of the town. It wasn't over him that people saw him out on dates, generally a different woman each time. He couldn't escape locals seeing him search for love. What was he to do, have every date in secrecy? Or stop searching?

"No." *She's none of your business.* "Just a friend." Was Laura a friend of his now? Despite their rocky start, it did feel like there was a certain level of comfort with her.

"Oh, that's nice." She took a seat beside her bag, a squished amount of space available for her. "You don't tend to keep those around for very long, either."

"Mom." He tipped his head back, frustrated. "You know, I'm the guy everyone knows, but nobody wants to know."

She made *tsk* sound with her tongue. "That's a bunch of hogwash. If you keep telling yourself that, you won't have any friends."

His excuse was partly true, as he had told Laura. But he'd also been quite the introvert in high school. His personality flourished and confidence blossomed in college and law school, a product he figured was due to the few years being away from the town, with a new set of people to get to know. Those here his age didn't get to see that side of him.

"I'm his friend!" Margaret yelled through the doorway from the front desk.

"Hey, this is attorney-client privilege," he shouted back.

"I approve of her knowing," Mom said, "and thanks for being my son's friend."

"You're welcome!"

Margaret chuckled just before the phone rang, and she answered it.

"This is why I need to get out of here."

"I also know about that. Margaret told me you had planned on leaving for Florida two days ago. You don't still plan on doing that, do you? And miss Christmas? When were you going to tell me?"

He snapped his briefcase shut, more of a metaphorical close on this conversation than a necessary item to bring with him. He had meant to tell her weeks ago, but if he had, that'd given her the time to wear him down until he canceled the trip altogether. "I have to go to the community center."

He threw on his jacket and swung around the desk as Mom stood. He touched her shoulder. "I apologize for not calling you back yesterday."

Her defiance at the abrupt end to their chat melted away. "It's all right. I'm sure you were busy. Calling your mother is only one thing on a long list of responsibilities for you."

He broke a smile to reassure her and walked alongside her to the front door. As she exited and neared her parked car, he turned to Margaret. "I'll deal with you listening in on that later."

She laughed. "Hey, you know Elizabeth is my second mom, right?" She winked, and he waved goodbye.

He headed west on Dowager Street, the morning sunnier than the past few days, although it didn't provide measurable warmth. Still, he enjoyed feeling it on his face during the brisk walk.

He stopped at the wrought-iron gate, parked cars overflowing from Dorset Drive to the intersection of Dowager. Although the community center offered Sunday morning brunch to those in need, he knew the crowding was from churchgoers. There were at least three churches he could think of within a few blocks, with overlapping service times. It made parking horrendous yet other parts of town still and quiet.

The gate doors were opened, and he walked up the sidewalk to the steps. Although the columns needed some masonry work, Ben and Tracy had done a great job cleaning up the overgrowth on the front lawn and porch. It was good to see a local landmark transform from ruin back to its former state.

As he walked through the front door, the smell of bacon, sausage, and hot maple syrup hit him. His stomach grumbled, even though he'd had a not-so-hearty breakfast of coffee and toast. Whose stomach wouldn't make noise with such savory delights?

"Good morning." A young receptionist stood at the front desk at the left side of the marble foyer. "Here for brunch?"

"No, thank you. Though it smells wonderful."

"Tracy made her famous French toast today. Third Sunday of every month."

"As delicious as I can imagine that tastes, I'm here to see Laura. Laura Crawford?"

"You may want to ask Ben or Tracy. They're out in the kitchen and seating area."

He nodded and headed in the hallway, between the rounded two staircases leading upstairs. The clattering and clinking of silverware and plates filled the quiet spaces between conversations.

"Steve!" Ben held two used plates in his hands. "I'll be right with you."

Steve nodded. He scanned the crowd, recognizing two children and their mom, as well as other familiar faces amongst the diners. Brunch was Tracy's idea of bringing the fortunate and less fortunate together at the same table, so to speak. There was a suggested donation amount per plate, and knowing Tracy, she didn't make anyone feel guilty in their decision.

Ben returned, wiping his hands on a towel he whipped back over his shoulder.

"You have a solid crowd out here this morning."

"Sure do. It's becoming more popular as word spreads." He leaned closer. "We were worried that we'd be competing with church services on Sunday morning, but many of these people come early to eat or after the service is over."

"That's great. It's good to see."

Ben nodded. "So, what can I do for you?"

"I came to see Laura. She said she'd stop by here this morning to talk to Tracy."

"She did, but she headed over to Moonlight Island already. What a great place for the event, by the way."

"The praise goes to Laura, trust me."

Ben pointed to a stack of three boxes over by the far wall. "Tracy and I found some decorations for her to use. Mrs. Bennett got in on it too. Tracy's supposed to message Laura about them."

"I can bring those out to the island." He looked foolishly at his briefcase, something he didn't need taking up a hand. "Can I leave this with you? I'll carry these out to Pearson's if they're not too heavy."

"I've got a dolly if that would help."

Steve nodded, and Ben retrieved the dolly, placing the three boxes on the wheeled cart. Steve took the dolly by the handle, keeping the contents tipped at an angle.

Ben stared at him with a grin.

"What?"

"Nothing." He grabbed the towel off his shoulder. "You seem quick to help out Laura."

"Oh, well, it's a good cause. Plus, the mother of that girlfriend of yours pressured me into it."

"When it comes to Beverly Bennett, my lips are sealed." He chuckled. "Is that all though? For real?"

Warmth returned to Steve's face with a vengeance. *A friend* was what he'd told Mom. Do friends linger in your thoughts at night? Was he ever simultaneously excited and nervous to see a friend? He didn't know what she was to him, but it certainly wasn't any kind of relationship he had with anyone before.

The dolly's weight thickened in his hand.

"Whoa there." Ben provided support in raising the cart back to a stable position. "You got it?"

"Yeah."

"A woman can do that to a person." Ben grinned.

"What?"

"Make your knees weak." He shrugged. "Or your arms."

"I don't know what you mean." He wanted to run and hide. "My grip slipped."

"Sure, it did." Ben slapped Steve on the shoulder. "I have to get back to busboy duty, otherwise there'll be a backup in the kitchen. No one wants cold french toast. Especially not Tracy. Be careful with that, and thanks for taking it."

"No problem."

"Bring her this too." Tracy, out of breath, appeared, holding a foam container loosely wrapped in a paper bag. "I'm sure she'll be hungry. There's some extra if you are too."

Steve took it with his free hand, nodding in appreciation.

"Did you tell him about tonight?" Tracy eyed Ben.

"Oh, right! I nearly forgot." Ben turned to Steve. "We're having a holiday dinner tonight with family and friends we've made along the way here. We'd love for you and Laura to come."

"Tonight?"

"Doors open at six," Ben said. "We'll probably eat six-thirty, seven-ish."

"Don't worry about bringing anything," Tracy said. "Just yourselves."

"Thank you for the invite. I'll think about it and let Laura know when I drop these off."

Ben and Tracy nodded in goodbye and returned to their work.

As Steve wheeled the cart out and rolled it clanging down the front porch steps, he shook his head. Two days ago, he thought he'd show Laura one, maybe two locations for the fundraiser and be done with his part, minus a few legal details. Yet here he was, on a Sunday morning, transporting Beverly Bennett's donated Christmas decorations across town to Pearson's Wharf while juggling lunch, to be boated over to Moonlight Island.

For Laura.

Yes, from his perspective, Laura was no ordinary friend.

Chapter Seventeen

Laura scribbled on the paper attached to the clipboard. "I've done the math. Given we have a thirty-AMP plug, and one thousand LED lights is sixty-nine watts..."

"LEDs? Not the traditional lights?" Valerie, head of the volunteers from Helping Hands of Waverly Lake, looked disappointed with the decision.

"LEDs are more energy efficient, and best of all, you can string many strands together without going over the AMPs." Laura went back to her scratchpad. "Using LEDs means we can have over fifty thousand lights on this island."

"That's a lot of lights."

Laura nodded. "The only thing holding us back is getting that many out here and setting them up."

"Don't worry about the setup." Valerie scanned the nearby volunteers, some on ladders stringing lights, others clearing the path Laura designed with their help. "Get us the supplies, and we'll make it happen."

"I cannot thank you enough."

Valerie laid a hand on Laura's elbow. "If we can get people out here and opening their pockets, that's enough thanks."

"This is quite some progress." Steve carried a box stacked on another.

"Let me help you there." She picked up the top box and set it down.

"I've got one more on the boat."

"What is all this?"

"Beverly Bennett's contributions to decorations."

Laura opened the nearest box. It was filled with neatly stacked unopened boxes of clear LED light strands. She flipped open the box Steve laid down. It was more of the same but multi-color lights. "Tracy must've told her about the need for LEDs. I can't believe it."

"The question is, did she have all of these sitting in her house, or did she clear every store from here to Wilmington?"

Laura chuckled. "I'm going to be grateful and not ask questions."

"Let me get the last one."

"I'll come with you." She followed Steve to the island's eastern coastline. A temporary wooden walkway was being built on the western shore, where the drop off was steeper and the boats could approach closer to the island. It wasn't finished yet, so all supply runs, and volunteer transportation still used the soft-sloping sandy shore.

He got in the boat and picked up the last box of decorations, handing it over to Laura.

"Did you come all the way out here just to deliver these?" The last box wasn't as heavy as the first, but any contribution to lights aided the cause. "Don't get me wrong, the volunteers were going to run out soon with the initial stash."

"I figured I'd better check everything, make sure you're not setting yourself up for a lawsuit."

"Always the optimist."

"Where'd the crew come from, anyway?" He pointed to another boat arriving, dropping off two more people.

"I ran into your friend George from the town council."

"You just happened to bump into him?"

She nodded. "It's easy to do when you go into Weeping Wares on a Saturday afternoon."

"Ah. So resourceful."

"I told him about what we're doing here and how I needed all the volunteers I could get. And apparently, I made the right choice because he informed me of Helping Hands. All he had to do was post on an app and set up volunteering times. Amazingly enough they filled up within hours."

"For all the negative impacts technology and social media have on us, there are some amazingly positive impacts." Steve took the box from her and switched it out for a bag with a hefty take-out Styrofoam container.

"What's this?"

"I figured, since I'm coming out here anyway, on legal business of course, and bringing supplies, why not bring some lunch?"

She smiled as full as her stomach was empty.

"I shouldn't take all the credit for it. It's from Tracy."

"I'll have to tell her thank you." Laura peeked into the bag, not seeing anything within the container but getting a better whiff of the intoxicating aroma. "Thank you for bringing it."

"No problem." He walked with the box back into the woods. "And before I forget, Tracy and Ben invited both of us for dinner tonight at the community center. It's some sort of holiday dinner with family and friends."

"Gosh. People really do make you a part of the family around here."

"Like technology, that also can have its positives and negatives."

They reached the other boxes, and he set the third one down. "How about we eat? You hungry?"

"I'm sorry? I couldn't hear you over my stomach growling." She continued westward carrying the food.

"Where are you going?"

"I thought we could eat out here." She led him to the west shore, the wooden planks forming the start of a foundation on land.

The rest of the planks were stacked in piles, and she sat atop one. Steve did the same.

"I'm hoping the majority of this will be done tomorrow for the soft opening, Tuesday at the latest." She opened the container, reveling in the smell from the sausage links, breakfast potatoes, and biscuits. Tracy had separately wrapped a cup of mixed fruit and mini cucumber sandwiches.

"If it's not done by then?"

She turned to him, scowling. "Again, ever the optimist."

"I'm only saying we should be prepared if things don't go as scheduled this week." He handed her a plastic fork.

"If we can't use this as the drop-off/pick-up point, then we can resort to using the east bank. It's not ideal, but nothing about this entire situation is ideal. That's why a soft open is a good idea. Gives time to work out any kinks before the larger crowds on the weekend." She poked a cube of breakfast potato and savored the seasoning, even though it was no longer hot.

"Besides, what do you mean *we* should be prepared? You've been a great help these past few days. But I have things covered from here on out. You can head off to that sunny beach you've been craving." Thinking about Steve leaving left her with a sinking feeling. It was nice to have someone with knowledge of the town and laws to lean on. But her discomfort, almost disappointment, was more complex than losing help. She'd miss this—eating a meal with him, although she did most of the eating when they were together the past two days, talking about the town. She'd miss his company. But she wouldn't dare ask him to stay. That would be unfair to him, and she didn't feel they were close enough to have the right to ask him to stay.

"About that." He stared at the water somewhere far off, his fork tapping the edge of the takeout container. "I'm worried about the operation here not being up to code."

The bite of biscuit had a hard time making its way down Laura's throat. "What do you mean? I thought you said as long as it's not a business, we don't have to be up to any official code?" She had worried about it yesterday after they discovered power on the island. If they had to get an electrician out, or inspector, or have a lower limit on the lights than their power limits, it could derail the event.

"I know. What I said is true. But there is an exchange of money somewhere along the line." The conviction in his words decreased. "We could be bordering on some legally shady area."

She smirked but worked to hide it. He was fighting for an excuse.

To stay.

"I mean, if you think there's a chance we're in jeopardy here, then you're right. It's probably best to stick around."

"I just want to make sure it goes smoothly. I'd hate to be hundreds of miles away if there's an emergency—a legal emergency."

She nodded, biting her lip. "Wouldn't want any legal emergencies."

"Okay, then." He nodded. "I should probably let Ben and Tracy know about dinner."

"If it's anything like this, you'd be a fool to miss it." She dipped a piece of biscuit in the container of sausage gravy. "I just hope this storm coming in hits their lower end of estimates. There's still a lot to do." She scanned the sky, a definite darkening gray to the west.

"You never know with these things," Steve said. "I think their predictions are about as good as guessing."

The soft hum of a boat grew louder. An aluminum jon boat slowed around the island, bobbing in the chop of the winter waves. It was just big enough to set out a fishing line on a lake this size, but too small to do much else. The operator sat at the helm, staring them down. He wore a heavy camouflage jacket, his face coarse with scruff and years of weathering. Laura would've smiled and waved hello, were it not for the obvious scowl on his face. Whether he grunted or she imagined it was up for debate.

"Who is that?"

Steve cleared his throat. "That's Erol Cavidge." He stood and waved. "Afternoon, Mr. Cavidge."

The boater gunned the motor and sped off to the south.

Steve sat back down. "That went well."

"What was that all about?"

"Mr. Cavidge started the first souvenir shop in town."

"That's how I knew that name. From the keychain at Winterfest."

"That still doesn't explain the hostility."

"The thing to know about him is, when a competing souvenir shop opened up, he somehow applied pressure and forced the owner to sell. To him."

"Now he owns two souvenir shops?"

He nodded. "The man is always on the lookout to snatch up land or office space for business opportunities. Right there was the reason I wasn't entirely happy about our discovery here on the island."

"What, you think he wants to start a business on the island? Was that an attempt at intimidating us?" The former would be difficult but not completely out of line. The latter was downright preposterous. What made this stranger want to intimidate her? If he knew her on even the slightest level, he'd know intimidation was not something Laura Crawford took well.

Steve shrugged. "You never know with that man. What worries me is that we may have worked ourselves out of code restrictions, but what if someone like Mr. Cavidge finds his own work-around to having a place out here? Or anyone else for that matter?"

"There's only so much you can do on the island," she assured him. "Limited power source, limited transportation across the lake. Even if he did set something up here, I couldn't imagine it being popular in the colder months."

She put down the remaining biscuit, stress overtaking her appetite. "I worry people won't want to come out here next weekend. It's a cold boat ride."

"But it's short," Steve said. "The destination will more than make up for any discomfort getting here."

"I hope so."

"Plus, it's for charity. You'd be surprised how much this town can come together for a good cause." He tapped her arm. "Look at the volunteers here on short notice. It's amazing. And what about how busy Winterfest was the other night?"

She backed away from the food, failing to hold back the moan of worry. "What am I thinking of trying to put on something at the same time as Winterfest? That's harder to get to." She buried her head in her hands.

"That's not why I mentioned Winterfest." Steve sighed, then rubbed her back. It was comforting, in fact, something she hadn't noticed until she did notice. Then her heart raced, and she couldn't look at him.

His hand stopped abruptly, as if he only now realized what he was doing. "It'll all come together, you'll see."

She nodded, finished with the food but not the company.

"I think going to this dinner tonight will be good for you. For the both of us." He took out his cell phone and dialed.

"Who are you calling?"

"Hey, Tracy...Yeah, I did, and thanks again. Listen, count both me and Laura in for tonight...great. See you then."

Laura folded her arms. "Making the decision for me?"

He grinned. "You can call her back if you don't want to go." He held his phone in front of her and raised an eyebrow.

She did want to go. Not solely for what was to be an excellent meal with overly generous people she'd met days ago.

She wanted to go with Steve.

Chapter Eighteen

STEVE STUCK A FINGER BETWEEN HIS SHIRT COLLAR AND neck. His heather sweater fit snugly over the button-down shirt, with his jacket over that. As he entered Woodman's Lodge, he began to regret the outfit choice. The fireplace roared, heating the room well beyond the seating area.

Aunt Dee came out of her office and greeted him with a smile. "Don't you look dapper."

He patted the crown of his head, the stray strands refusing to obey. "Going to dinner over at the community center." It struck him how Aunt Dee belonged in the family category of guests, as Tracy's great-aunt. "Are you not going tonight?"

"I am, but I have a few loose ends here before I can leave. Besides, I know how they can be, not serving food for the first hour."

He sincerely hoped not as his stomach pangs intensified. Tracy had provided them with a hearty lunch for sure. But he hadn't planned on staying on the island all afternoon, stringing lights on trees, up and down the ladder. It was the most calories he's burned in one afternoon since who knew when.

Not that he minded helping out. The trip to Florida was a distant memory at this point. Certainly, there would be other opportunities to borrow Margaret's aunt's place. He was needed here, and it felt good to be needed for something beyond his legal expertise. The law moved slowly, and sometimes he'd forget to embrace the victories, or even just the settlement of a case. The reward took long to achieve and oftentimes didn't feel climactic. Today, he was using his hands, physical labor, and the reward was immediate. He could see how far they had come as a team, and how much they had left to go before the fundraiser began.

What he didn't enjoy much was standing inside Woodsman's Lodge. The brown wooden hotel, with its soft, musty smell mixed with cedar, drew him right back to October. He'd met Rachel for their blind date right there, seated by the bookshelf, taking in the fire's warmth.

"Can you tell Laura I'll be out on the porch?" He moved to the door.

"It's so cold out there tonight. Supposed to be the coldest so far this season." Aunt Dee turned to the stairs. "I bet that's her coming down now."

She was right. Laura stepped down, wearing a sleek black sweater dress, along with those same boots from the other night she pulled off so well. Her hair was curled in loose spirals, one side pinned back with a silvery clip.

"Sorry if you were waiting long," she said.

"Not long at all."

Aunt Dee smirked. "He was about to freeze his butt off outside waiting for you."

Laura looked at him quizzically.

"It's just a bit warm in here, that's all."

"You and I both know your feelings about the lodge." Aunt Dee pulled a piece of lint off Laura's shoulder. "I'd better get ready myself. You two be careful driving. They're saying this snowstorm isn't something to take lightly."

"You be careful too," Steve said. "See you there."

"You're coming?" Laura put on her coat, careful not to smoosh her hair.

"There aren't many events I plan for to take the time off. But this holiday dinner is one of them. See you soon."

Steve held the front door open, and Laura stepped onto the porch. Big, wet flurries glided through the stiff air.

"Any update on how much snow is expected?" Laura held out her hand, catching a snowflake before putting on her gloves.

"I'd say we already got half an inch." The roads to Woodsman's Lodge had a light dusting but nothing to worry about. Yet. "They have us in the one-to-three-inch band but keep sliding the three-to-five-inch band closer."

He registered the worry on her face. "The town is pretty good at clearing the roads whenever we have a storm. It's more the auxiliary roads that don't get the attention." It was also the winding main roads circling the lake, but Laura didn't need to know that right now. No sense in worrying her more.

This was time for her to forget about Moonlight Island and relax at the dinner.

They got in his car, the passenger door slightly sticking with the thin layer of ice forming along the door frame. The temperature had dropped in the past half hour, which wouldn't be a problem if the initial snowfall hadn't melted to any degree. If it did, it would freeze and form a sheet of ice on the roads.

They buckled and headed east, swerving along with the road around the lake.

"What was Aunt Dee talking about back there?" Laura rubbed her gloved hands together. "With how you both know how you feel about the lodge?"

He shook his head. "Just an old lady ranting," was what he wanted to say. But for some reason the truth came out. "A little event called Lovetoberfest."

"What did you have to do with that?"

"You know about Lovetoberfest?"

"Just the basics. Aunt Dee told me it had to do with pairing guests together for dates around the town."

He nodded. "Believe it or not, I was one of the guests that participated."

"Really?" Her eyes perked open wider, meeting his gaze. He appreciated being the driver, having an excuse to keep his focus elsewhere. "That does surprise me."

"Me too." He smiled, and this time he let them connect glances for a second before pulling back. "The thing is, the past year or two, I'd go on date after date."

"Oh? Ladies' man?" She giggled.

"No, not like that. I'd meet someone, or so-and-so had a friend of a friend they thought I'd like, that sort of thing. I had been on so many first dates I was beginning to believe the problem was me."

She quieted, staring at her hands on her lap.

"Anyway, when Aunt Dee approached me to look over some documentation for the event, she suggested I give it a try." He shrugged. "Between the not-so-great dates and not wanting to let Aunt Dee down, I figured, why not." He huffed. "Unfortunately, I learned why not."

"Was it that bad?"

"The event itself wasn't bad. Of course, it's a bit awkward to stay in a place with a bunch of single people, all looking for the same thing. But the dates were fun, even when the company wasn't so much. It was my third date, Rachel."

The automatic wipers kicked in on steady, low speed, the snowfall picking up, hitting the windshield harder. "We hit it off great. I thought we had a connection, and we hung out together in our spare time the rest of that weekend. The problem was that I thought it was real, something that could last. But the longer we were away from the lodge, and past that weekend, the less I heard from her. She made me feel like the weekend put a spell on her or something. Does that make sense?"

"She got caught up in the moment?"

"Something like that. For her it wasn't as deep a connection as it was for me." He sighed. "Hence the slight discomfort being inside the lodge."

"Aunt Dee knows about it all?"

"Of course. She kept in contact with the three couples that formed from the weekend. I think she wanted to be able to say she had success with Lovetoberfest. That it worked for at least one couple."

"What happened to the other two couples?"

"I haven't asked. To be honest, I was a little embarrassed Rachel and I didn't last longer. I didn't really care to hear if the others had better luck, while I was wallowing in misery." He smirked. It wasn't entirely miserable they hadn't worked out. At least not now, after some time. After meeting Laura. If he were with Rachel, he probably wouldn't be driving Laura to this dinner.

"I almost feel like I'm doomed, living in Waverly Lake. Everyone I know with a lasting relationship is with someone they've known for a long time, or even grew up with. I was too shy in high school to have a girlfriend, and too busy studying beyond that. I never really had a first love."

He couldn't believe the last words escaped his mouth. He swallowed, the heat in his cheeks rushing down his body. He turned the heat dial lower, anything to distract him and not look at her.

"First loves are overrated." She gave a gentle smile. "Especially when they propose to you, convince you to move into their apartment, then fall for someone else."

Steve nearly slammed on the brakes. "Are you serious?"

She nodded slowly, examining her naked ring finger. It was the first time she'd realized she hadn't sought out the feeling of the band with her thumb or glanced down to see the sparkle of the diamond for an entire day.

"The worst part about it—well, I take that back, it's not *the* worst part, but it's up there—is that I'm still living in that apartment. I just can't bring myself to move out. I tell myself it's convenient for work, which it is, and that I wouldn't find such a great deal on rent living on my own, which is also true, but..."

She bit her lip, the muted rose lipstick smudging a tiny bit on her front tooth. It was adorable. "I think a part of me is holding out hope things will go back the way they were. He'd come back, we'd forget about all of this hiccup on our journey to the altar and move forward."

"Is that what you want to happen?" It hit him then, harder than the impending snowstorm, as sure as the darkness of the night. He knew what he wanted her answer to be.

And he wanted her answer to be an astounding, solid no. He was falling for her, this assertive, confident, never-say-die woman he'd met two days ago. Their time together felt like ages, in a good way. As if they got to know each other in fast forward.

She closed her eyes. "I'm sorry. I'm just thinking aloud now, aren't I?"

"Don't apologize." *She didn't answer the question.* "I told you about Lovetoberfest, and my own mother has been trying to get that information out of me for nearly two months."

"You mean your sailing partner?"

"Yeah, exactly. Even she doesn't know the number Rachel did on me." His joking died down. He wanted to say something to let Laura know that Rachel posed a sore subject nowadays mostly due to his embarrassment. He wanted—he needed—to convey Rachel remained in the past. That his future was open. But he didn't have the words.

"It sounds like whoever this guy is—what's his name?"

"Logan."

"Ugh, Logan. He just sounds like trouble."

She chuckled, and he winked. "Logan sounds like he's made the mistake of his life. I mean, to have a relationship with you, someone who is focused and compassionate." *And beautiful.* Why couldn't he say it? "To be engaged to you, then to blow it. He's gonna be kicking himself if he hasn't already. I guarantee it."

"Part of me hopes that." She stared out the window with her elbow on the door, chin in her hand. "That he regrets it, only to find that I'm already happily married."

"That's the spirit," Steve said. "To a billionaire."

"With a fabulous yacht." She smiled and it was golden. "With a personal chef."

"Endless caviar and freshly caught seafood."

She shook her head. "Honestly, I'd prefer a good burger over any of that."

"I like the sound of that." How, in all his dating career, had he never met anyone like Laura? He had never connected with anyone the way he meshed with her. Then again, he'd thought he had connected with Rachel that weekend. Maybe that was his problem. Did he fall too fast, or misinterpret interest for something more?

No, this was different. He could spend the whole night driving around. As long as he was with Laura.

Billionaire or not, no amount of money could buy the feeling he had.

Chapter Nineteen

ALTHOUGH THE SNOWFALL HAD PICKED UP, LAURA FELT safe with Steve driving. Even if she hadn't, the talk was distraction enough. She couldn't believe she had opened up to Steve about Logan. The only people she really talked to about him were Kim and her parents. And Mom and Dad didn't know the full story—she'd told them he was sent off for work in the hopes it would all clear up quickly. When it hadn't, she had to tell them they broke up, but she softened it by saying the distance was too hard. In a way it was, for him. Too hard to keep his hands to himself.

They parallel parked along Dorset Drive and walked around the corner of Dowager Street to the front gate of Phillips Community Center. The sidewalks were glazing over, the snow crystals freezing on the open gate creating shimmery crystals.

"This is going to sound crazy." Steve walked with his hands in his coat pockets and shoulders up near his ears. "But I feel nervous for some reason."

Who knew how many cases went to court for Steve, having to speak in front of a judge and everyone else in the courthouse. Why would a dinner party make him nervous? Yet after he said it, Laura's stomach tumbled, increasing her nerves.

"At least you know more people than I do."

"I can introduce you if you'd like. Although I doubt I'll know everyone." He paused, then chuckled, his warm breath billowing white in the freezing air. "Then again, this is Waverly Lake. I'll probably know everyone."

Steve meant it in the sense of the community, and his position in it. If Logan had said that it would've been out of arrogance. It felt good to have spoken with Steve about him, like affirmation she recovered from their relationship and was ready to move on. The words *with Steve* snuck in her thoughts. She slapped them right out of her head.

Clear lights bedazzled the doorway of the community center. Green garland spiraled around its white columns, and an enormous wreath hung above the doorway between two windows.

Laura walked up the front steps, the low din of Ella Fitzgerald's jazzy *Have Yourself a Merry Little Christmas* mashed with the chatter of guests. Her foot lost traction on the third step, and she grabbed Steve's elbow for support.

"You all right?" Steve's hazel eyes pierced through the cold.

She nodded and as she was about to unleash her grip on his arm, he placed his hand over her glove. They walked together like that up to the door, calming and exhilarating her nerves at the same time.

He moved to knock but the front door swung open. It was Danny Bennett, his unzipped down jacket covering a blue button-down shirt. "Oh, sorry. Didn't know you were there. Glad you both could make it."

"Leaving already?" Steve asked.

"Ice run. Apparently, the machine gave out, but Tracy won't let me lay a finger on it. Something about boat motors not being the same thing." Danny grinned, his smile handsome. "Ironic we're getting dumped on from this storm, yet we don't have enough ice for drinks inside." He patted Steve on the shoulder. "I'll be back in a few. Go ahead and make yourselves at home. Ben and Tracy are in the kitchen." He walked down the stairs and onto the path leading to the gate. "Maybe they'll realize you're here by the time I get back."

Laura wondered what he meant by that. It didn't take but a minute or two inside to understand—there had to have been close to fifty people, with no sign of Ben or Tracy in the foyer or dining room.

"Can I get you a drink?" Steve nodded to a room off to the right.

She followed him. A man and woman dressed in black collared shirts stood behind a high table covered in white linen. The woman wore a headband of felt reindeer antlers and the man a necklace of chunky, colored light-up bulbs. A few bottles on the table displayed the options for red and white wines, while two printed placards listed other alcoholic and non-alcoholic beverages, with names like Yule Log Warmth and Candy Cane Juice.

The woman took their order.

"White wine please," Laura said.

Steve opted for a specialty drink called Red-Nosed Rudolph. Laura laughed at the fact he had to say it out loud.

He shrugged. "When in Rome."

They got their drinks and walked to the dining room. Four large tables seating twelve each were beautifully decorated with red tablecloths and silver accents—table runners, napkin rings, chargers. It sparkled in festive holiday elegance.

"I didn't realize it would be this big," Steve said.

"I had no idea what we were coming into. I guess that's why I was a bit nervous too."

Steve smiled.

She wanted to hold his hand, let him know they were in this together. But she didn't have to. The look in his soft eyes and the warm glow of his face said he felt the same way.

They carried their drinks through the converted house. Steve told her how Ben inherited the property, something most residents had wanted for years before his return. She met folks from all walks of life around the town and spread the word about the fundraiser kick-starting tomorrow.

It was hard to believe they had something up and running in

such a short amount of time. Were it not for the unique circumstances of Moonlight Island, and the willingness of volunteers to dedicate their time, she would've had bad news for Beverly Bennett. It was good she didn't because Beverly approached them as they moved to the dining room.

"Is everything ready for the soft open tomorrow?" No use for formalities in greeting with Beverly. Right to the point.

Laura sipped her wine, its warmth oozing down her throat. "We made great progress today with the displays and clearing pathways. We just have some finishing touches tomorrow on the display and loading dock and will set up the hot chocolate truck on the island and the ticket booth at Pearson's Wharf."

"I certainly hope it all works out. To have a fundraiser event on Moonlight Island, well, I wouldn't have believed you! It's absolutely marvelous. My biggest concern, though, is getting folks out there and back."

Steve finished a swig of his Rudolph drink, wincing as he did after every sip. "We hired Harjeet, with the same company—"

"That does the regatta in the summer." She nodded her head. "Very clever."

"He's bringing a fleet of three boats. Said he'd either leave tonight or tomorrow depending on the weather."

Beverly glanced across the room, through the windows. The snowflakes grew hefty and round, clinging to the tree branches. "Let's all hope the weather won't be an issue."

Steve raised his glass as if toasting to the thought.

Beverly smiled and made her exit from their corner.

Laura took another taste of the wine, holding back drinking the whole glass. She hadn't thought about Harjeet towing three boats out here in this weather.

Steve touched her shoulder. "Let's just enjoy the night, okay?"

He knew what she was thinking, and he knew what to say to pull her out of it.

A set of bells jingled and jangled, and the crowd turned to face the kitchen. Ben stood atop a step stool, wearing a red Santa hat and a burgundy flannel, sleeves rolled up. For as warm as it was in the dining room with the number of guests and food cooking, it had to be sweltering in the kitchen.

"I wanted to thank you all for coming out tonight, especially on a Sunday night. But hopefully, it's a great way to start off your week." There were chuckles in the crowd, and Tracy appeared from the kitchen, standing on the floor next to Ben.

"I can't say I fully appreciated growing up in this house when I was a kid. But my parents tried to instill in me the importance of two things—family and giving back. Every year they hosted a Christmas dinner. Since they didn't have much family between the two of them, and certainly not locally, they invited their friends and even strangers from town. Those special dinners stayed with me, and I knew when I signed the papers to this place that I wanted to give back. I wanted a place people could go to and feel like they had a family, even if not by blood. I couldn't have imagined having such a big family of wonderful people."

His voice cracked and Tracy leant out a hand, squeezing his.

"All right," Ben shouted. "Enough of that! Food is served!"

The crowd clapped.

Laura tapped her thigh with her free hand in applause.

Guests began to line up in two queues along the row of serving tables.

She and Steve got in line. He handed her a plate as they reached the front, giving her a warm stare that heated her core better than the wine.

"You made it!" Tracy stepped into line, hugging Laura and patting Steve in the chest. "Are you all settled at Aunt Dee's?"

"Yes, it's wonderful. Thanks again for organizing that, and for the food earlier today. And inviting us tonight." As the list came out of her mouth, it was clear she owed a lot to Tracy and her boyfriend Ben. For them to help out a near stranger as much as they had was endearing.

"Don't even think about it. It's my pleasure." As quickly as she appeared, she hopped to other guests farther back in line.

Laura and Steve stood with their plates, examining the seating at the tables filling up. "Over here you two." Aunt Dee stood, waving them over.

They looked at each other, registering the dismay and the fact they had no choice out of respect for Aunt Dee.

Aunt Dee slapped the seat next to her and Danny Bennett filled it right as they walked up to the table. He gave a wink, and they moved to the other side, sitting next to each other and opposite Aunt Dee and Danny.

"I don't know if you've met, this is my girlfriend Kara." Danny stretched his arm out over the young girl's head and tapped the woman with long dark hair two seats over. "And my daughter Hannah."

"I remember meeting Hannah." Laura smiled at the brown-haired girl, whose food selection included macaroni and cheese with a side of macaroni and cheese. Depending on how ASD manifested, it could be difficult to find foods that kids especially agreed with.

"How are you? I heard you really love Christmas trees."

Hannah's attention turned towards Laura for a second, then back at her plate. "I like the ones with all the colors."

"Oh, me too. It's like seeing a rainbow wrapped around a tree." She winked at Hannah, who again looked up for a second. "I don't know how much your dad told you about what we are doing with the fundraiser, but I think it's right up your alley."

Danny rubbed Hannah's back. "Go ahead and eat your macaroni."

"How is the fundraiser coming along?" Kara asked the question of the night.

Laura took in a breath to give her the same answer she gave Beverly when Steve pulled out his phone.

"So sorry." He stood up from the table and pressed his hand over his free ear to hear better.

Laura's appetite vanished. The worried look on Steve's face when he saw the caller could not have meant good news. She contemplated getting up and following him but faced the guests at the table instead.

"Probably Ned Wellington wanting to sue Doug Chambers over who gets to decorate that darn weeping willow on their property line again." Aunt Dee shook her head, and Danny chuckled.

Steve returned, all delight of the night washed from his face. He sat next to Laura.

"Well?" She anxiously awaited.

"That was Harjeet. He decided to leave this evening to get here before the brunt of the storm. But one of his trailers jackknifed when exiting off 40."

Laura gasped. "Is anyone hurt?"

"No, luckily. But the boat suffered damage. And unfortunately for both parties, he had to turn around."

"What about tomorrow?" Laura asked. "Maybe he can send the other two."

"He says the roads are worsening, and he can't let his guys out driving in it."

Laura worked on keeping the little food she did have in her stomach down. "What do we do now?" Her voice shook. "How are we going to get people to the island?"

"I can help," Danny said.

Laura looked at him, pleading, hope sweltering in her eyes.

"Working at Pearson's, I know who has boats in the water right now. I can round up some volunteers."

Kara got out her phone and pushed on the screen. "We can get volunteers through the Helping Hands app. Ask them to meet first thing in the morning, at town hall?"

Danny checked the time. "It's gonna have to be tonight. More people will be home and available now than on a Monday morning."

"I don't want to interrupt Ben's dinner," Laura said.

"Yeah, you don't have to do this right now," said Steve.

"You need boats, and you need boat operators by tomorrow night, right?" Danny awaited their answer.

Laura looked at Steve, hesitancy and desperation in his eyes. No doubt her face read the same way.

She nodded at Danny, and Kara typed away.

Steve leaned close to Laura's ear, the smell of bergamot mixed with cinnamon from his drink fluttering her heart. She could almost feel his lips on her skin. "At least we got out of dinner with Aunt Dee."

She smirked, looking at Aunt Dee who hadn't heard a thing. Or at least didn't act like it.

His fingers found hers under the table. As if completely natural, and not awkward or too soon or overly complicated, his hand clasped hers, their fingers entwined.

Regardless of the drama that unfolded tonight, she felt calm.

Chapter Twenty

THE NIGHT WOULD'VE BEEN PERFECT. THE FOOD WAS amazing—the drink not so much, but that was likely due to his poor choice—and the company even better. Every now and then, he caught Laura glancing at him, holding back a smile, and she'd catch him doing the same with her. Except he wasn't so successful holding back his feelings manifesting on his face. He even managed to grab ahold of her hand, soft and delicate in his. He didn't want to let go, but they had work to do.

Because of the imperfect part of the night. Had it not been for the major setback of losing their planned transportation, they could've stayed at Phillips Community Center longer, enjoying more drinks and dessert. But the impromptu meeting at Town Hall was going to start in ten minutes.

Steve helped Laura with her coat in the foyer. Danny had kissed Kara before leaving her with Hannah, already on his way to the meeting.

They stepped outside, the temperature noticeably lower than earlier in the evening. The snow had accumulated nearly half a foot.

"I'm not sure the weather report got this one right." Steve glanced at Laura, who tested her foot on the stairs. "Here, take my arm again." It was the gentlemanly thing to do, but he was happy to have the excuse.

Until he thought about how the storm did not bode well for them. It already rendered their transportation plans dead in the water. Even with Danny's plan, this much snow could deter people from volunteering at all. And if it didn't let up into tomorrow, there may not be guests for the soft open.

He had to shake off the list of problems. Right now, they had to get to town hall. If people didn't show up tomorrow, that was okay. They knew they'd have to work out issues the first few days before the big weekend.

"You're being awfully quiet." Laura kept her eyes focused on the ground, her feet sinking into the snow-covered sidewalk.

"I was having a Laura moment." He smiled.

"And what would that entail?"

"Oh, you know. Thinking of a string of negative things that could happen and overly worrying about them."

She smirked and squeezed his arm tighter. "Worrying is not always a bad thing. It helps to be better prepared."

"Did I say it was a bad thing?" He raised his eyebrows. *Nothing she did was bad.* No, that wasn't true. It was that kind of thinking that got him into the mess with Rachel. Nobody is perfect. Everyone has some kind of flaw, if not many. It was loving the person completely, flaws and all, that made for a strong relationship. Not that he had the experience.

"No, but it can be a bad thing." She sighed, her breath a crisp white cutting through the darkness of the sky. "Worry too much, and you fail to see the good things, the things that didn't go wrong. When I look back on past events I've worried about, generally everything worked out. Yet I work myself up with the next thing."

"I can promise you, this fundraiser—despite the fact that just about everything has worked against us—is going to work out."

"I know neither of us can tell the future, so why do we try?"

"This time may be different than others," he said.

She stopped at the gate, and he wrapped his hand around the

wrought iron. The cold seeped through his glove, the frozen crystals of ice sticking his hand briefly to the gate.

"You have me helping you." He grinned, showing his teeth, before getting more serious. "You also have this town behind you. We—all of us—won't let you fail. We won't let this fundraiser fail." As he said it, he hoped to everything holy that there were warm bodies awaiting the meeting's start at Town Hall. Or his speech was for naught.

She reluctantly accepted his confidence with a nod, and they walked to his parked car. It was covered with a layer of snow. As he brushed off the windshield, a thick layer of ice was exposed. It would take a bit of warming up for it to defrost.

"How are you feeling about walking in this to the hall?"

She looked over her shoulder, as if town hall would appear in her line of vision. "How far is it?"

"A few blocks over and down." He looked at the frozen BMW and traced his finger along the doorframe. There was a good chance it was frozen shut.

"I think I can handle that." She started tromping through the snow on the sidewalk. "Probably a good thing I didn't wear stilettos."

He chuckled, although picturing her in strappy high heels was not an unpleasant image.

She popped up her coat's hood, preventing any more snowflakes accumulating in her hair. Steve didn't have a hood. Besides, his hair was beyond keeping dry now. At this point, it crunched when he pinched strands.

They walked down Dowager Street. Hardly any pedestrians or drivers were out on the sidewalks and streets. The shops were shut down, some with signs of early closure. The lamppost lights were all that lit their way, which was plenty with the reflective white wonderland the storm provided.

He guided her to the right, up a side street and ahead lay the front steps of the town hall, albeit covered in snow, looking puffed up like squishy marshmallows.

They held onto each other going up the steps and reached the front door. Danny should've arrived already, along with—hopefully—the volunteers. Another person behind them worked his way up the steps.

At least there's one.

Steve opened the door, a squeaky creak in the quiet of the snowfall. Heads turned toward them. Several heads. Steve counted at least eight people awaiting the meeting.

Laura took off her hood and shook out her hair a little, clumps of snow and ice falling onto her jacket and the floor.

When she looked up, she smiled. "Are you—is everyone here for the meeting?"

It was the town hall, a building that wasn't open twenty-four seven, and mainly used for meetings. He didn't say it out loud, though. It could've been that the doors were open, and these folks were caught in the storm, seeking shelter for a while.

"Not my usual way to spend a Sunday evening," Mr. Nichols, the owner of the pharmacy, said. "But you call for an emergency meeting for all boat operators, I'm gonna show up."

"And I'm all grateful you all did." It was Richard Carter, Danny's girlfriend's father. He must've left with Danny from the community center. If Steve remembered correctly, he owned a motorboat and a sailboat. Or that was, until Danny acquired the sailboat.

"Come up front, you two." Danny stood in the front row, urging them forward.

Steve and Laura walked up the aisle. He looked at her as she looked at him, wondering who was going to speak first. He took the initiative. As a lawyer, he spoke in front of people all the time. Who knew how comfortable Laura was, though he imagined she had the confidence and ability to do just as well as him.

"Thank you all for coming out tonight, especially on such short notice with this storm acting up."

Some of the men—and two women—nodded in acknowledgement.

"I don't know how much you all know of the situation. Laura is from The Learning Center for ASD and has been tasked via Beverly Bennett, with planning a fundraiser locally for the organization."

Danny stood back up. "It will go to help other kids like Hannah get the help and support they and their families need." He took a seat again and nodded to Steve.

"That's right. The event is being held on Moonlight Island, a spectacular walk-through Christmas forest light display. We had hired Harjeet Barsar with his fleet as our transportation for folks to and from the island. However, there's been an accident with one of his boats, and they can't make it out here with this storm."

"What is it you want, Steve?" Donald was married to Carly Fletcher, the owner of Dye Happy Salon. They were regular participants in the Annual Regatta. "All I have to do is let Carly know and we'll have triple the amount of people here."

Steve smiled briefly. It was funny but it was true. Carly Fletcher's network reached far beyond any app in Waverly Lake.

"We need volunteers to bring people from Pearson's Wharf out to the island and back. The more we have, the shorter the wait for guests, and the fewer trips you'd have to make."

Laura stepped forward. "While we can't get the deposit back with Harjeet, the rest of the money we would've spent will go towards your fuel costs, so we can at least cover that."

"How long are we looking at here?"

"We'd need volunteers starting tomorrow evening," Steve said. "Every weekday night this week, six to nine. Next weekend, we expect the bulk of our guests and are open six to ten."

Richard stood and scanned the room. "We're going to have to get the word out. The eight of us—"

"Nine." Danny interjected.

Richard affirmed him with a nod. "The nine of us won't be enough. We can't all work every night for three, four hours at a time."

"I can ask around," Mr. Nichols said, "but I know for sure two of my neighbors have their boats out of the water for the winter."

Danny raised his hand. "I may be able to help with that, getting them up and ready, and winterizing again when this is all over. I can talk to Pearson about temporarily letting them dock at the wharf." He looked at Mr. Nichols. "If they're willing to help out."

"I'll certainly try."

"Danny, you've done so much already." Laura almost pleaded with her eyes. "Don't overextend yourself for us."

"It's not for you. It's for Hannah." He winked and turned to the crowd. "I can't begin to tell you all what TLC and the ASD community has done for my family. But it's enough for me to feel passionate about helping. If you find people who can help and are hesitant, have them give me a call. Or heck, give me their number or address, and I'll approach them."

Laura nearly had tears in her eyes. "Thank you all again for coming out." She rifled through her purse and passed out her business card to each volunteer. "You can communicate through the app or contact me directly."

"Or me," Steve added.

"Same," said Danny.

"Now get back to your families before we're stuck here with this storm." Steve looked at Laura, who nodded she was finished.

Steve shook Danny's hand as he walked out the front row. "Again, we appreciate your help."

"No problem." He leaned closer, out of eyesight of Laura. "You'd better get her back to the lodge, or else you might be stranded on the road. Not that such a predicament would be a terrible thing." He winked.

Steve shook his head in embarrassment before looking back at Laura, who didn't appear to have heard anything. Did Danny pick up on their chemistry? As in, it wasn't all in Steve's head? Or was it obvious what Steve thought of her? There was no time to ask now, and he didn't want to ask either. Rather sit and stew over it than verbally acknowledge the truth.

Laura bundled back up, putting her hood over her mostly dried hair.

"Ready?" Steve followed her out, two other stragglers lingering behind. One of them likely had the key to close up, and if not, there wouldn't be a whole lot of people roaming town this late in this storm.

"Are you going to be okay driving in this?" she asked, taking his arm for assistance down the steps. She chose to make new footprints on fresh snow, a smart choice with the old footprints icing over.

"Should be." Although his BMW was not all-wheel drive. He had passed on the expensive addition considering he lived in North Carolina, and snow and ice were few and far between. A decision he regretted every now and then, on nights like tonight.

"I hope so," Laura said. She looked at him at the bottom of the steps. Her perfect pink lips curled up into a smile. "Wouldn't want to be stranded on the road with you."

Steve's jaw dropped along with his stomach. She *had* heard what Danny said. "That wasn't—I mean, Danny—"

She giggled, her head tipping back. Snow fell on her nose and rosy cold cheeks.

She was beautiful and laughing at him, and he didn't care one bit about his embarrassment.

Chapter Twenty-One

Monday, December 19

LAURA RUBBED HER GLOVED HANDS TOGETHER, MORE due to nerves than the cold. Although, it was mighty cold. The snow had abated by morning and the afternoon sky was clear and blue, but the temps hadn't worked their way up enough to make a dent in the accumulation.

The island seemed colder, more exposed in the middle of the lake. The westerly shore had nothing to break the wind, but once amid the trees along the walking path, it wasn't so bad.

She waited at the dock, sun beneath the mountaintops, greeting the first groups of guests as they arrived. She wouldn't be a greeter the entire time or every night, but it was the next boat's passengers she wanted to catch.

After the meeting last night, the volunteers got to networking, just as they promised. Between them and their friends, they secured at least three boats rotating at a time per hour shift, for the weeknights. For the weekend, they upped it to five. The sheer volume and enthusiasm of volunteers in this town was amazing.

The maroon and navy fiberglass boat pulled up, driven by Mr. Nichols. As it slowed at the temporary dock, Laura could make out the face of Beverly Bennett, hood wrapped tight around her head. Her husband James helped her off the boat, and four other passengers disembarked.

"Hello!" Laura stretched out her arms in cheerful greeting. It was the first time the Bennetts had viewed the event, and a positive tone hopefully would carry through their first impression. "I couldn't let you visit without having a personalized tour."

"Lovely," Beverly said. James warmly smiled, and the two followed her off the dock to the stand near the start of the pathway.

"Care for some hot cocoa?" With the limited amps supplied to the island, she had to balance out the magnitude of the light display with the availability of food or beverages. Luckily, she found Hot Choco-latte, a local food—mostly drink—truck business with their own generator that would last through the evening. She'd secured two more vendors for the weekend, wanting it to be more impressive for the larger crowd.

James' eyebrows raised in delight.

"I'm good, thank you." Beverly continued walking along the path. The look of disappointment on James' face lay plain as day.

Laura waved at the truck attendant Marie to get her attention, then held up one finger. She hastily grabbed the covered cup of hot chocolate and met back up with the Bennetts.

She stopped them beneath the entranceway, a lit-up sign overhead spelling out the moniker. She toiled over whether to change the colloquial name of the island, but Steve convinced her the change would be temporary. Not to mention it adequately described the event. "Welcome to Christmas Island, your holiday oasis in Waverly Lake." She felt silly adding the last bit. The Bennetts didn't react either way. "Shall we start?"

She handed James the hot chocolate with a wink, and he happily accepted. They stopped at a post, a printed sign with instructions. "Rather than blast music on the island—and take up power—the local radio station *Wavy 98.5* came to our rescue. They agreed to play non-stop Christmas music during our operating hours that you can stream on your cell phone through their website or app."

She demonstrated, opening the app, and turning the volume up slightly. Beverly gave her the sense that loud music, even Christmas music, was not appreciated.

"How clever," Beverly said. "That way you don't pollute the island with loud noise. Before the regatta, there's a DJ at Lakeshore Park and it gets abhorrently loud."

James shook his head in agreement with her. "We tend to stay away until the race starts."

They walked along the path. She, along with the volunteers, worked on clearing the pathway through the afternoon. Although the snow had melted close to the trees, the more open spaces had been blanketed enough to lose track of the original path. They shoveled and laid down more pine straw, creating a crunchy path to prevent slipping.

"The pathway is approximately half a mile round-trip, which may not seem that long. But I like to think with the twists and turns amid the various scenes, it's more than enough for guests to be satisfied." *Hopefully*.

They traveled through the first portion of the walk, trees lit up in alternating red and green lights. Shiny giant golden bows were tied along the branches.

"This is darling," Beverly said. "Has Hannah come out to see it yet?"

Laura shook her head. "I don't think so. Danny had said something about bringing her around Wednesday night."

"I'll definitely have to come back with her. She's going to love this."

Laura smiled, genuinely. It was what she hoped, more so for Hannah than Beverly. She wished all the children from The Learning Center could make it out here to see this.

They walked over a make-shift candy cane bridge, the lighted canes crisscrossed on either side and into the next phase.

"I call this part Winter Wonderland." The next set of trees were adorned in clear lights and silver bows, beads, and garland. Laura insisted on keeping as much of the snow untouched here as possible, as it gave the whole area a soft glow, glistening on the ground and the branches. On the left, a few volunteers had made a family of snow-people, fully decked out in scarfs, vests, and top hats. *So much for leaving the snow.* But how could she be upset about it? They were adorable and added wonderfully to the scene.

"Look there, that one has an actual smoking pipe!"

It was the first thing she'd heard James say. Perhaps ever. The man seemed delighted among the trees, sipping his hot cocoa. She suspected he knew more about Waverly Lake and its people than he let on. He was an observer, and people like him took in everything, and tended to remember everything.

They passed through two more scenes—pink trees with peacock-color accents, and blue trees, Laura's second favorite area. Being surrounded by the soft blue, amid the dark greenery and white snow, calmed her. It also sat along the northeastern section of the island, a quieter place all around.

"Here we are at the grand finale." Multi-colored lights tied the whole walk together. Some flashed, some faded then brightened, while others rotated entire trees through the color wheel, one color at a time.

Beverly gasped. "These are some of my lights, aren't they?"

Laura nodded. "Yes, and thanks again for that donation. We couldn't have done this part without them." The boxes of lights Beverly donated weren't just LED lights, but ones that were controlled by remote for different settings. It made for a crazy, sensory overload finale, that while Laura was thinking about it, didn't quite fit the mold for children with ASD. Some would endure it, but others, like Hannah, might find it too flashy.

She typed a note in her phone to reconsider the settings. At least Beverly saw them in their craziness. But that was why she had scheduled the soft opening, to work out any kinks and listen to feedback.

As they finished up the walk, Laura stopped them by the hot

chocolate stand again. "Well, what do you think?" Had it been what Beverly envisioned? Was it enough? Even though Laura questioned herself, her mind also brought her back to the achievements made in such a short period of time. Finding the venue. Discovering power on the island. Getting volunteers to decorate and provide transportation. It was a downright Christmas miracle the Bennetts had a fundraising event to walk through tonight.

"It's absolutely fantastic." Beverly nearly squealed.

"It's beautiful. Well done," James said.

"We couldn't be prouder to have our names on this event as sponsors. You've really done a wonderful job." Beverly stretched out her arms and stepped forward. Laura accepted the hug, relieved at her reaction but also feeling awkward at the display of emotion.

Beverly let go. "Danny's not allowed to bring Hannah without me coming as well. I must see her reaction to all of this."

Laura smiled and the next boat pulled up, dropping off five passengers.

"Did you want to stick around for a while?" Laura asked. "Another round of hot chocolate?"

James' eyebrows raised in consideration.

"We'd better head back." Beverly held onto James' arm, and Laura walked with them to the boat. Two other passengers had already boarded.

"Room for two more?" Laura asked.

"Hop on in." Laura didn't know the name of this volunteer. It would do her some good studying the volunteer schedule. They all deserved to be noticed.

Laura waved goodbye to the Bennetts as they veered off, the boat turning around and heading back to town.

She sighed, a long, breathy let-out-the-warmth-of-her-lungs sigh. She actually had sweat forming down her neck and under her arms, courtesy of the anxiety of pleasing the Bennetts.

"Are you Mrs. Crawford?"

Laura turned around to see a woman in her thirties, two

children holding her hands. "I'm Miss Crawford. But please, call me Laura."

"We just wanted to tell you how lovely this was. The kids loved it, right?" The boy and girl at her side smiled shyly.

Laura crouched lower. "I'm so glad you liked it. And you know what—if it's okay with Mom—you can go right over there to the hot chocolate stand and tell Marie I sent you. She may have a little something special for you." She winked and they smiled in wonderment.

The mother took them to the hot chocolate stand, and Marie handed each of them a candy cane.

"Well, don't you have all the tricks?"

Laura turned around and saw Steve, wearing a puffy vest over a flannel shirt. It looked more like something from Ben's wardrobe than Steve's.

Why wouldn't Steve wear something like that? Just because he dressed up for work didn't mean the guy didn't know how to relax. Heck, he was the one who tried to get her to relax.

"Care for a drink?" He raised two champagne glasses in one hand, a bottle in the other.

"Looks like you're the one with the tricks."

It felt unbelievably satisfying to see him. He helped out as much as he could earlier in the day, but she missed him most of the afternoon. Then her nerves kicked in, flying awry in having to entertain the Bennetts. Seeing his familiar face had a way of instantly calming her.

She followed him, walking in the opposite flow of traffic on the walkway.

"I'd say the first night has been a success," he said. "Everyone coming off the boat that picked me up said it was great."

"That's good to hear."

"Do you still doubt it?"

She looked around at the twinkling lights, the revelers pointing and oohing and ahhing. "I want to say no. It definitely looks like the feedback is positive."

"Why so hesitant? What you did here was amazing."

"I don't know." She shrugged. "I guess whenever something is good, I just wait for the ball to drop."

"The only ball that's going to be dropping is the New Year's one, in twelve days. Which brings me to something..." He stopped as they reached the blue section. Did he know she found that section calming, or was it a coincidence?

He weaved between two trees. "Come on."

She followed him, and he led her to two lawn chairs, set behind the last of the lit trees, overlooking the lake northward. "You brought all this with you?"

"You can't have a glass of champagne sitting *in* the snow."

She took a seat, and he poured the champagne, handing her a flute.

"To many more wonderful nights."

She clinked, wondering if he meant the fundraiser, or them. She swallowed it, the bubbles as cold as the snow but refreshing.

"Thank you for this."

"No problem."

Their chairs were close enough that she leaned her head onto his shoulder. "It sounded like you wanted to talk to me about something?"

Steve stayed quiet for a second. She almost lifted her head. Maybe it was too much, too soon. Or he didn't care for such affection. But *he* had reached for *her* hand under the table last night, right?

"It's nothing. Let's just stay like this for now."

It wasn't too much, too soon for him.

Laura savored the closeness of the moment. She slipped her phone out of her pocket, the radio station playing *I'll be Home for Christmas*, and turned it up.

Steve chuckled. "Looks like I'll be home for Christmas after all."

She lifted her head and looked in his eyes. "Sorry to sabotage your plans."

His eyes softened, a few wrinkles crinkling next to his eyes lit a dark amber with the reflection of the lights. "I'm not."

He leaned in closer, and her heart pounded, thundering in a wave over the music. She closed her eyes, not caring about the Bennetts, or the fact she'd have to go back to Charlotte soon. His soft breath tickled her mouth, and she parted her lips slightly. He reached for her, cupping her head in his hand, pulling her closer.

She wanted this, wanted to be close with him all day. It had ached to be away from him for the afternoon, and she pushed away the knowing pain she'd feel when they'd have to go their separate ways. It was bound to come soon, with the fundraiser settled.

It didn't matter. That was later, and there was only now—his warm breath, his lips, his hands in her hair—

Honk! H-h-h-honk!

The boat horn startled them apart. She squinted, looking out on the water.

"I asked Mr. Nichols to come by after the last of the passengers." Steve shook his head.

Laura bit her lip and softly nodded. "I guess we'd better—" She nodded her head in the direction of the entrance.

"Yeah." Steve stood and folded up the chairs.

Laura carried the champagne and glasses as they walked to the west end of the island. They walked in silence, meeting eyes every now and then, smiling and even letting out little giggles.

After spending so much time worrying over it, wanting it over, the night had ended up a success. And Laura didn't want it to end.

Chapter Twenty-Two

Tuesday, December 20

THE ONLY PART OF STAYING IN TOWN OVER THE holidays Steve regretted was the visit to his law office downtown. While he wasn't getting a break from Waverly Lake, he realized he certainly needed a break from work. The fundraising event, even though frustrating at the start, made for a great distraction. It felt rewarding to accomplish something that brought joy to people and raised money for a good cause.

The next big ticket on his docket was a custody case that would play out in February. He figured he'd get a jumpstart on the research aspect. With the tinsel and garland strung in shops around town, and Margaret playing Christmas music softly at the front desk, motivation ran low. Could it be he'd actually caught the Christmas spirit this year?

Or did it all have to do with Laura? She renewed in him the true meaning of the season and his faith in people of the town. Maybe even his hope to find love.

She occupied his waking thoughts, wondering where she was— the island—and what she was up to—adjusting the display.

Knowing the answers to those questions didn't stop his lack of focus on his work.

Margaret knocked on the door. What she needed to do was knock on his brain and tell him to get back to reality. He was thankful though for the disruption in his mush of thoughts.

"Mr. Cavidge is here to see you." She pressed her lips into a straight line. "I don't think it's for anything positive."

Steve shook his head and ran his hand through his hair. "I wouldn't expect it to be, coming from him."

Margaret smirked, peeking behind her as if Mr. Cavidge could've heard Steve.

"Send him back."

Margaret left and Mr. Cavidge appeared, wearing the same bulky jacket and boots he'd worn on the boat the other day when half-stalking them on the island.

Steve stood from behind his desk and extended a hand. Mr. Cavidge denied the shake and Steve sat back down. Sure, it was rude, but Steve expected as much.

"What can I do for you, Mr. Cavidge?"

"I'm letting you know that if you don't stop this nonsense on the lake and at that island, I'm going to file a complaint."

Steve put his hands on top of his head, elbows out to the sides. "On what grounds, may I ask?"

"Boat traffic."

Steve chuckled. "You do realize there's less boat traffic out there for this than there is during an average summer day?"

"Exactly. We have to endure the boat traffic in the warmer months. Winter is the quiet time around here, and you're ruining that."

Steve focused on the next few breaths before speaking. It was important to set the right tone, with the appropriate mix of legal authority and friendliness. "Everything we are doing there is legal. You have the right to make sure of that, and feel free. I would imagine you wouldn't have the time on your hands, managing two souvenir shops."

Mr. Cavidge shook his head, clearly irritated. "It's not fair. Either anyone can use the island for commercial purposes, or no one."

"It's for charity, Mr. Cavidge. No one is out there profiting off the event happening there."

"I know some food truck owners that might say otherwise."

Steve held back a smile calling his bluff. "We have three vendors set up for this weekend, and all three have agreed to donate their profits to TLC. Now, I can maybe see the argument that they'll be exposed to more people, and indirectly benefit from the exposure further down the road. But that will not hold in a court of law as commercial profit of the fundraiser."

"It...it just isn't right."

Mr. Cavidge's case was no case at all. It came down to his hatred of knowing someone else used a piece of property he could've used to expand his pocketbooks.

"Honestly, I think you owe thanks to Miss Crawford and The Learning Center for ASD, and even the Bennetts for sponsoring this event."

"And why would I do that?"

Steve stood from his desk, hands on hips. "It's bringing in more people from out of town, and those already visiting for Winterfest are staying longer. Which benefits your shops. Indirectly, of course." It was a dig at him wanting to shut down the vendors on the island. But it was also true. Rooms continued to be filled up around town, with the highest demand ever for room shares in locals' homes leading up to the weekend. And guests were booking more than one night. Social media blasts, local gossip of the event, and the network of donors and friends the Bennetts had acquired made sure of that.

Mr. Cavidge stood there, hands balling into fists in frustration.

"Now, was there anything else you needed to discuss?"

He stomped to the doorway and turned around, pointing a finger. "This isn't over."

Not until Sunday, Steve wanted to say. Instead, he let the man vent and storm out.

Steve shouted from his office after he heard the front door shut. "Next time, maybe offer him some coffee?"

"That man needs way more than coffee," Margaret yelled back.

The front door opened again. Maybe Mr. Cavidge came up with a stronger comeback after some thought. Poor guy.

"I just wanted to talk to Steve for a minute."

It was Laura. He nearly jumped out of his office but didn't want to chat in front of Margaret. She would undoubtedly see the redness in his face and hear the eagerness in his voice.

Margaret approached the doorway. "Miss Cr—"

He nodded, rummaging through papers on his desk. It was an illusion of business, one Margaret found amusing.

Laura entered the office, jacket buttoned up and a cross bag over it.

"Hey." He greeted her with a grin. He wanted to run to her and hold her in his arms. It felt inappropriate in his office. And with their relationship.

Relationship. He blacked out the near kiss of last night, the haunting, excruciatingly beautiful memory of her seated next to him, head on his shoulder, then lips drawing close.

"I thought you were at the island."

"I was, just for a few minutes. I told the volunteer team what to adjust and they're taking it from there."

"It's fortunate to have such a team."

"I'll say." She nodded, the movement slowing and the corners of her mouth dropping. "It's partly why I can head back to Charlotte now."

He about choked on his spit. "What? You're heading back?"

She gestured to one of the chairs, and he nodded. She sat, leaving her jacket buttoned and purse on. "I knew I wouldn't be staying for the entire event. I actually stayed longer than planned." She shrugged her shoulders and cracked a smile. "It's only so long a non-profit can afford to keep me here. Plus, we have a system in place, and it should run smoothly from here on out."

He chewed on the inside of his cheek, mind busy coming up

with a business excuse to keep her. "You'll miss Hannah seeing the display."

"I know." She looked at her hands on her lap.

"And the big crowds on the weekend."

"Kim—my boss—says she'll send me back next week to manage the tear-down, and I have to make sure the volunteer boaters are compensated for the gas, as promised. We're already talking with Beverly Bennett about making this an annual thing, so we may store all the supplies locally."

"So, I'll get to see you next week?"

Laura half-smiled. "I'm sure we can arrange something. A lunch maybe?"

"I'd like that." Steve's fake happiness faded. *I'd like that.* What were they, business colleagues?

"I feel terrible about leaving on short notice like this. If I could..." She shuffled her feet on the floor and managed to meet his eyes. "Especially since you changed your vacation plans."

He waved a hand in the air. "Don't worry about that." He had changed his plans, because he wanted as much time with her as he could get. Couldn't she see that? Couldn't she sense how his actions revolved around time with her?

"Anything else, before I go?"

Yes, Laura. I'd like lunch with you. And awkward invited dinners and Winterfests and sailing and all the things. Every day.

Would telling her that be enough for her to stay? Of course not. Why would this woman, this gorgeous, perfectly imperfect woman upend her career and uproot her home for a lawyer she worked with for a few days?

If he said no, she'd leave. He wasn't ready for her to walk out of his office. Not yet.

"Oh, I should tell you." Perhaps Mr. Cavidge had been a blessing in disguise, if only for giving him another talking point to keep her here a minute longer. "Mr. Cavidge came by before you arrived. He threatened to file a complaint."

She rolled her eyes. "I swear, that man has it out for me without ever meeting me."

"You know, you have a point there. Maybe if you stayed and chatted with him, it would help."

She smirked, smart enough to catch on to his hint. "What would he complain about?"

"What wouldn't he complain about?" Steve folded his arms, leaning against his desk. "Boat traffic is his angle, for now."

"Is that really a thing?"

"Nothing you need to worry about. I just figured you'd like to know." *And I wanted to see your face a second longer.*

"Would you like a glass of water?" Margaret stood in the doorway. "Coffee perhaps?"

Yes, Margaret. Keep her here.

Laura stood, straightening her coat. "No, thanks. I'd better get going. Rather be driving during the daylight back."

"I understand." He stared at her. It was hard not to look at her, and she stood there, as if frozen, not daring to move. What did she want of him? Was she asking him something without actually asking it? It certainly felt that way. "Please be careful."

She snapped out of her stillness. "I will." She walked to the doorway and Margaret rushed back to her desk.

Margaret probably thought him a fool. But that wouldn't be entirely new.

Steve followed her out of his office, to the front door. She turned, giving him a last smile.

"You take care of yourself. You have my number." It felt odd leaving it at that. "In case you need me to go to the island, or anything."

She nodded. "You have mine. I'll be in contact with the volunteer teams, but if there's something I should know..."

"I'll let you know. I'll keep watch for you."

"Thanks." She gave a slight wave to Margaret and looked directly at Steve again.

This was it. This was the time to just go for it, to kiss her. Even if it was a goodbye kiss, at least they'd have that moment to hold onto.

But the more he thought instead of acted, the more she slipped out the door until she was gone. The door closed, and he stared through the glass.

Like an idiot.

He turned around and Margaret quickly looked down at her desk.

"Don't say anything," Steve said.

Margaret looked up, eyes full of pity. "That was—"

"Not a word!" He hurried back to his office, closed the door, and plopped into his desk chair.

Anything Margaret would say would be true. And he wasn't ready to hear it. Not when Laura Crawford just walked out of his life.

Chapter Twenty-Three

LAURA TRIED TO BLOCK OUT THOUGHTS OF STEVE THE entire drive back to Charlotte. The way into Waverly Lake hadn't seemed that long of a trip, yet returning to Charlotte never ended.

There were things she wanted to say in his office, things she wanted to hear from him. They had nearly kissed last night, for goodness sakes. Why was it so hard to address it? The fact she had to leave half pulled her to forget about it and half pushed her to take the chance while she had it.

She listened to the first half, yet the forgetting part proved tough.

He *had* wanted to say more to her, didn't he? The look in his eyes when she walked into his office...

It didn't matter now. As soon as she confirmed the soft opening went smoothly, Kim wanted her back at the office. As hard as she tried, she couldn't justify the company paying for her stay any longer. It was true what she had told Steve. They had a system in place, and she didn't need to be there twenty-four-seven.

She parallel parked on the street in front of her apartment. Normally she'd drive in the alleyway to the resident lot behind the building, but she only needed to pop into the apartment and take inventory of the food situation. She'd drive to the office to catch up with Kim and pick up groceries on the way home.

That was one thing about living in the city. People had this idea of how great it would be to walk to the local supermarket. It worked when she was out of a condiment or wanted to buy some fruit. But to do a full-blown grocery session, she needed her car to haul the groceries home.

She walked up the stairs to the second floor and turned the key in the lock, but the bolt already sat retracted. Had she forgotten to lock up when leaving? That didn't sound like her. Then again, falling for someone she had known for a few days didn't sound like her either.

Did someone break in? The door remained unmarked, with no signs of force. Should she call the police? She swallowed hard and slowly turned the knob, poking her head in.

Her heart dropped to the floor.

Logan stood across the living room, a big smile on his face. "Hey, Laura." He slipped his hands in his pant pockets. He stood there, awaiting her response, as if she was the unusual thing in the room.

"What are you doing here?" She scanned the room. The couch, bar stools, the two house plants—items she could remember offhand he'd picked—remained. Maybe he was waiting to ask if it was okay to pack them up.

"Kim said you'd be back in town today."

And? So? "You spoke with Kim?" He wouldn't speak with her, but he'd talk to her boss? Was that why Kim insisted she come back, because she knew Logan would be waiting for her? Kim had always disliked Logan. Why would she help him?

Unless Kim hoped she'd throw him out once and for all.

She held up a hand. "Just tell me what you're doing here. You've come to reclaim your stuff? That's fine, take it. I really don't care."

"It's over." It came out of his mouth with a deep sigh, as if this burden he had been holding inside released. "With Annette."

The sound of her name pinched Laura's nerves. It was funny

how names could be ruined for people throughout their life. Kristen was ruined because it belonged to the bully who'd pestered her through sixth grade. She would never name a future child or pet of hers Kristen.

"You mean for now." She set her crossbody bag on the console table.

"I mean for good."

"Until the next Annette comes along, right?"

"Laura, I'm back to tell you I made a mistake." He held up a hand. "I know, a major mistake. You and I had something real and great, and I blew it."

Hm. Not everything out of his mouth was a lie.

"I want us to be us again. I want to try to mend this, to move forward."

She couldn't help but *tsk* in reaction. "Did you think I was just waiting around for you to come back, to come to your senses? That I would welcome you with open arms, and thank the heavens you've come back?"

At the start of it all, she did wait around. She did want him to come back and grovel for forgiveness and vow never to hurt her again.

"I don't expect anything from you. I know I hurt you. I...hoped. I hoped you would consider giving me another chance."

"Why would I do that? Honestly, what reason do I have to do that?"

He walked around the sofa and sat, urging Laura to do the same. She unbuttoned her jacket but left it on and sat on the far opposite side of the couch.

"I know I broke your trust, and that's on me. What I hoped was that you'd remember our good times, how we spent most of our days together. We have a history, Laura. Just think of how well we know each other."

"You mean how I *thought* I knew you."

He shuffled in his seat. "Is this what it's going to be like? Me constantly apologizing for my mistake?"

The audacity of this man—no, *child*. "Are you already irritated by that? It's going to take a lot more work than a five-minute conversation to mend the wound you inflicted. Honestly, I don't think you have the patience or desire to put in the work. And that's if it's mendable at all." She shook her head. "I can't believe you."

She didn't want to look at him in her fury. But he sat there, sad eyes and pitiful stare. He almost looked moved to tears.

"There's another reason I came back." He turned his gaze to nowhere in the room. "It's my mother. The cancer is back and more aggressive. There's nothing the doctors can do for her except help with any pain or discomfort."

He still knew how to stab her in the compassion nerve. "I'm sorry to hear that. I really am. You know how much I respect and admire your mom."

He nodded and wiped his face harshly with his hand. "That's why I need to ask a favor of you."

She took in a breath. Of course. That's what this was all about. He needed a favor. Why not butter her up with an apology first?

"I haven't gone to see her yet at the hospital. I was wondering if you'd come with me. I don't think I can do it alone."

Curse him for stringing her along, for making her feel pity on him. But she had no qualms with his mother. They had always gotten along, and Laura admired Betsy for her brave stance during chemo and radiation. She even gave her rides to treatment a few times.

"Fine." She held up a finger. "But I'm only doing it for your mother, not for you."

He nodded. "There's something else you need to know, then."

Laura closed her eyes to keep herself from screaming. All he ever did was ask too much of her.

"You know my mom adored you, right?"

She didn't respond. *Out with it already.*

"She thought you were the best thing that ever happened to me." He chuckled, then quickly stopped. "I agree. You are the best thing."

Laura wanted to roll her eyes. "Logan, flattery isn't going to get you anywhere."

He nodded quickly. "Right. Well, I didn't quite have the opportunity to tell Mom that you and I had…"

"You didn't tell her you cheated on me?"

His mouth remained agape. It must've hurt his head thinking over what to say. "She doesn't know we had a falling out, no."

She stood, the fury unable to stay seated. "You're asking me to not only go with you to the hospital, but you want me to pretend we're still together? That everything is fine?"

That couldn't possibly be what he was asking for, because only a conceited selfish jerk would ask that.

He stood, arms pleading with her. "It'd just be for one visit. That's all."

Laura shook her head in disbelief, palms to her forehead trying to contain the rage. "Do you realize what you're asking of me?"

"I do!" He stepped back and calmed down, tears forming in his eyes.

"You're not doing this to me. I will not—"

"She's dying, Laura. I came to see her one last time. And I'm asking, I'm begging—please come with me. Please, just this once, lie. You don't have to do it for me, like you said. But for my mom."

Her phone buzzed in her purse. She welcomed the distraction and retrieved her bag. For a split second, even through all the ridiculous discourse with Logan, or perhaps because of it, she hoped the message came from Steve.

To see his words on the screen, even if a simple hello, or that she forgot something in his office. Anything. To know he was thinking of her would've helped her get through this awful afternoon.

But her phone only delivered disappointment.

"It's Kim. She's asking how soon I'll be coming around."

"I don't want to take up any more of your time." Logan neared, headed for the front door. "Would you please just think about it? I was going to go this evening before visiting hours finished up. I'll give you a call before I do."

She didn't dare look at him as he slipped out the front door.

Laura clutched her phone, frozen in the apartment. Her body couldn't decide what to feel. Or maybe it was shutting down all together.

She waited a few minutes, knowing Logan would be out of the building, out of the parking lot. But not quite out of her life.

She texted Kim back saying she'd be on her way in ten minutes. That gave her time to drag her feet through the door and to the car. Her mind rewound what had just happened, and it wasn't any easier to comprehend a second or third or tenth time.

It settled on knowing two things for sure. One, that Logan was a terrible person. How could she have dated him as long as she did? How did she not leave him before he'd cheated, let alone hoped he'd come back after?

The second was that she knew she'd regret not saying her goodbyes to his mother. She would have to suck up her pride, her disdain for Logan, and go to the hospital this evening.

A third surety crept up, courtesy of Kim's text. And that was how much she already missed Steve.

Chapter Twenty-Four

Wednesday, December 21

"Go home, already." Steve stood by Margaret's desk in the front office of Albertson Law.

"I know, I know." She moved the mouse and clicked a few times, the computer monitor switching to its background of Yosemite's El Capitan. "I wanted to finish up that document so I'm all caught up on paperwork."

Her chair rolled away from the desk, and she stared at him. "I also stayed longer because I wanted to make sure you're okay."

"Me?"

She angled her head, eyebrows raised, as if nothing got past her. That was because nothing ever did get past her.

"I'm fine." It had been barely over twenty-four hours since Laura had left, but it felt like twenty-four days.

"I know you're gonna say it's none of my business." She stood, putting on her coat. "But I'd like to think you see me as a friend, beyond being a coworker."

"I do, really."

"You miss her, Steve. It wouldn't hurt anybody for you to call her and let her know how you really feel."

"I don't know how I really feel."

She gave him the stare down again.

"Scratch that. I know for sure I'm an idiot. Either I'm an idiot because I only spent four days with Laura and fell for her, hard. Who does that? Who meets someone and thinks days later they may have made the connection of their life with them?"

"You can't control the whos, whats, and whys, or any of the other 'w's' of love. You can try to help it along, but sometimes it just happens."

"Well, I'm still an idiot, then. Because if what I feel is really true, if it's the real deal, why couldn't I tell her yesterday? Why couldn't I just come out with it when she was sitting here in the office?" It was the question he'd asked himself all night and day. So many dates he'd been on, so many tries at finding love. When he found it, had it in his grasp, and could've done something about it, he didn't.

Margaret shrugged. "You were scared." She slipped her purse over her shoulder. "The good news is, it's not over. If you don't want it to be."

He studied her face, wondering if she meant what he thought she meant.

"Just call her." She shook her head. "Or you can stay in this moping state and always wonder what would've happened, what could've been. She's only a phone call away, Steve."

He digested her words, staring at his feet before meeting her gaze again. "You make it sound so simple."

She chuckled. "Because it is. Technically speaking." She stared at the framed pictures on her desk. "Love is a powerful emotion and can make us behave in ways we never imagined. It can make hard things like giving up a vacation to spend time with someone easy, and easy things like dialing the phone hard."

"Are you sure you're in the right profession?"

She stood tall. "Yes. Because if I didn't work here, you'd be spending your Christmas knee-deep in paperwork."

"True." He smiled. "Good night, Margaret."

"Night, Steve." She strolled out the front door, looking back at him in pity.

He waved her off. "I'll be fine."

He waited for the click of the front door and locked it behind her. He wasn't quite ready to go home but didn't want locals wandering in, thinking he extended his operating hours into the evening. Word would spread fast, and he'd be eating dinners at his desk in no time.

He moseyed back to his desk and sat in the chair. His cell phone sat atop the desk, taunting him. No notifications, no missed calls. Why did he put the onus on her to call him? She came into his office to personally say goodbye after all.

He clicked on the green call icon and closed it again. If he wasn't ready to call, he wasn't ready to call. There was consolation in knowing that she'd come back after the weekend to help organize the teardown of the display. But it seemed foolish to wait until then to have at least a little bit of a chat or text, or some kind of contact, in the meantime. First and foremost, they were friends.

Someone pounded on the front door.

Steve stood, hurrying to the front office. A man leaned against the window, hands over his eyes to peer in. He registered seeing Steve and hurried back to the door handle.

Steve recognized him as one of the volunteers. He unlocked the door and let him in.

"I'm so sorry to bother you. With Laura gone, I didn't know who to go to." His words came out rushed and his breaths were quick and short.

"It's okay. Have a seat." Steve guided him to one of the chairs. "What is it?"

"The power is out. On the island. We were fine all day until—"

Steve checked his watch. The first round of boats were supposed to bring people out in less than ten minutes.

"Come on." He rushed out of the office, the volunteer behind him. He didn't bother bringing a jacket, but his adrenaline and quick steps kept him warm enough for now.

"Was a fuse blown?" He managed the words out of his quickening breath.

"We thought the same thing at first. We can't find anything wrong."

Steve took note of the streetlamps lit, the lights in store shop fronts twinkling. "Is it out anywhere else in Waverly Lake?"

"That's the thing. As far as we can tell, it's only the island."

They reached Pearson's Wharf in what felt like record time. A line of visitors had already formed at the edge of the dock at the pickup location.

Out on the lake, the island was dark. So dark it looked like it absorbed light from the few boat lights and fading sunlight.

He reached his pocket for his phone, but it was empty. He pictured it on his desk, waiting for him to be brave enough to call Laura.

"Do you have your phone on you? I'll call the power company."

"Sure." The volunteer handed over his phone, unlocked.

Steve searched for the number and dialed. He sat through a portion of options before dialing zero, hoping it would send him to an actual person.

"Hello, Lorain Electric, may I please have your name?"

"This is Steve Albertson. I'm calling about a power outage on Christmas Island—er, Moonlight Island."

She put him on hold. Every second that ticked by was an hour. "I'm sorry, your name isn't listed as the account name."

"I know, it's listed under The Learning Center, TLC. I'm their legal representative on this. I spoke with a Charles, or Charlie?"

She placed him on hold again.

The wait was maddening. The queue was getting longer, the crowd getting too large for the end section of the dock. Mr. Pearson appeared, guiding the line to stretch out, giving people space and distributing the weight on the dock. The last thing Mr. Pearson wanted, or anyone for that matter, was for someone to fall in the chilly winter waters of the lake.

"Okay, Mr. Albertson," she returned on the line. "What can I do for you?"

"The power to Moonlight Island is out. Our volunteer team said there's no blown fuse."

"It looks like the power was turned off."

"What? Why was it turned off?"

"There's a note here saying that there is, and I quote, an inquiry on the legality and safety of the underwater cable."

"An inquiry? What kind of inquiry? I'm a lawyer for goodness sakes. I need to see whatever documents were delivered to you."

"I am not aware of any documentation. My boss Charlie would be the one to talk to on that."

"Yes, he's the one I spoke with about setting up this account. Please put him on the phone."

"Unfortunately, he's out of the office for the evening. You can try again tomorrow morning."

"You can't keep it on until the morning when he gets back?"

"I'm afraid there's nothing I can do right now. Is there anything else I can help you with?"

He wanted to throw the phone in the water. As he hung up, he realized it wasn't his phone to chuck, and he handed it back to the volunteer.

"What is it?" he asked.

"Someone shut us down. At least for the night, until I can sort this out in the morning."

"The whole night?" The volunteer's hopefulness melted off his shoulders. "Who would shut down a charity event? What are we going to do?"

"I don't know." Steve shook his head. "To both of those." He rubbed the back of his neck, assessing the growing line at the dock. Who knew how much money they were going to lose tonight. Already it looked like the biggest crowd so far. And would these people come back tomorrow after being let down tonight? That's if he could get the power back on tomorrow. What if he couldn't get it back on ever?

"We're going to have to tell them," Steve said. "Come on."

He walked with the volunteer along the dock, past the guests in the line to the front. Two volunteers were holding off people getting into the first boat, one of three that waited for passengers.

Steve turned to face the crowd. "Everyone, if I can have your attention."

The chatter calmed. "As you can see, we are having an issue with power on the island. Now, we could boat you out there, and hand you some flashlights to go at it, but you wouldn't be able to fully experience the holiday extravaganza we have prepared for you. Unfortunately, we will have to cancel all visits to the island tonight."

Groans and chatter built up. "We are so sorry for the inconvenience. Please know you may use your tickets on any other night of the event."

"How do we know it's going to be working tomorrow?"

Steve's throat clenched. It was the same thing he wondered. "I will be addressing the issue first thing in the morning with the power company in order to give you all a great time on Christmas Island and raise money for a wonderful cause."

"We can't wait around another day," a guest said. "We check out tomorrow morning."

"Yeah," someone else yelled. "What about a refund?"

So much for reminding them about the charity part. "If you truly can't make it another time, you may get a full refund at the ticket booth."

The crowd turned around, slowly leaving the dock.

"That's not very encouraging." The volunteer pointed out the new line forming at the ticket booth near the main building.

"I'm going to get to the bottom of this," Steve said. "I promise."

As people slowly poured back onto solid ground, one figure stood still, facing the lake.

His arms were crossed, and he stared right at Steve.

"I think we have our answer on the *who*."

The volunteer looked at Steve, then followed the direction of his stare to the man standing firm in the crowd's tracks.

To the smiling face of Mr. Cavidge.

Chapter Twenty-Five

Thursday, December 22

Laura sat at her desk at The Learning Center for ASD, double-checking dates on the new year's calendar. Every quarter she had to hand in the next quarter's plans for community outreach. Although the planning for January through March had been finished before Halloween—at least in terms of dates, activities and mainly school venues—she had put off the quarterly write-up. Kim set high expectations on logging details of every happening, which was a good thing running a non-profit.

Cindy popped her head in after a knock. "Phone call for you, line two."

Laura sat up straighter and took a breath. Speaking of next quarter's events...

It was probably someone following up. People tended to get nervous when things were planned out months in advance, like she'd forget they had planned it by the time it rolled around.

Or maybe it was Steve.

She shook her head. Why would Steve call her work number? A simple internet search would be easy enough to find it, but he had her cell number. Maybe he got a new phone, and his contacts were messed up.

She ordered her nerves and silly thought distortions to realign with reality and picked up the phone. "Hello, this is Laura."

"Laura, please don't hang up." It was Logan. How dare he call her on her work phone. "You won't pick up on your cell phone, so I had to call here."

"I won't pick up because I told you the other night after the hospital it's over with us." She had met him at the hospital Tuesday night, feigned a smile when in his mother's room with him, and said her goodbyes. It was more of a conversation with Betsy, to make her feel like it was old times and not a forever goodbye. She deserved to have a few minutes of happiness seeing them together in her last moments, even if it was a lie.

"I thought that—"

"You thought what? That because I went to the hospital, that meant we were back together?"

"You were so convincing around Mom."

"That's because you were right about one thing—she didn't deserve to have more heartache to bear in her last visit from either of us."

"Can't we just talk a little more about it? Over coffee? We at least need to discuss the apartment situation."

Even though they did need to discuss the apartment, that wasn't why he mentioned it. It was his lure, his way to entice her into one more conversation, one more outing together so he could try to charm his way back into her life.

"Logan, I'm not doing this right now. And don't call me here again." She hung up, staring at the phone in anger, as if the device had some control over Logan's behavior.

"That was impressive." Kim startled her from the doorway.

"I didn't know you were there."

"I'm kinda glad I was. Not to be nosy." She moved to a chair in front of Laura's desk. "I never said I'm sorry I told Logan about your return. I thought it would be like tearing the Band-Aid off. That you'd have one meeting to get it out, and that would be it. I had no idea he'd be like this."

Laura shook her head. "That's because you weren't the one dating him." She took a breath and cracked a smile. "It's okay. Really. His mother could go any day now, and I'm glad I had a chance to end that at peace. And every time he calls me, I get another chance to tell him it's over."

Kim chuckled. "I know it takes effort, hon. But eventually he'll get the picture. I will help in whatever way I can to get him to understand that." She eyed the doorway. "Which starts with Cindy screening your calls."

Laura shook her head. "She didn't know."

"I know, but she will right after this meeting."

They sat there, two girlfriends content in silence for the moment. Laura could feel Kim analyzing her, mind busy.

"Are you going to tell me who this mystery man is?"

Laura snapped to attention. "What?"

"The man, back in Waverly Lake."

I don't know what you're talking about. She could've said it, but it would've been wasted words. Kim knew her too well. Either that, or she sent spies to keep track of her activity.

"I hate to admit you're right. And don't ever tell me how you know. I may have to stop working for you."

"You're different." Kim disregarded the *don't ever tell me how you know* part. "I mean, you're doing your work, but there's an underlying..."

"Confusion? Disorganization? Lack of focus?" She lifted papers from her desk, tasks she had yet to complete, and let them fall back down.

"I was going to say moping."

"I'm not moping." Laura crossed her arms over her chest. Who knew, though? Maybe it was moping. She kept checking her phone, as if contacting Steve herself was not a possibility. And she followed up with the volunteers enough times to hear if they mentioned Steve that they stopped taking her calls yesterday afternoon.

"His name is Steve."

"Yes." Kim scooted the chair closer, laying her elbows on the desk and chin in her hands.

"He's an attorney in town. The Bennetts wanted him to help me find a venue, get to know the town."

Kim gave her a sly look. "And throughout that you got to know each other."

She tapped Kim's forearm. "It's all crazy. We were around each other for a few days."

"But..."

"But..." She sighed. "I was a completely terrible person to him at the start and realized I was wrong about him. He's amazing." She stared off. The gray wall staring back had no answers for her. "The last night there, we nearly kissed."

"Laura." Kim slapped the desk. "So, what's the status now? Are you going to pursue a relationship with him?"

She shrugged. "The job is almost over. I told him I'd be back to help with teardown, but honestly the volunteers have it all managed. There's no reason I need to go back."

"Except for him." Kim sat up, elbows off the desk. "You do realize that's a good enough reason, right? If you feel for him the way I think you do."

"Is it, though?" She leaned back in her chair. "And then what? Stay there? Quit this job? Do you really want me to leave for a man I've known a few days?"

"I want you to be happy. I'd love you to work here forever," Kim said. "But if you're not happy." She scolded her with her eyes.

"I'm happy with my job. I really am."

"It's not just the job I'm talking about. I mean the bigger picture."

It wasn't that Laura hadn't thought about it. She'd thought about it too much. On the one hand, she loved her job. On the other, she lived in Charlotte in her ex's apartment. The same ex who didn't know himself enough to know he'd cheat on her again and again. And how could she move to Waverly Lake? What would she do there? Especially after Logan, it didn't feel right moving to another town because of a man she knew, a man she fell for, for a few days. Would a long-distance relationship work? Was a four-hour drive long distance?

"I know," she said. "The bigger picture is harder to figure out."

Kim nodded. She placed a hand on Laura's. "I'm here if you need anything." She stood and straightened her well-tailored jacket. "I'll start with Cindy screening your calls."

"Thanks."

Laura's cell rang and her organs jumped. She scanned the caller ID. "It's him."

Kim gave a thumbs up with a smile and hurried out of the office.

Laura shuffled in her seat, like he was about to step into her office instead of chat on the phone. "Hello, Steve?"

"Laura, hi."

Hearing his voice was like feeling a cool breeze in the heat of summer.

A myriad of questions invaded her brain. *Are you okay? What've you been up to? Why on Earth did you wait this long to contact me? Do you miss me as much as I miss you?* She fished for one and ended up with a safe bet. "How are you?"

"I must admit," he said, "it's good to hear your voice.

She smiled, the cool breeze effect overruled by the flush in her cheeks.

"I'm sorry to call you like this. The volunteers came to me since you're back in Charlotte."

She straightened, worry washing over her body. "What is it?" She set aside the thought that the volunteers probably had enough of her phone calls to begin with.

"Last night, right before the first shift of boat rides out there, the island lost power."

"Oh no. Was it the changes I instructed?" After Monday night's walk-through with the Bennetts, she came up with alterations to the grand finale to make it more ASD-friendly. If the changes were to blame, though, a blown fuse would've happened the previous night. Unless they took longer than expected to make the changes.

"It wasn't the fault of any of us. It was purposely turned off. By Mr. Cavidge."

"What? Why—how could he do such a thing?" Her anger swelled. Last night was Wednesday, the night Danny was going to bring Hannah to see the display. The night Beverly Bennett wanted to attend again, to see what joy Hannah would offer up on the island.

"Was the whole night lost?"

"Unfortunately." Steve paused. "I'm not sure if I can get it back up and running by tonight either."

"I'm on my way."

"You don't have to come out—I mean, that would be nice to see you again, but—"

"Don't be silly. I set up the event, and if it's not actually happening, I need to be there." Her mind wasn't going to change. She had wanted an excuse to call him, to talk to him, to see him again. But this was not the kind of excuse she had hoped for. "I'll call you when I get into town."

"Okay. Be careful."

"I will." She hung up and grabbed her coat and bag. She stopped at the doorway, Kim standing in the hallway.

"I guess the job isn't finished after all?" She looked stern, then her mouth softened to a smile.

"I'm sorry."

"Don't be. Go do your job."

"I'll pay for the hotel myself." Though she doubted anything would be available. Hopefully, Aunt Dee had a room, or maybe she could ask Tracy for a favor and stay.

"I can cover one more night. If you need longer..."

Laura understood. It was Kim's way of saying it was time for Laura to choose what made her happy. In more than just her job.

She wasn't sure now and didn't know when she'd be sure.

She had to focus on her job. Right now, that meant she had an island to power again.

Chapter Twenty-Six

STEVE WIPED HIS SWEATY PALMS ON HIS PANTS. THE front door opened, and a familiar voice greeted Margaret.

"It's good to be back, although not under the best circumstances."

"I understand. Steve is in—"

"Right here." He stood in the doorway between his office and the front entrance. He tried not to show his absolute delight in seeing her, the way her lovely, angled cheeks and dazzling eyes lifted his worries.

"Hey." She smiled, frozen in front of Margaret's desk.

They remained like that, staring at each other for an uncomfortable amount of time. At least to Margaret apparently, because she cleared her throat. "I've got some more research to do here." She returned to her monitor, typed a few keys, then looked at the two of them. "I think you two had better work out the power situation..."

Steve snapped out of the trance. "Right. Come on back."

Laura followed him and sat in the same chair she had said her goodbyes in two days ago. Steve walked around his desk.

"What's the situation now? Are we still out of power?"

"Unfortunately." He moved a file folder over, not necessary or useful in any way except to busy his hands. "I threatened Mr. Cavidge with an injunction. He agreed to back off on the power company."

"That's good news, right?"

"Yes." He sat in his chair. "And no. The good part is that Lorain Electric will be turning the power back on. The bad news is that there are sequential steps to make it happen, to officially dismiss his claim. Therefore, we won't have power for tonight either."

She shook her head, eyes wary.

"I'm sorry," he said. "I haven't even asked about your drive in. Everything okay? You must be exhausted, not having planned on making this trip."

She sighed and leaned back in the chair. "It was fine. I think the adrenaline of the situation fueled me to keep going instead of making the one or two stops I would've taken."

"At least you got here before sunset."

She scoffed. "Just in time to see the visitors get a dose of disappointment." She sat upright again. "Have you told them anything? Contacted the volunteers and ticket office?"

"I informed the volunteers. Looks like another night of refunds. I'm not sure if people will stick around another day. Some of today's crowd is from yesterday. With a track record like this, no one will buy tickets for tomorrow in the first place."

"I just don't understand." She unbuttoned her coat. "What compels someone to shut down a charitable event? Does he really think he's losing money from the visitors here?"

"I've tried telling him that before. Right here in this office. He's convinced that he could be making money on the island, ever since he learned about the power supply. Therefore, every day he's not using it, he's out the money he potentially could've made."

"That's ridiculous."

Steve shrugged. "Trust me, I'm in full agreement with you. But I don't know how we solve this problem, if he intends to keep interfering with our goal."

"He's going to run out of days to interfere with soon enough."

Steve moved around to the front of his desk and leaned against it. "I'm really sorry about this."

"It's not your fault. You're only trying to help." She tucked a lock of hair behind her ear. "Without your help we may not ever get power restored."

"Still, it pains me to see Mr. Cavidge's behavior."

"He's one bad apple," she said. "Think about all the good ones we've encountered. All the volunteers on the island, the ones using their boats to transport everyone. The donations of decorations."

He nodded and the door swung open again. Steve checked his watch. *5:58 p.m.*

"I'd better tell Margaret to get going. It's the second night in a row she's been working late. It doesn't help that people see her and think we're open this late."

Margaret knocked on the door frame.

"Margaret, why don't you head on home? Nothing could be this important with all the hours you're putting in."

"I was just finishing up. But one of the volunteers is here."

Steve nodded and walked to the front office, Laura following him. Margaret packed up her things and waved as she exited.

"Mr. Albertson, you have to come out to the dock right away."

Steve glanced at Laura, her eyebrows tight and lips curved in confusion. "What is it? Are all the visitors requesting refunds? Did some of them show up and not know it was cancelled this evening?"

"That's the thing," the volunteer said. "It's not cancelled."

"What do you mean it's not cancelled?" Laura asked.

The words were stolen from Steve's mouth.

"I think you need to see it to understand." He stepped out of the office, holding the front door open.

Steve and Laura met eyes for a second in hesitation. Laura clutched her coat together and followed the volunteer out.

"Let me grab my jacket." Steve retrieved it from his office and locked up the front door before hurrying to catch up with Laura and the volunteer.

"I'm not sure if I can handle another major problem on my

plate right now." He spoke to Laura, who shook her head no. She couldn't either.

"I don't think you'd classify it as a problem." The volunteer crossed Dowager Street. His elusiveness was making matters worse. Why couldn't he just come out with it?

They hurried to Pearson's Wharf. Steve didn't have to walk out on the dock to see what the volunteer meant.

People lined up in the queuing spot at the end of the dock, waiting their turn. What they awaited took his breath away.

Five boats, two under full sail, were decked out in lights. One had strands blinking on and off, each strand a different solid color. Another boat had clear lights all around the gunwale and up the mast.

"Come on." The volunteer edged them across the dock.

Another boat appeared at the front of the line, multi-colored lights and three mini-Christmas trees on deck, similar to the Winterfest saplings.

They neared the volunteers helping passengers board and disembark.

"What is all this?" Laura asked.

Valerie, the lead volunteer for Helping Hands, stepped aside. "Miss Crawford. I didn't expect to see you here."

She hinted at a smile. "I can say the same for all this. What is going on?"

"When Mr. Anderson here asked us to inform the scheduled boaters that tonight was off, some of them hadn't heard about last night. They didn't want yet another night of losing fundraising, so they came up with an alternative instead."

Steve looked out across the water. The island was indeed still dark, but the lit boats crisscrossed the waters of Waverly Lake.

"They figured, they dedicated this time to take passengers out on the water, so why not still do that? They came up with the decorations on their own. I kinda think they started to see it as a competition, who has the best mobile light display."

"It's absolutely amazing." Laura's face glowed from the lighted boat filling with passengers.

Steve stood close enough to graze his fingers along hers. Their hands wrapped around each other's, and they stood there, awed by the volunteers making lemonade out of lemons.

"I don't know what to say," Steve said.

"Just say you'll do what you can to get that power back on," Valerie said. "We're not sure the novelty of this will last more than a night."

Steve nodded. "I promise."

Laura squeezed his hand tighter.

He looked into her eyes, the lights reflecting off the water making them twinkle. "Come here."

They kept their hands together as he led her away from the queuing crowd, down the dock to the parking lot of Pearson's Wharf.

"I wanted—there was something I wanted to tell you, to talk to you about the other day, when you came by to say goodbye." He still didn't feel brave enough to get it out, but if he didn't, he wouldn't sleep tonight knowing she was in town, and he'd chickened out. Again.

She looked down at her feet, corners of her mouth curling. "I'm sorry, I was being awkward. I should've told you something too, but I was leaving. I didn't know exactly what or how I wanted to say it."

He studied her face. Could she have been thinking the same thing he had? That there was something between them, a chemistry, that he'd never felt with anyone else?

"Okay. Perhaps you first."

"No, go ahead," she said. "You started this conversation, after all. I don't want to hijack it."

"You're not hijacking it." *Stop stalling. Just tell her.* "Okay. Well, I know we haven't known each other for a long time. Even a short time." He laughed nervously. Why was this so hard to get out? "I told you about my dating history. How I'm the king of first dates."

Her mouth softened to a larger smile.

"You even know about the embarrassment of Lovetoberfest."

She placed her other hand on top of the one she held already.

"I just—I wanted to tell you—"

"Laura!"

He looked to his right, breaking his sorry excuse for a speech.

"Logan?" Laura's hand slipped out of his. "What are you doing here?"

"The other day, before we went to see my mother in the hospital. You said that you didn't think I'd put the work in. For us." He touched his chest then reached out to her. "Well, here I am, putting the work in." He grinned.

Laura's face was blank. Steve couldn't read happiness, joy, anger. Only shock.

The man looked Steve up and down. "Aren't you going to introduce me?" He stepped closer and extended a hand. "I'm Logan. Ainsworth."

Steve reluctantly shook it, confused as all get out. The name struck familiarity, but he couldn't think straight.

"Laura's fiancé."

Steve's hand recoiled. It naturally formed a fist, desiring to make contact with Logan's face. The man who cheated on Laura and broke her heart. What was he doing here? What did he mean by the other day? Had she gotten back with him?

His guts dropped, his legs not wanting to support his body. It was what she had hoped. He had returned, wanting her back. Of course, he did. Who wouldn't regret leaving Laura and want her back?

"Logan, you can't be here."

He chuckled and put his arm over Laura's shoulder. "I know, it's a big surprise. I can't believe I never tried to surprise you like this before." He leaned in closer to her ear. "Don't worry, I'll add it to things I'll make sure to do in our future together."

"How did you even know where—"

"I spoke with Cindy. Claudia? Someone with a C at your office. She said there was some emergency out here. I don't really understand what's so emergent to make you pick up and leave Charlotte. But I figured if there really is an emergency, maybe I could help with that. I know I didn't take much interest in your work before, but I'm here now."

Steve felt his insides shifting beyond their place, up into his throat. "I'd better leave you two alone."

"Steve." Laura reached out her hand. "Don't go. He's the one—"

He held up a hand and feigned a weak smile. "It sounds like you two have some catching up to do." *We had catching up to do. But I didn't get it out in time. I failed again.*

But this time, it really was too late. With Logan back in her life, he wouldn't get another chance to fail. Or succeed.

"I'll see you back at the office tomorrow morning." The words came out shaky, his nerves playing with him from head to toe.

He managed to look her in the eyes for a brief second. What he read was pity.

She felt sorry for him. She knew what he was going to say, and she was going to let him say it, even knowing her fiancé was back in the picture.

"Good night, Laura." He turned away, heading for Dowager Street.

"Steve..." she pleaded once more. Logan whispered something to her, and she mumbled something back. Through the muffled air in his ears, he heard her last words, voice tiny and weak.

"Good night."

Chapter Twenty-Seven

THE LAST FEW MINUTES HAPPENED IN SECONDS. STEVE was about to tell her something, something hard for him to confess, she could tell. She wanted to tell him it was okay, caress his face, let him know he didn't have to be nervous to tell her anything. She was there for him, and if he meant to say what she thought he meant to say, then she would have told him she felt the same way.

But then Logan showed up, and now she stared at Steve's back, getting farther away with each step. He was out of reach, his absence leaving her empty. Leaving her longing for him and angry with Logan.

Laura dipped, unraveling the grasp Logan had on her shoulder. "What are you doing here? Do you know how crazy you look?"

He backed up a step and looked around, as if his presence was obvious. "I told you. I'm showing you I'm willing to put in the work for this. For us."

"I can't believe you. Whoever Annette was, she must've really done a number on you. For you to come groveling like this, across the state." She shook her head in disbelief. This wasn't happening, was it?

He closed his eyes and shook his head. "I knew you wouldn't answer your phone, and I didn't want to send it in a text."

"Send what?" She crossed her arms. This had better be good, but she doubted it. Another sorry. Another promise to never cheat on her again. More of the same old Logan.

His face sobered, the congenial excitement of surprising her wiped away. He scratched the back of his head, staring at nothing, then at her, then nothing again. Something wasn't right.

"What is it, Logan?"

He cleared his throat. "Mom passed away." His voice came out soft.

The wind knocked out of Laura's lungs. She unfolded her arms, not knowing what to do or say. They both knew it was coming. She knew Tuesday night was her last goodbye, but it still hurt to hear. "I'm sorry for your loss, Logan. I really am."

He rubbed his shoe on the dock, looking forlorn. "I didn't know where to go. I didn't want to be alone. You're the only person I know that truly knew her." He shrugged. "You may have known her better than her own son."

Laura walked over to a bench, bolted to the dock at the back of the main building, and took a seat. He followed her, the overhead light above giving off a little steam from its heat. The boats continued to pick up visitors, the line getting longer. She briefly wondered how long they took out each group, what path they traversed on the water. But it didn't matter. What mattered were the happy faces disembarking, and the fact people got some use out of their tickets. Any fundraising on top would be miraculous.

She didn't want to be here. Not on this bench, at the dock, with Logan beside her. But perhaps it was for the best. It gave her a chance to say what she needed to say, and maybe it took a trip out here for him to listen to her words, not just hear them.

"I know you loved your mother. She was a great woman, and it's hard to think she's not with us anymore."

He nodded, face solemn.

"Please don't take this the wrong way, but I can't be what you want me to be for you anymore. I can't be the crying shoulder you're seeking. I've been your go-to person for so long. If you had a bad day at work, you leaned on me. When you gave up your dog Riley, you leaned on me." As she remembered the times she assumed the role of his rock, the times he relied on her to pick him up from the bottom, the more evident his narcissism. The situation with Riley should've been enough to question his loyalty. Who gives up his dog after three years? He claimed he had to because the apartment didn't allow dogs. So why move into that apartment? Find one that does. Riley should've meant more to him than a zip code.

"It's always you leaning on me, and not the other way around."

He angled more to face her. "Because you always have your stuff together, Laura. You never need it. Do you know what it's like living with someone who never makes a mistake? Who is always composed?"

She wanted to cry. All those times she needed someone, why couldn't he see it? Like when her aunt died and he downright refused to go to her funeral, or when she moved out of the apartment she had adored not for its grandeur, but because it was her first that she paid for on her own, to go live with him. She could easily come up with a dozen times she'd needed someone but wanted *him*. She'd desperately wanted him to console her, to say everything was okay. Even just a hug to recognize her needs.

This man wasn't worth her tears. "How could you say that to someone, especially someone you supposedly love? Everyone needs somebody now and then. Nobody is perfect. I pull myself together because I have to, not because I want to. It's what you do as an adult, but it's a lot easier, freeing even, to have someone there to lend support. Someone who gives me the opportunity to let go, who listens."

"I'm listening to you now." He grabbed her hands and held them.

She pulled them away. "Too little, too late, Logan." Or never. She couldn't believe any of his newfound promises. She couldn't trust the changes he displayed would hold up in the future. He presented himself the way he wanted to be seen for now, and it would all wash away when they were back to reality in Charlotte. "A relationship is give and take. All I do is give, and you take. That's not what that expression means."

"That's not true. That can't be true. I'm sure I've given."

"The worst part is, after all the giving of myself to you, it still wasn't enough. You had to run off with someone else." She finally looked him in the eyes. "Until their giving dries up, and you come back to me."

His foot tapped up and down, then he stood. "If we're going to move on, make this happen together, you have got to forgive me. I've said I'm sorry and promised I will never do that again."

"Yes, you have." She stood. "But what you haven't done is listen to a word I've said."

"I have listened."

"I'm done with this, Logan. Done with *us*."

"No, Laura, you don't mean it."

"I am truly sorry about your mother. Please know that. But you have to let me go. Here, and right now." She shuffled through her coat pocket.

"If you could just—"

She held out a key, the key to his apartment. She had taken it off the keychain this morning and placed it in her pocket to remind her to give it to him. Then she received the phone call from Steve and came straight here. Not exactly straight here. Not before she packed up her clothes from the apartment and dropped them off with Kim first. She was grateful he wasn't around when she did.

Then again, if he had been, they could've avoided this whole scene.

He stared at it dumbfoundedly. Attaching it to her engagement ring gave it a finality and extra punch at the same time.

"Please take it."

"We can work this out, Laura."

"Take it, or I'll throw it in the lake, and you'll have to make another copy from your key and lose your chance to return the ring."

He submitted and took the key from her grasp.

"Keep whatever furniture you want. All of it, I don't care. I've already packed my clothes."

"Was it my cheating? Is that what changed you so much?"

She was almost as dumbfounded with the comment as he had been seeing the key. "Who said I'm the one who changed?"

"But you have. You're more...sure-footed. Assertive, even. You're actually more beautiful now than ever."

She wanted to punch him. Strangle him. Smack the bad pieces of his personality out of him and only leave the good. Yes, there was good in there, deep down. But she was tired of shoveling.

"I met someone. And I think I love him."

"What? Who? That guy I just met?" It was a joke he found laughable until he registered the look on her face. "It is, isn't it? You can't be serious."

"Why not? Steve is incredibly kind, smart, and handsome. But above all, he cares about people, and he cares about me. Enough to really listen to what I have to say and consider my ideas."

He slipped his hands in his pockets. "What are you gonna do, Laura? He's here and you're in Charlotte. Are you going to quit your job?"

"I don't know."

"Are you moving here?"

She shrugged. "I don't have the slightest idea. All I know is that I feel for him like I've never felt for someone before, and I hope—I mean, I think he feels the same way for me. I have to at least try."

Steve had wanted to say something to her at the dock. It sounded like he was going to open up, tell her how he felt. It ached to watch him struggle with his words and not blurt out how she felt. But she had enough respect for him to give him time, to let him speak, to listen to every word—fumbled or not—he had to say.

Then Logan showed up.

Oh no. What was Steve going to think about Logan's visit? If he mustered up the courage to tell her how he felt...

"I have to go."

"This can't be goodbye, Laura."

"I'm sorry again, about your mother. But I need to go. And you should go home, back to Charlotte. There's nothing here for you, Logan."

Her heart pounded as she walked away from him. Stronger and assuredly, but also mixed with flutters the closer she stepped to Albertson Law. What were the chances he went back to the office? What if he wasn't there? She had no idea where he lived. But she had a network of friends in Waverly Lake.

She shook her head. She'd cross that bridge if she couldn't find him. What worried her more was his reaction.

Had he thought she took Logan back? She rubbed her forehead, rehashing the conversation. Logan mentioned the other day, and the hospital. What was Steve to think? Did Logan do that on purpose in front of Steve, to make it look like they were back together?

Her anger towards Logan rose. Even when she cut him out of her life, cut the cord for good, he still affected her emotions.

She needed to tell Steve the truth about what happened when she returned to Charlotte. How he ambushed her at the apartment, guilted her into seeing his mom. That he meant next to nothing to her now.

Steve helped her see that. His kindness, his tender heart that he unsuccessfully tried to conceal, showed her that not only men like that existed, but she had found one.

She'd found the best one.

She slowed her near-jogging to a fast walk, going over how she'd say what she was going to say. As the words piled up in her head, she knew anything she prepared would come out wrong. She'd have to speak from the heart.

Maybe if she did, it would be easier for him to do the same.

Chapter Twenty-Eight

Steve locked himself away in his office.

He could've gone straight home, but he wasn't thinking, not about where he should be and what he should be doing. His stomach grumbled, but the last thing he wanted to do was eat. He had no desire to work on anything, yet he needed a distraction.

He busied himself with the pitcher of water Margaret had left out, with two serving cups. He filled one and drank it, the ice still chilling it enough to help cool his fire-hot emotions.

His thoughts swarmed over Laura, about how he fell for her and almost had the chance to tell her. No wonder people were bah-humbug about love. Because it was cruel and unfair. Why couldn't she have told him about Logan? All it would've taken was a text.

Easy for him to say. He'd chickened out calling or texting her.

Was this his fault? Was it his cowardice, his shrinking away from his feelings that pushed her away? If he had just checked in with her. A simple I'm thinking of you, or I miss you. Heck, a simple hello. None of it would've been wrong because he did think of her, constantly, and he missed her with everything in him.

No. He got caught up in the moment. That was it. This past week was a compilation of moments he took for more. Visiting venues, attending Winterfest, wine at the island.

And tonight, the community of volunteers pulled together to make something out of nothing. It was a beautiful sight, seeing the boats lit up, people happy and content with the surprising alternative. The warmth they showed heightened his senses, led him to want to connect with Laura, kiss her, tell her she had stolen his heart.

Good thing he didn't tell her his thoughts.

Someone knocked at the glass door, and he jumped out of his seat for the front door.

Laura.

After everything—his near-confession, the humiliation he experienced with her fiancé showing up—the sight of her still made his heart leap. But for a second he contemplated whether to open the door. It was a callous thought, leaving her out there, but it wouldn't have been to hurt her. Not directly, at least.

It would've been to spare himself more hurt.

She knocked again. "Please," she mouthed, the word muted through the glass. She bounced up and down on her tiptoes, as if the matter required urgency. Either that or something excited her.

He opened the door and stood behind it, a see-through shield protecting him.

Laura turned around, standing in the middle of the room, facing him.

He let the door slowly swing shut but kept his footing.

She clapped her hands together as if in prayer. "I'm so sorry, Steve. I didn't know Logan would show up like that. Honestly, I had no idea."

As he filtered through his words carefully, she continued.

"You don't have to apologize." Not for Logan showing up. That wasn't her fault. Perhaps. But not telling him her fiancé was back in her life? Yep, that was her fault.

"We were talking, you and I, on the dock. You were going to say something to me. I think"—she placed her hand on her chest—"it may be what I need to say to you. Something I should've said Monday."

Could Logan have contacted her Monday? Was that the real reason she went back to Charlotte so suddenly?

She smiled as she said it. How could she be happy about what went down minutes ago? How could what he needed to say be anywhere in the proximity of the same thing she wanted to tell him? Did she think he'd tell her that a former flame of his was back in his life? To not pursue this anymore—if it was a pursuit to begin with.

That's the funny thing. He hadn't been pursuing her. He didn't ask for this or seek it out, unlike the embarrassing number of first dates or Lovetoberfest. Sure, she had struck him with her beauty the first moment they met, but her tongue struck harder with her assumptions. He agonized over having to spend the day with her, until he saw who she truly was. Or who he thought she was.

Why was it harder to lose her, someone he hadn't seen coming into his life, than any of the other dates?

He rubbed his forehead before raking his hand through his hair. "I'm not supposed to be here right now. Six days ago, I was supposed to leave town for a vacation, something I haven't had in forever. But I stayed."

"I know, and I'm so grateful you did."

"I stayed, Laura. I'd like to think that it was because what we were doing was for charity. Because the Bennetts asked me to help, and you needed my legal help. It was clear after the first few hours you needed more than my legal help, what with the short deadline and venues booked up or not appropriate."

"You've gone above and beyond for me, for all of this."

He didn't absorb her kind words. "I've bent over backwards on some of the work I've done here. This nonsense with the electric company is just part of what I've had to deal with. And I was doing part of it for charity, but..."

"But what?" Her eyes pleaded for his confession.

He walked over to the chair, sat, and leaned on the arm rest as if everything were too much for his body to handle.

I stayed because of you. He hadn't admitted it to himself until now. After all the excuses he told himself the past few days, it took the threat of losing Laura to fully realize it.

"I didn't understand why you had to go back to Charlotte so soon, before the event was over."

"I told you, Kim wanted me back, and she couldn't fund my stay forever."

Laura could've funded her own stay. Heck, she could've stayed rent-free with any of the volunteers, or Tracy, or even...

He shook his head, climbing himself out of the what if hole. "It's all clear to me now. You had to go back because of him, right? You two have a long history together, the kind of history I said I wished I had with somebody. A solid foundation to build a lasting relationship. So I get it. I can't say I'm happy about it, but I do get that part of it."

She shook her head. "Steve—"

"Please know I wish you well. I hope he comes to his senses, which he has partially if he came back after what he did to you." It pained him knowing what a jerk Logan was. At least Laura framed him that way days ago. That was the part he didn't understand. How could she take him back? Her confidence and certainty of herself shone throughout this whole process, yet when it came to love she lacked those qualities. Did she not feel she deserved better? The best?

"I hope he treats you the way you deserve to be treated."

Laura bit her pink, beautiful lip. Her eyes welled with tears. If it noticeably pained her to make this choice, why was she making it? Did she realize, deep down, staying with Logan equaled the wrong choice?

Or did she pity Steve for breaking his heart? If so, she would've assumed she had his heart in the first place. If she knew, why not address it?

But maybe she had. Holding his arm, clasping her hand in his. The near kiss on the island on opening night. Was she showing him she knew? That she felt the same way?

How he wished he could sort out reality versus his mind playing tricks.

"Is that all you have to say?" Bitterness cut through her voice.

No. She doesn't get to be the bitter one. All I have to say? What did she expect, a confession of undying love for her? Did she want him to beg, to plead with her to choose him? Because he wasn't going to do that. Love shouldn't require a plea.

He rubbed his hand across his mouth, back and forth, feeling the stubble across his chin. He hadn't shaved since Laura left. He immediately remembered he hadn't when she had shown up at his office this evening, but the joy she brought him in seeing her face, the delight he saw in her eyes, said it didn't matter what he looked like.

But he saw what he wanted to see.

"Yes," he let out. Anything more, and he would've fully released the anger, the hurt. The embarrassment.

She sniffled and wiped the corners of her eyes with her delicate fingers. "I see." She took a few breaths and stared out the front window facade. The streetlamps lit Dowager Street with a soft glow, the dusk sky turning into solid night, a deep blue above the shops. Passers-by clung their coats close to their chest, a stiff wind picking up, as if Steve's tumultuous feelings manifested itself in the evening's weather.

Laura adjusted her bag, clinging onto the straps. "What about the charity event?"

"What about it?" Now he sounded the bitter one and didn't care. He had every right to let some of the scorn show.

"Tomorrow is a big weekend night, with the finale Saturday," she said. "We've pre-sold more tickets for those two nights than all other nights combined."

"I'm sure Mr. Cavidge will find some way to restrict what our boat volunteers did tonight, however amazing it might have been. He'll shut that down before we can do anything about it, and I'm pretty sure the power won't be restored in time for tomorrow."

It was the most negative scenario he could think of. He had no evidence Mr. Cavidge would argue, although history did show his grudge ran deeper than being upset. The restoration of power was a little more ambiguous. Earlier this evening he gave it a fifty-fifty chance. But Laura didn't know that, and no sense in having her hope for the best when that wasn't likely to happen.

"So, what are you saying?"

He stood, legs gaining their strength, his posture and confidence regaining its backbone. "I'm saying it's over." He shot her a glance, straight to her eyes. It stabbed her resolve, the tears reappearing and lips quivering.

He wanted to take it back. All of it. Every word he had just said. He fought the urge to comfort her, to wrap his arms around her and apologize. Tell her sorry in her ear over and over and kiss her cheek and her lips.

They'd work something out if Mr. Cavidge hit them with something else. And he'd take a thousand knives to the gut before letting her take Logan back into her life. He'd give him a ride or pay for a bus or plane ticket back to Charlotte himself.

Instead, he simply opened the front door.

"I see." She nodded, his words bruising her to her core. She walked away and paused in the doorway.

Tell her. All the things.

He heard her sob deeply before she walked out, not turning back to catch a last glimpse of him.

It *was* over. His motivation to keep the fundraiser going was next to nil. They'd exhausted his energy, overworked the volunteers, and squeezed out what little they could from the visitors' pockets. It was time to end it.

Worst of all, the statement applied to more than the fundraiser. In less than an hour, his hopes to be with Laura, to possibly spend the rest of his life with her, were over.

Chapter Twenty-Nine

"It's so good to see you again. I heard something about you coming after the event. I didn't know you'd be back this soon."

Neither did I.

The drive to Woodsman's Lodge was a cloudy one, Laura blinking back her tears at the way things ended with Steve. She didn't consider calling Aunt Dee about availability. She just drove. If she had called, she probably would've been a sobbing mess anyway.

"There was a bit of an emergency with the event. I thought it best if I came to check it out myself."

"You mean the power outage?"

Laura nodded. "Unfortunately, it doesn't look like my presence will have any effect on that."

"Shame." Aunt Dee shook her head. "Well, hopefully Steve can make things happen quickly."

"Yeah, hopefully." She flinched at hearing his name. He wasn't going to make things happen. But why tell Aunt Dee that? It wouldn't change a thing, except make her feel bad. Misery did love company, though.

"Your same room is open one more night. No one rented it

since you checked out, but I'm afraid it's booked for the weekend." Aunt Dee handed over the key. "I'll see what I can do about finding you another place."

"Don't worry about that." *I won't be staying longer.* "You have enough to take care of here than worry about me."

"Honey, it's in my nature to worry. You won't be changing that habit of eighty odd years."

Laura cracked a smile that faded as quickly as it appeared. "Thank you so much for the room, especially on such short notice."

"You are always welcome. I wish I could help you out more."

There was no way for Aunt Dee to know what happened with Steve, unless he called her right after, which did not seem in his nature. Although his reaction tonight didn't seem in his nature either. Yet the sympathy in Aunt Dee's eyes told Laura she knew something was amiss. Not hard to miss when it was written in the tear tracks down Laura's cheeks and her red eyes.

"If you need a late-night snack, I've got some chopped fruit in the fridge, and I can fix you up hot tea." She scanned Laura again. "I didn't tell everyone this, but I also have some chocolate pudding stashed away. Sometimes you just need a little pudding." She winked.

"Thank you." Even though her stomach growled not having eaten dinner, the thought of food was repulsive. "I think I'm just going to call it a night."

"Good night, then."

Aunt Dee dialed a number on her cell phone, and Laura took her luggage upstairs. Despite the circumstances, being back in Woodsman's Lodge comforted her. She dropped her bag near the door and plopped face first onto the bed. Between the frazzled drive across the state, confronting Logan and getting an earful from Steve, her nerves were shot. The tiredness crept through her muscles down to her toes and fingers. She could've slept all night were it not for the knock on her door.

Laura jerked up, checking her phone. She had been out for forty-five minutes.

More knocking.

"Coming." Maybe word had traveled to Aunt Dee, and she was checking on her. That was the kind of person Aunt Dee was, aunt to everyone, a consoler and straight talker when you most needed to hear the hard truth. Or maybe she was pushing the chocolate pudding on her. Also, very Aunt Dee.

Laura rubbed her eyes, not caring about the disheveled state of her hair. She opened the door.

Tracy stood in the hall, hands on her hips. Her curls tied back in a ponytail, the ringlets around her face escaping the hair tie. She wore a navy hoodie, powdered sugar, and something maroon splotched on the front pocket, as if she had dropped berry pies or Christmas cookies in mid-bake to come out here.

"Tracy?"

"Aunt Dee thought I could be of use." She walked into the room, and Laura didn't put up a fight. She shut the door, Tracy sitting on the edge of the bed, and Laura remaining on her feet.

"What's going on?" Tracy asked. "I didn't know you were back in town." She scowled, a small expression of being slighted Laura hadn't called her. To be fair she hadn't called anyone.

"I left Charlotte today. Steve called this morning and told me about the power outage on the island. I came right away." After she gathered her belongings out of the apartment. "I didn't even have time to find a room. I went straight to Steve's office."

"I'm guessing you couldn't get it fixed, judging by how dark it was on my drive over."

She shook her head. "No. I—" She rubbed her hands together in a fret. "I don't think we'll be able to do anything about it in time. I think it's over." Repeating the last words Steve had spoken choked her up again.

Laura dabbed her eyes and sat next to Tracy. "How did you know to come here?"

"Aunt Dee's sixth sense." She chuckled lightly. "She called me and told me you checked in. That you didn't look okay. I came over as soon as I could. And from what I see, she's right."

Normally, she'd curse Aunt Dee or anyone for that matter for interfering in her personal life. What if Aunt Dee had been wrong? She got Tracy to come all the way out here for nothing.

But it wasn't for nothing. She was glad Tracy was next to her, lending an ear. She had no one else to talk to.

"What happened?"

"We were talking about what could be done about the power, then a volunteer told us to come out to Pearson's Wharf."

"You saw the boats? It was pretty amazing, wasn't it? Danny is kicking himself for not being available tonight to participate. Hannah would've loved it if he decorated *Kare Bear*. I can see him still doing it anyway."

"It was amazing. And Steve pulled me aside, wanting to tell me something. I thought, or maybe I just hoped, he was going to tell me he has feelings for me, beyond the friendship we've made over these past days."

"But he didn't?"

"He didn't get the chance because Logan showed up."

"Logan?"

She realized the only person she had told about Logan was Steve. "I was engaged to Logan, back in Charlotte, until he left me for someone else."

"I'm so sorry to hear that. I had no idea."

"I know. I haven't exactly been an open book."

"Did Steve know?"

"He knew most of it—that at first, I had hoped Logan would come back, see the error of his ways. But after some time apart, I had stopped hoping. Honestly, I think it was my time here that opened my eyes. Steve showed me that there were nice guys out there, who were respectful and kind and listened. Who would never behave like Logan."

"If it was over, why did this Logan guy show up?"

"That's the thing. When I went back to Charlotte, he was waiting for me at the apartment. He kept calling my cell, my work, pleading for me to take him back." It wasn't exactly pleading.

Somehow, Logan made it seem like she was doing the wrong thing, that he was in the right. "I gave him no indication that I wanted to work it out, which apparently wasn't enough."

"So, he showed up here, hoping you'd take him back?"

She nodded. "The worst part is, he showed up right when Steve was opening up. Logan acted like a real jerk, and Steve—wrongfully—assumed I took him back." She sighed and stood up again. "I made it clear to Logan this time. I told him I've moved on and gave him my ring and key to the apartment back. I told him I fell for someone else. For Steve."

Tracy's eyes widened. "What does that mean, Laura? Where will you stay? What will happen—"

Laura held a hand up. "I don't know, that's the thing. It was spur of the moment, but it also was a long time coming, telling him off. I think in that moment, I had chosen Steve, chosen Waverly Lake, over him, over Charlotte, even over this job if that's what needs to happen."

"But that's amazing, Laura!" Tracy jumped up from the bed, holding Laura's hands in hers. "You acted out of the heart. Sometimes you need to do that, and the brain will follow and make it happen."

"The problem is that when I went to tell Steve everything, he put up a wall. He pushed me away and wanted nothing to do with me. I had never seen him so upset." She placed a shaky hand on her forehead. "I don't know what I'm going to do. I have this place for a night. Maybe I'll drive back tomorrow."

"You can't go back to Charlotte now. Not after all of that."

"What am I going to do?"

Tracy paced the room and finally took a seat on the bed. "I'll talk to Ben. Maybe you can help at the community center for a while until we figure this out. And Danny!" She pointed a finger. "Yes, Danny has plenty of room at his house. You can stay there."

"This is just too crazy. I can't ask that of you all."

"You're not asking. We're offering." Tracy flashed a smile. "All I know is, you care about Steve enough to give up your life as you know it. That's a good enough reason for me to help you. For all of us to help you. Heck, even without that, you've helped raise money for ASD, and that's enough reason."

"I'm going to have to break the bad news to your parents." Her stomach spun and heart sank. "Oh God, I didn't even think about that until now. Your mom is going to be devastated. I've failed her."

"Are you kidding me? You haven't failed in the least bit. You've given us several nights of fundraising and those visitors several nights of holiday spirited fun. The only person who failed us, who failed Waverly Lake, was Mr. Cavidge."

Laura looked Tracy squarely in the face.

"Oh yeah, we all know it was Mr. Cavidge who sabotaged your event. There'll be a reckoning someday, I promise you."

While it may take some time for that to happen, Laura had no doubt Tracy meant it. Getting on Tracy's bad side was not something to strive for. At the same time, it would be too late to make any difference in having to cancel the event.

Tracy slapped her hands on her thighs as she stood. "Okay, so we've sorted out where you'll stay and some work for you. Have I convinced you not to leave tomorrow morning?"

Laura ran through her job obligations. Although she had chosen this world over her old one when cutting it off with Logan, that didn't mean she had no obligations to Kim. Her heart still pulled to her job. She did love it, and despite acting in a role she wasn't qualified for, it led her to Steve. Could she give up the career that did that for her? Was there any way to live with both her career and a relationship with Steve?

Who was she kidding? Steve wasn't even talking to her right now.

"What about Steve?" It rushed out of her mouth. "I mean, I don't even think he'll see me." Her eyes started up again, and she willfully held back the tears. "I would've felt better if he had yelled or screamed at me, but instead he gave me nothing. Like he was emotionally empty."

"It's a simple case of misunderstanding that I'll personally help you sort out." Tracy walked to the door, opening it part way.

"What kind of sorting out? What will you do?"

"Just promise me you'll stay tomorrow, and you won't have to worry about it."

That only made her worry about it, but what else was she to do?

"I promise."

Chapter Thirty

Friday, December 23

STEVE WIPED HIS EYES WAITING AT THE COUNTER AT THE Cake Zone. Sleep was not something he accomplished last night. At least not consistently or for long enough. He replayed stumbling to tell Laura his feelings at the dock, the sight of Logan, and nearly kicking her out of his office. Had he been too harsh?

He hadn't let her speak or explain herself. He didn't want her to talk her way back into his heart. *As if she left it.*

She needed to figure out what she wanted, and it was best for him to step aside. Being out of the picture made the process less complicated. He was doing her a favor, really.

So why did he feel terrible?

"Here you are."

He grabbed his hot coffee cup and nodded in thanks. It was going to be a long day, not just because of his utter exhaustion. Even though he told Laura the event was over, he still wanted to see where they stood in getting the power back on. It didn't hurt to try. He nearly laughed at himself. Everything hurt right now.

His cell phone buzzed, and he checked the ID. *Tracy.*

He sighed. He would have to break it to her and Ben and the

Bennetts the likelihood things didn't work out for this weekend. Now was as good a time as any.

"Morning, Tracy."

"Hey Steve. Do you have some time to spare this morning? A few of us are at the center and wanted to chat with you." She paused. He wasn't sure if he should answer or if she was thinking. "About the fundraiser."

"I'm nearby at The Cake Zone. I can walk over there now if that works."

"That'd be perfect. See you in a few minutes."

He dreaded this talk, with every step closer to Phillips Community Center. He didn't like letting people down, especially ones who relied on his expertise, his knowledge and ability to get things done. A client a few years back reminded him of his grandmother. She had clearly been taken advantage of with a contract she signed. He knew it was a longshot to win the case going in, and consistently reminded her of that fact. Regardless, when they lost, it stung.

He walked through the open gates and up the stairs to the front door. A handful of elderly folks sipped coffee and played cards in the room to the right of the foyer, the room that served as the bar during the holiday party. It was nearly a week ago, yet it felt like yesterday he and Laura laughed over his Red-Nosed Rudolph drink choice.

"Steve." Tracy stood in the hallway, waving him over. "Thought we could talk in here." She led him to a table in the corner of the dining area. It looked cafeteria-like compared to the other evening with full decorations.

"I see you kept the centerpieces out." He pointed to the silver and gold pieces on the tables.

"I wanted to keep it all out, keep the place festive. But it was impossible to keep the tablecloths clean."

He nodded, not having the experience but imagining that would be the case. "What's going on? Why the call?"

Tracy leaned back and folded her arms. "You tell me."

He looked at her, befuddled. "You mean with the power to the island?" That was not the vibe she gave off, but he went for it anyway.

"You know what I mean. With Laura. We had a chat last night at Aunt Dee's."

He wondered if Laura found a place to stay in town and felt relief hearing so. Why he felt that way, he didn't know. He kept imagining she left with Logan after his words last night in the office.

"She told you, then, about her fiancé coming back? You didn't know she was engaged, did you?" He ran his fingers along the edge of the table.

"She told me about Larry."

"Logan." It pained him to correct her.

"Whatever. I'm guessing she didn't tell me about him earlier because she's not engaged."

He shook his head briskly. "She gave me that story too. He left her—the jerk he is—and she waited for him to come back." He waved his finger, his blood getting worked up again. "Just when I was starting to think—starting to believe she was over him."

Two men seated three tables down glared at him. He reined in his volume.

"Did she tell you what happened with Logan? After you scurried off to your office?"

"She came by." He had reviewed the conversation enough times to remember what little she said. And didn't say.

She hadn't said what happened.

He assumed what happened and didn't give her a chance to tell him.

He sulked, shoulders slumping. "What happened?"

"You know, she vows you're a good listener, but I'm not so sure." She shook her head, irritated with him. "I thought you'd like to know she told him off for good. She gave him the key to his apartment back. And the engagement ring, which by the way, she hadn't worn the entire time here. That should've told you something right there."

His stomach jumped a little, though he suppressed showing a speck of hope on his face. "Good for her. She deserves better than that creep."

"Yeah." Tracy nodded vigorously. "She does. And I'm starting to think she deserves better than you."

"Me?" His feigned surprise was laughable, even to himself. The two men stared again, grabbing his attention.

"You're a really bad liar, which is either a good thing or a terrible thing for a lawyer." Tracy turned around and waved a hand. "Hey, Snoop and Snoopier, a little bit of privacy here?"

"Hard to not hear with all the shouting," one of them said.

"I'll try to keep him in check, okay?" Tracy winked and turned back around.

Steve glowered and leaned back.

"Now where was I? Lost my train of thought."

"You were just telling me how bad of a liar I am."

"Oh, right." She smirked before getting back to business. "Laura not only kicked Logan to the curb, she told him she has feelings for someone else. She named you, Steve. She loves you."

That was it. The words reverberated, hurting his head.

She loves you.

His insides somersaulted, the unexplainable guilt from last night crashing down on him. If he had just let her speak. If he sat and listened. If he had gotten his feelings out before any of this...

"It's too late."

Tracy's hands flung in the air. "What are you talking about, too late?"

"When I saw her with Logan, it...it hurt too much. I can't take being in love if it means having to ever feel that bad. I understand why they call it heartbreak now." He clutched his chest. "It literally hurts to breathe." All last night his chest was caving in, his blood pressure raging. His body acted as if it didn't know how to function anymore.

"How many break-ups have you endured?"

"They're not much of a break-up if you've only gone on a date or two."

"Exactly. How many first dates, second dates have you gone on? Lord knows all of Waverly Lake has seen you with someone or other. There goes Attorney Steve, trying his luck at love again."

He was trying to understand what she was getting at. Maybe he didn't want to know. "Do people really call me Attorney Steve?"

Tracy waved her hand. "What? No. That's not the point."

He didn't believe her, but in this town, his nickname could've been a lot worse.

"Think of all the dates you have been on, the start of relationships you've had that ended. They've never made you feel the way you feel now."

"If they did, I would've stopped a long time ago." After the falling out with Rachel, he thought he had experienced heartache. But now he recognized it as embarrassment. He had wanted Lovetoberfest to work so badly he compromised his feelings. Rachel hadn't been right for him, but he clung to her so as not to fail in the eyes of Aunt Dee, or the people in Waverly Lake who knew he participated. To not fail himself. The fear of looking like a failure ended up embarrassing him more than actual failure.

Tracy worked herself in a frenzy, clenching her fists and loosening them open again. It looked like she stopped herself from shaking him. Knowing Tracy, it took control. "You feel so terrible because you finally found it. You found love. You've looked for so long and hard, and now it's in front of your face, and you're letting it go."

He fidgeted with the cardboard slip on his to-go coffee cup, the coffee down to lukewarm through the cup.

Laura had done it. She stood up for herself and threw out the toxicity in her life.

And she loved him. *Him*. If only he hadn't added to the toxicity last night.

He wiped his face in his hands, breathing a deep sigh. "You tricked me into coming here to tell me I'm an idiot, basically?"

"Basically." Tracy smirked at seeing it had sunk in his thick skull. "And to tell you we have your back. Obviously, hers too."

He nodded, ashamed of his actions, his words. How he treated her.

"Now, what do you plan on doing about it?"

He chuckled, but Tracy's deadpan stare said she wasn't joking. "What am I supposed to do about it? I told her the event was over. She's probably leaving today if she hasn't already. That doesn't cover the mess that is this weekend. I came over here to tell you about shutting it down—"

Tracy held up a hand. "I just told you. We have your back."

He wanted to throw out the whole thing, be done with it. But she commanded his attention. "Who is we?"

Tracy rose from the chair, and he followed her to the conference room, the same room he had met with the Bennetts and Laura the first day they met.

She stopped him at the closed door. "Now, before we go in, tell me straight up. Do you want to work things out with Laura?"

If she had asked him ten minutes ago, the answer would've been a resounding no. He saw no way it would work out. He had doubted her feelings for him, pictured her happy with Logan until he hurt her again, leaving him out in the dust in Waverly Lake. Even when he wanted to tell her how he felt, he wondered what it meant for their futures. Would he stay here? Was he willing to leave? Where would she be and what would she do?

But as she asked him now, there was only one word that came to mind. No doubting. No wondering. No what-ifs.

"Yes."

Tracy touched his chest and looked into his eyes. "You promise?"

He nodded. "I don't care what happens afterward. I have to tell her sorry, and how I feel about her."

"Which is?" Tracy looked at him as Mr. Nichols had the time he tried to steal a piece of candy at the pharmacy, waiting for a confession.

"I love her." It came out in the open, and he wished it hit Laura's ears instead of Tracy's.

"Okay, then." Tracy opened the door and a rush of voices silenced as they entered the room.

There were ten, twelve of the volunteer boaters from this week, including Danny and Kara's dad Richard.

"What's all this?"

"It wasn't entirely under false pretenses that I had you come out here. We do need to solve the problem of the power outage." Tracy shrugged. "Didn't think it'd hurt killing two birds with one stone." She leaned over and whispered. "You know, you and Laura, and the island."

He nodded, understanding yet not having a clue what they had in mind.

"How do you plan on doing that?"

Tracy placed her hands on her hips and nodded to the volunteers. "Let him hear it."

Chapter Thirty-One

AFTER A LONG NIGHT OF NOT SLEEPING, THEN SLEEPING through breakfast, Laura spent the day battling over staying or leaving. Part of her wanted to run away, leave this town in her rearview mirror. But after handing over the key to the apartment, she had to work out where she would go.

She briefly considered going back to Lake Norman. Moving back in with her parents, even temporarily, felt like an admission of defeat. Kim would happily house her, at least for a short while.

But the other part of her wanted to stay, holding out hope that things would clear up between her and Steve. Tracy was convinced Danny would let her stay at his house. Did she honestly feel comfortable doing that? Staying in the house of a client?

And what about her job? Was temp work at the community center something she wanted, even in transition, over her current work? Could she ever find something as fulfilling?

What was taking Tracy so long to contact her?

Laura officially checked out of her room at noon. It wasn't right to keep occupying it when it needed cleaning for the new guests tonight. She ate lunch with Aunt Dee at a table by the mural, Aunt Dee squeezing morsels of gossip about last night out of her, and Laura consistently changing the subject.

By early afternoon, she was ready to call it quits and leave. Of course, that's when Tracy called.

"I think it's time for me to move on, Tracy. I have to get back to my life and sort some things out."

"Are you sure? Because Danny is all in with you staying, and Ben said he could use the extra set of hands."

"Please don't take this as me not being appreciative. You have gone above and beyond. All of you, and I'm so grateful. But it's not in the cards for me here."

"You can't—" Tracy's voice quivered, urgency in her voice. "Please, will you at least come by the community center to say goodbye before you go?"

Laura sighed. Tracy would take it as one last opportunity to convince her to stay. It was bad enough having to tell Beverly Bennett about the cancelation of the event this weekend. At least that took place on the phone this morning. If it had been in person, Laura wouldn't have been able to hold back the tears in her disappointment. Although, Beverly took it surprisingly well.

Laura gave the only answer she could give. "Of course."

"Oh, good. Swing by any time after six o'clock. Ben and I have something to attend to this afternoon."

"Six? But I was going to leave—"

"See you this evening!"

Tracy ended the call. It approached four, and that put her driving in the dark for the second half of the drive back. Waiting that late forced her to drive the entire way in the dark, including the twisty mountain roads out of town.

Besides, what was she to do until then? There were only so many books in the Woodsman's Lodge lounge, and she had gotten bored well over an hour ago. If she had artistic talent, she could recreate the mural down to the last tree after staring at it for so long.

Aunt Dee came out of her office, having taken a break from the check-in desk. A wave of guests checked in near the start of check-in at three, followed by a lull.

"Should I plan on you staying for dinner?"

Although it would give her something to do, and everything that came out of the kitchen was beyond delicious, lunch lingered in her stomach from sitting all afternoon. "No, thank you. Tracy called, and I'm going to see her as I head out." She stood, making her move to exit. It was too early, but she couldn't stay here one minute longer.

"Please don't be a stranger." Aunt Dee extended her arms, and Laura accepted the hug.

"Thank you for your hospitality, again."

"Don't mention it."

Laura broke from the embrace and grabbed her bags. She walked around the desk to the front door. "Is it true you can get to town heading west out of here?" She had only ever gone east past the orchard or across the lake by boat.

"Yes, just keep on the main road. Whenever it forks, stay left and you'll wrap around the lake. There are some pretty overlooks on those side roads though if you want to take your time."

There it was again. Like Aunt Dee knew the goings on before Laura did, yet she played it off like she was making a friendly suggestion.

"I haven't really been up to those points during winter in a while. But with the bare trees, you'll be able to see for miles."

Laura nodded. "I'll have to check it out, then." She waved goodbye as she exited the lodge and carefully walked to her car.

She followed Aunt Dee's advice on her drive back to town. She took her time, meandering off the main road and taking pictures at overlooks, eating a snack of chips she had left in the car, and even hiking a short quarter-mile loop to a landmark where one of the first settlements had been established. The roots of the trees kept the snow at bay on the trail, and she managed to keep her boots mostly clean, the mud too hard to smoosh onto the soles.

As the sun lowered beyond the western range of mountains, she approached town. There was a line of cars heading into town, and she sat through a bit of traffic—nothing like Charlotte's—before she reached the community center. It was Friday evening after all, during the holiday season. They were probably shoppers and visitors for Winterfest.

At least she was able to find a parking spot on Dorset Drive. As she got out of the car, she realized she stood in the spot she had met Steve.

She shewed it off and clasped her coat, walking through the gate to the porch of Phillips Community Center. The front door was locked. In her haze of memories, she didn't realize until now the lights were off on the first floor.

She retraced her steps, then stopped halfway down the sidewalk. She looked up at the second floor. Two windows shone soft light. Maybe Tracy was up there.

She hurried back to the front door and knocked. After three rounds, she gave up. Tracy nor Ben had arrived back from whatever errands or business they had this afternoon.

Was it normal for them to close the center at his hour? Should she wait here? She paced on the front porch, concluding she'd wait in the warm car after her fingers registered the cold. At least the parking spot offered a view of the intersection so she could see when they'd arrive.

She walked back through the gates and realized a line of people were gathered across Dowager Street. The line wrapped along the sidewalk into the souvenir shop.

Mr. Cavidge's souvenir shop.

She crossed the street, a car driver honking at her through the line of cars. She held up a hand. "Sorry," she mouthed.

She approached a woman in line. "Excuse me. What's all this for?"

The woman put her hand on a little boy's shoulders standing by her. "For the event at the wharf." She pointed down the street.

People exited out of the souvenir shop, and the flow of pedestrians overwhelmingly headed east.

Laura walked in the same direction, her steps quicker than the crowd. She weaved through people, sometimes stepping over the curb into the street to work her way around them. When she got to

Pearson's Wharf, she stopped, catching her breath. Yet what lay before her took it away.

People aligned in clusters from the sidewalk to the dock, all the way to the pick-up and drop-off point. Boats waited in a queue for passengers. In the distance lay the island.

In all its holiday brightness.

It couldn't be. This was cancelled. She had told the Bennetts it was over. The tickets were to be refunded. And yet...

She worked her way along the dock, some guests not happy with her cutting in line. "Excuse me. Sorry. I'm the organizer. Pardon me."

She reached a bolus of people at the start of the line and stood on her tiptoes. She couldn't make out anything up ahead. "Please, if I could get through."

"Let her up here."

She recognized the voice. The smooth, solid voice of Steve.

The crowd parted, and she made it to the front. Steve stood on a boat whose bow pointed away from the dock. Another boat's stern was at its bow, and a line of boats continued bow to stern, all the way out to the island.

"What is this? What's going on?"

Steve held up a cord, a long wire that strung from his boat to the next. As her eyes focused further out, she could barely make out the cord running along the stretch of the boats.

"Is that—"

"Extension cords. Pearson's letting us use his outlet. I figured if we couldn't use the underwater cable, why not above water?"

She didn't know what to say. It was the craziest, dumbest, most beautiful thing she had ever seen.

"You know, I've been telling people, I'm the most known guy in town with the least amount of friends. Tonight, I stand corrected." He grinned, yet an underlying sadness bled through. "I was wrong about Waverly Lake. About the people here. They're exactly what this world needs, and it was about time I saw that."

There were too many thoughts to get out. "I can't believe it. I saw the crowds at the souvenir shop."

"Mr. Cavidge had a change of heart." He chuckled as Laura's eyes widened in shock. "He rescinded his complaints after I offered for him to partner with us selling tickets in his shop. He couldn't pass up the foot traffic in his store."

"You solved everything, then. The power outage, Mr. Cavidge." She shook her head, wanting to shout with joy and cry from the overwhelming feelings of it all.

"Almost everything."

He stepped up on the dock, his other foot wobbling on the rocking boat. Laura grabbed his arms and helped him up.

"Last night I—" He shook his head. "I heard what happened." He stared into her eyes and started over. "I've circumvented what I need to say for too long, so I'm just going to say it. I love you, Laura. I know it sounds crazy, and it may scare you off, and I wouldn't blame you because I was such a jerk, especially last night."

Laura grabbed his hands in hers. "It's okay." She looked into his eyes. "I wanted to tell you last night too. I love you, Steve." She bit her lip and giggled. "But you didn't let me get it out."

His forehead touched hers. "Can you forgive me?"

"Of course."

He reached his hands to her, touching her face, to the back of her neck. Although his fingertips were cold, they sizzled her skin. She leaned in, wrapping her arms around his waist. Their lips touched in a soft kiss, her pulse quickening, a flash of heat warming her core. His hunger intensified, and she pulled him in harder, the kiss blissfully dizzying.

She didn't want it to stop, but the cheers of the crowd grew more audible. He pulled away, nothing but a smile on his lips and glee in his eyes.

"Wait a second. How did you know what happened with me and Logan?"

Steve looked out to the line of boats.

A woman waved from the next boat down—Velma from the

library. Beyond her was Richard Carter, and she just barely made out the curly ringlets of none other than Tracy with her brother Danny.

"Tracy. This was all a setup, wasn't it?" That's why Tracy wanted her to stick around until dark. To see this.

Laura shook her head then waved back.

"Hold on." Steve got back in the boat and bent down. Laura couldn't see what he was doing. He popped back up, a bottle of champagne in his hand.

"What do you say we take the next boat out there? I have the chairs in the same spot."

Laura smiled, forever grateful she'd talked herself into staying. Grateful to Aunt Dee, to Tracy, Ben, Danny, the whole crew of volunteers. Even to Mr. Cavidge for coming to his senses. But most of all, to Steve.

"I'd love to." She took his arm and they walked to the boat awaiting passengers, hungry for another touch of his lips, eager to be alone with him on the island, in their private nook. It didn't matter what her next move would be, where she would stay, how she would make a living. What mattered was right now, this Christmas miracle, this town that pulled together out of love, and the man she fell in love with.

She stared at him with a grin. "But this time, no boat horns."

Epilogue

Monday, January 30

"Good morning, Regional Liaison."

"You don't have to keep stating my title, as if I'm royalty or something." Laura chuckled into the phone, sitting in the conference room at Phillips Community Center.

"It just has a nice ring to it, though," Kim said.

After Laura spent Christmas in Waverly Lake, she worked it out with Kim to remain connected to the community while still keeping her job. She'd work part of her time in Charlotte and part locally in Waverly Lake, as well as the surrounding Appalachian communities. She wanted to keep the outreach program up and running in western North Carolina, but her main project got her more excited than any other job had before.

"I'm calling because I need that list of accommodations for the summer camp. We're getting the major items worked out but wanted to double check."

Aunt Dee had been more than enthusiastic about using Woodsman's Lodge one week in the summer as a camp for kids with ASD. It would be a place where the kids and their families could stay and enjoy all the outdoor activities like any other camp while offering the guidance and augmentations to the activities to suit their needs.

The end of June seemed like a long way away, but five months was a short window to get the plans sorted. Not as short as the holiday fundraiser, though.

"We will have to revisit the budget too," Laura said. "Looks like the work on her dock may be more than we expected. I'm planning a workaround for it, just in case."

"If there's anyone who can find a way to make it happen, it's you. Or should I say, Steve?"

Kim had heard all about the world's longest extension cord stunt during the final days of the fundraiser, plus the surprise visit from Logan and the fallout afterwards. Either Steve had won her over with his big gesture, or her disdain for Logan was so great, or both, but Kim took a liking to Steve, albeit they hadn't met in person yet.

"Speaking of."

Steve walked into the conference room, making sure to keep the door's opening and closing as quiet as possible. He carried a white unlabeled box, but Laura knew it was from The Cake Zone. He opened it and revealed the powdered-sugar pastries inside.

"He brought me breakfast."

"If you don't bring him around soon, I'm going to start believing you're making him up."

Laura held out the phone to Steve.

"Hi, Kim."

She put it back to her ear.

"Believe me now?"

"Hired work is what that is."

Laura giggled. "All right, I'll catch up with you later."

She hung up and turned her face to offer a cheek. Instead, he turned her chin and kissed her on the mouth, the faint taste of warm coffee and sugar on his lips. She could live with mornings like this the rest of her life.

"Any luck with that office space?"

"They're supposed to call back today."

She'd been trying to find a shared office space in town. For now, Ben was letting her use the community center. It was good in that she met more locals each day, but she needed dedicated space, especially if she moved forward with establishing a branch of The Learning Center here in Waverly Lake. That was the long-term goal, at least.

Laura took a pastry from the box. It was still warm, crunchy on the outside and soft on the inside. "What's the occasion?" Powdered sugar emanated from her mouth in little dust clouds.

Steve chuckled. He kissed her again, and when he pulled back, white powder covered his mouth.

Laura laughed and took a swig of coffee from her mug.

Steve revealed a folder underneath the bakery box. He held it with both hands, tilting it side to side. "It's official."

"Really?"

He nodded. "Moonlight Island cannot be used for commercial or residential purposes. It will be registered as a historic landmark and can only be used for historical tours and charitable events approved by the town council."

It was an amazing win, something that would calm the worries Steve had about their discovery. "The teenagers won't be too happy about that."

"There are plenty of other islands out there for them to sneak off to." He sat on the desk, taking a pastry for himself.

"What about the campaign?"

"I go this afternoon to set up the account."

After the power fiasco, the power company investigated the safety of the underwater cable. Due to its age and the liability, they insisted a new cable must be laid as well as newer junction boxes on the island. If they were going to replace the cable, they might as well power the island with all they could. That way the historic tours could provide restrooms, and the holiday event could have speakers for music, more outlets for lights and displays and more vendor possibilities.

It sounded wonderful, but the new cable and boxes would cost upwards of fifty thousand dollars. So, Steve made it his second mission to organize a fund. It may take months, years even, to raise the money, but she had faith the town would pull together to make it happen.

It felt good to have that hope. To know that there was a community here, cheering her on, supporting each other no matter the petty squabbles of day-to-day life.

How was she able to have such hope?

She looked at Steve, who dunked his pastry in his coffee. It dripped down his chin, and he caught it with his coffee cup. She beamed with contentment. Some would call it luck or fate they were together. They'd be wrong. The reason for such hope, such optimism in her life, in *their* life, was clear as day. The town somehow pulled together the heartbroken charity worker from Charlotte with the notorious lawyer who couldn't find love.

That's how she knew anything was possible in Waverly Lake.

***

Thank you for reading! Did you enjoy? Please add your review because nothing helps an author more and encourages readers to take a chance on a book than a review.

And don't miss more from Mary Shotwell coming soon!

Until then read more great books like EIGHT DAYS OF CHRISTMAS, by City Owl Author, Starla DeKruyf. Turn the page for a sneak peek!

Also be sure to sign up for the City Owl Press newsletter to receive notice of all book releases!

Sneak Peek of...

EIGHT DAYS OF CHRISTMAS BY STARLA DEKRUYF

Isabella Whitley gripped both armrests and prayed she wouldn't die in a fiery plummet to the earth. Only clouds filled the view out the plane's window, but the aircraft jolted sideways and up and down, so vigorously that she closed her eyes and did the most ridiculous thing given her situation.

She *laughed*.

The irony of the moment was almost as painful as it was comical. Because wasn't this what her life had become now? A life in complete disarray and full of turbulence?

Bob—the complete stranger in the seat next to Isabella who'd talked non-stop since the wheels lifted from the JFK runway—cleared his throat. "I-it's going to be okay. We-we're going to be fine. Promise."

Isabella rolled her eyes and glanced down at his fisted hands in his lap, his knuckles white. What did Bob know? How did he know everything would be okay? And why was he so positive anyway? He'd already confessed that his girlfriend had dumped him, moved out and taken their cat with her, and his father died after choking on a shrimp—all in the last few weeks.

The plane rocked angrily, and Isabella inhaled a sharp breath. Sure, her life currently sucked, maybe not as bad as Bob's, but she definitely didn't want to die by way of a plane crash.

"H-hey, you've been letting me talk your ear off," Bob mumbled. "Besides your name, I don't know anything about you. How 'bout you tell me about yourself?"

Isabella didn't open up to just anyone. And on an airplane

headed back home for the first time in ten years definitely wouldn't be one of those times. People often mistook this as a sign that she was a good listener—people other than her ex-boyfriend, Harrison Blake, anyway.

Harrison used this as one of the reasons to end their relationship. His exact words had been: *It's like you've built a wall around your heart, and after four years, it's still impossible to get in. Someone broke your heart. Broke you. And I can't help you. If you ever want me to commit, you gotta figure this out.*

Technically, their relationship hadn't ended. Harrison asked her to move out of his modern apartment and suggested they *take a break*. But who really knew what that meant? Was this a Ross and Rachel break? Or were they free to see other people?

As the floor beneath her feet continued to rumble, Isabella found herself asking, "What do you wanna know, Bob?" If she did die today, she refused to prove Harrison right.

"So, you live in New York?"

She nodded, picturing Central Park, and took a calming breath.

"And w-what do you do for a living?"

"I'm a journalist. At *The New Yorker*."

Bob exhaled a low whistle. "Impressive."

Gah, had she said too much? She tried not to be paranoid, but with her career, she'd met an unsuspecting creep or two in her day. The few things Bob knew about her could be enough for him to locate any of her social media profiles or find her bio on *The New Yorker*'s website for that matter. From there it would only be a matter of time before he had her address.

Except as of now, she technically didn't have a home address. The thought of Bob showing up at Harrison's apartment provoked the bubble of a laugh in her throat. *Joke's on you Bob*. She didn't live there anymore.

Something inside her withered. Not having an address linked to her name was the opposite of funny—it was disturbing and downright pathetic. She'd worked tirelessly to reach her current position at *The New Yorker* and what did she have to show for it? A new popcorn maker she'd left at Harrison's apartment and a strict wardrobe of blazers and designer boots.

Since living in Manhattan for the past ten years, she'd relied on city transit and subways, so she didn't even have a car. She didn't own a single thing with her name attached to it. Currently, Isabella was crashing on Margo and Todd's old, lumpy couch. Her friends from college had a two-bedroom apartment with each of them occupying a room.

She wasn't complaining. She was grateful for a place to stay, even if it was a slightly dilapidated apartment building just outside of the city, while Harrison's modern and recently renovated building was in the heart of NYC.

Isabella couldn't dwell on the issue of technically being homeless, which was how she knew Dad would label it.

Dad. She probably missed him the most. He'd been so supportive and encouraged her to follow her dreams and attend Ithaca College. But when fate threw a wrench into Isabella's plans and she never returned after graduation, he'd been the most resentful toward her.

Scratch that—second most resentful. She'd have to wait to figure out a more permanent living situation after she returned to New York. Right now, her only focus was surviving the next eight days.

The aircraft rattled and Isabella clutched the armrests again. A baby cried somewhere toward the back of the plane.

Bob patted her shoulder. "Everything's gonna be alright." His stale coffee breath emitted across the small space between them. "Tell me why you're headed to Colorado?"

The plane leveled and Isabella exhaled a breath through her nose. She wasn't typically a nervous flyer. She flew often for work. But a lot was riding on this trip to Colorado. Her family was counting on her—Norah was counting on her.

Maybe by her opening up to Bob, she'd be on her way to proving Harrison wrong. She didn't *always* need to be one of those tough nuts to crack; she could be chatty and charismatic like Norah.

"My sister is getting married," she said. To little Landon Hoffman from next door. Isabella was still trying to swallow that news.

"That's nice. Good reason to travel at Christmas. Unlike me, who has to attend a big pharmaceutical conference..." Bob rambled on.

When Isabella had agreed to be Norah's maid of honor, she had no clue Norah had chosen the week of Christmas to get married. If she'd known, she might've said no. It was almost like Norah chose a Christmas Day wedding on purpose. That way Isabella would be forced to return to Pineridge, not only to celebrate her only sister's new marriage, but to endure the holiday as well, including Eight Days of Christmas—a Whitley tradition where they performed a specific holiday activity each day for eight days leading up to December twenty-fifth.

Norah had left Isabella no choice but to return home and withstand the eleven million questions from her family. No choice but to face Landon's older brother Leo—the boy who held the key to her heart for more years than she could count.

She glanced out the window. Ready or not—she was headed home.

Or maybe not.

Static blared through the plane's overhead speakers, followed by an announcement.

"Good afternoon flight 434, this is your captain speaking. I'm afraid I have some less than exciting news. Due to the snowstorm Denver is currently experiencing, ground control has directed us to make an emergency landing in Omaha, Nebraska."

"What?" Isabella flung herself forward in her seat as groans, disapproving comments, and moans echoed through the cabin. "Is he for real?"

"I'm 'fraid so." Bob gave her a soft smile.

"At any rate," the captain continued, "the good folks at American Airlines customer service will be more than happy to assist you with accommodations. Hopefully the ice and fog will let up in Denver so we can get you all on your way real soon. American Airlines thanks you for flying with us and, as always, don't forget to fill out a customer service survey online and give us a top-star rating."

Just how in the hell was she supposed to make it home now? The plane descended quickly, giving Isabella that queasy feeling in her stomach she despised. This was seriously happening. The pilot was actually landing the plane in Omaha, Nebraska.

"This can't be happening." Isabella closed her eyes, pinching the bridge of her nose.

"Omaha, huh?" Bob said. "Never been here before." He pulled his phone from the front pocket of his laptop bag, ready for when he'd have service. "Better check Yelp for the best places to find some grub."

As if this little emergency pit stop was the best thing to happen to him. Then again, maybe it was.

All around her, phones chimed, signaling service. She exhaled a few deep breaths before slipping her phone from her purse. She pushed her hair behind her ear and scrolled through her notifications. There was a missed call from Dad, a missed call from Norah, and several unanswered texts from Margo and Norah. But the text that stood out the most was from Harrison.

Harrison: Did you want the Pampered Chef cheese grater? Or the popcorn air popper? I know how much you love popcorn. But I did buy it.

Isabella's eyes burned. She squeezed them tight enough to see floating black spots behind her lids. He was really doing this now? He had some nerve. Dividing their things the week before Christmas? When she wasn't even in town?

Even though he'd sent the text two hours before, Isabella opened her eyes and tapped out a reply.

Isabella: Keep them both.

Isabella: On second thought, no. If you can't wait until I'm back to divide our things, then I want them.

She inhaled a deep breath, holding it in.

Isabella: I didn't know we'd made a decision yet. To divide our things. To be completely over.

She didn't expect a reply, at least not so soon. But regardless, it came.

Harrison: Just figured it would be easier this way.

Isabella: You mean easier for you.

Harrison: Why make it harder than it has to be?

Isabella: After four years together, breaking up shouldn't be easy.

No response—no surprise.

Isabella sent a quick text to Dad to let him know about the flight's detour to Omaha, and to assure Norah everything was fine and not to worry. She'd figure something out.

Eppley Airfield was fully decked out for the holidays. Garland dangled above wide windows, and glimmering lights wrapped around fake trees that lined the walls. All it did was cause a tight pressure in Isabella's chest. By the time she—along with her rolling suitcase and overstuffed carry-on—made it to the customer service for American Airlines, there was already a long line.

"Well, would you look at that line," Bob said, hot on her heels.

"Right?" Isabella huffed. "This is going to take forever."

"Why don't you come with me to get a bite to eat and then we can make our way to customer service afterward."

Isabella glared at him. "I don't have time to get a bite to eat. I have to get on another plane. And fast." In truth, missing the first few days of Eight Days of Christmas sounded amazing, but Isabella's family already saw her as the daughter and sister who abandoned them. Storm or no storm, she had to make it home within the next twenty-four hours.

"Whoa, okay." Bob put up his hands. "I'm sure you'll get on another plane. But not anytime soon. You heard the captain. There's a winter storm rolling through Denver. It's probably gonna be a while. Maybe not even until tomorrow."

Isabella grunted. She rubbed at the tension building between her eyes. She didn't have time for Bob and his rational thinking. Or this line. Or to be in the Omaha airport at all. "You go ahead. I'm gonna wait."

"Alright, alright. I think I might just do that." He backed up, and Isabella exhaled her relief. "Check you later, Miss Bella." He tipped an imaginary hat at her.

"It's *Isa*bella," she said flatly as he, thankfully, walked away. Despite it being Isabella's unlucky day, the customer service line for American Airlines moved swiftly. When it was her turn, she stepped up to the counter and held her head high. She needed to put on her game face. The one she used in the office. The one she used to get the story. The friendly-but-don't-mess-with-me face.

"Good afternoon, welcome to American Airlines. How can I help you today?" The customer service representative—Ben, his name tag read—had too big of a smile plastered on his face for how distraught Isabella felt.

"Hi there. My name is Isabella Whitley. I was on flight 434 en route to Denver, Colorado, but we were rerouted here due to the snowstorm. The reader board," she pointed above Ben's head, "shows all flights to Denver are canceled. But are you sure the info has been updated? Because I need to get on the first available flight. Please."

"I do apologize, ma'am. But as you just said, all flights to Denver have been canceled."

She gritted her teeth, resisting the urge to raise her voice. Ben was only doing his job, but desperation tingled through her unforgivingly.

"Right. I understand that. But when will the next one take off? I need to get on that flight."

"Again, I do apologize. However, I'm unable to give you that info."

She exhaled. "And why not?"

"Because I'm unable to see the future." His smile turned into a smirk.

Isabella recognized a smirk when she saw one. And he was definitely smirking at her now.

She narrowed her eyes and leaned across the counter. "I have to get to Denver. Today. Whatever you need to do to make that happen, *Ben*, do it." She forced out a strangled, "Please."

"Since it's already late afternoon, what I *can* do for you, ma'am, is give you a hotel voucher and hopefully we can get you on a flight tomorrow morning."

She leaned in closer, heat crawling up her neck and spreading into her cheeks. "I don't *want* a hotel voucher. I *want* on a plane."

He rearranged his expression into a jackass blank stare, as if looking straight through her. "Like I said, let me get you that hotel voucher and—"

Isabella slapped her hand on the counter. "Ben, I'd like to speak to your manager."

"Izzy?"

Isabella sucked in a breath. Her back went rigid while her stomach plummeted to the floor. "Oh please, oh please, oh please, no."

She turned around, slowly.

But nope, luck was still not on her side today. Because when she turned, she knew exactly who would be standing there. Not only because his voice was as familiar as her own skin, but because he'd called her *Izzy*. Besides her family, only one other person in this world called her by that childhood nickname.

Leo Hoffman.

"What the hell are you doing?" Leo stood in the customer service line a few patrons back, hands stuffed in the pockets of his black peacoat.

She swallowed, uncertain if she could find her voice to reply. "Leo?"

She had to still be asleep on the plane, having a nightmare. There was no possible way her luck was this bad.

"You think yelling at customer service is actually gonna get you to Colorado faster? Man, you haven't changed a bit." His face, while the same, was older, all sharp lines and dark brown scruff. And too beautiful to even be fair.

She could wake up now. Any minute.

"I just thought...I was just hoping...I," she mumbled, her mouth going dry. This was real, and she sounded like a blubbering idiot instead of the accomplished woman she'd grown up to be. His words registered. "Wait. Haven't changed a bit? What is that supposed to mean?" She glared. "And what are you doing here?"

"What does it look like?" he snapped.

Her brows pinched together. "You're flying somewhere?"

The Leo she knew never left Pineridge.

His gaze shifted to the people who had their attention trained on the two of them. "Just take your hotel voucher, Izzy. You're holding up the line."

Isabella reluctantly faced Ben and forced a smile, her heart raging against her chest. After all the ways she'd thought about avoiding her ex once she arrived in Pineridge, he was here. In freaking Omaha, Nebraska. With her.

"Look," she said to Ben. "I'm sorry. I know you're just trying to do your job. But you don't understand. I need to get home to Colorado today." She pushed back her unexpected emotions and cleared her throat, feeling the bizarre urge to open up to this guy and win him over. "My little sister is getting married on Christmas Day and—"

"That's still a week away, ma'am. I can guarantee you'll be there by then."

"But you see, my family has this tradition..." She pinched the bridge of her nose, her back absorbing the scrutiny from the other fliers. "They call it Eight Days of Christmas. They expect me to be there." She leaned forward and whispered, "I haven't been home for Christmas in ten years."

And the stupidly handsome ghost of her past had clearly appeared to remind her of that fact.

Ben inhaled a sharp breath. "Ten years? What kind of person doesn't go home for Christmas for ten years?"

Isabella's jaw dropped, and her first instinct was to give in to the fantasy of clutching the navy-blue tie around his neck and choking him with it. But she couldn't be angry with Ben, because he was exactly right. What kind of person didn't go home for Christmas for ten years? What kind of selfish person did that?

Her—that's who.

"Damn it." Leo groaned, now suddenly standing at her side, sporting that sexy, scruffy beard. "What are you gonna do, tell him your life story? It's a little late to get sympathy when you've already pissed someone off." He leaned over the counter, his phone in his hand. "Excuse me, Ben? Where's the airport's car rental located?"

Ben proceeded to give Leo directions while Isabella remained quiet, trying hard to be annoyed with him while also admiring his broad shoulders and obvious fit physique. He smelled good, too, like pine and citrus, and all man and... Jeez, this was a really bad scenario.

Leo took a few steps sideways, hiking a duffel bag over his shoulder. "You can either come with me and rent yourself a car and drive to Pineridge, or you can stay here and harass this nice guy and embarrass yourself further." He held up a palm. "Your choice."

"Whoa, hold on a sec." She shuffled next to him, getting out of the customer service line. "How far is it from here to Pineridge?" Isabella hadn't driven a car since she moved to New York. The thought of driving, especially through a snowstorm, caused her stomach to flip-flop.

"About six hundred miles."

She gasped. "Six hundred miles?"

Leo blew out an exaggerated and annoyed breath. "Yep. And you might want to hurry. Before all of the cars are gone." Leo stalked away from her, his attention fixed on his phone.

Isabella stood there stupefied, staring after the man who had once been her everything.

Pressing her lips together in a grimace, her mind battled over her options: remain stranded in the airport alone or chase after Leo and somehow persuade him to let her catch a ride with him.

With the flight information screens displaying *cancelled* for nearly every departure, her chest tightened while imagining driving through a death-inducing blizzard. In the end, the panic won.

She bit the inside of her cheek, gripped the handle of her rolling suitcase, and stomped off after Leo.

Don't stop now. Keep reading with your copy of EIGHT DAYS OF CHRISTMAS, by City Owl Author, Starla DeKruyf.

And don't miss more from Mary Shotwell coming soon!

Don't miss from Mary Shotwell coming soon and find her at www.maryshotwell.com

Until then, discover EIGHT DAYS OF CHRISTMAS, by City Owl Author, Starla DeKruyf!

Ready or not, Isabella Whitley is returning to her snowy hometown of Pineridge, Colorado for her sister's Christmas wedding. She wants in and out unscathed. Unlikely. A decade ago, she headed to New York and hasn't looked back. Now she must explain her disappearing act to not only her family, but the high-school sweetheart she left behind as well.

Enter Leo Hoffman. He's frosty after striving—and failing—to forget Isabella, the only woman capable of jingling his bells. Since his brother is marrying her sister, Leo is forced to celebrate Eight Days of Christmas with Isabella and her family—a tradition where they perform a different holiday activity each day leading up to December 25th.

Soon, their close proximity brings back memories—and the inability to keep their hands off one another. There's only one problem. Isabella's ex unexpectedly enters the equation, and she faces a difficult choice. Listen to her heart or her head? Isabella will need to decide, once and for all, where she belongs.

All reviews are **welcome** and **appreciated**. Please consider leaving one on your favorite social media and book buying sites.

Escape Your World. Get Lost in Ours! City Owl Press at www.cityowlpress.com.

Acknowledgments

The series has been near and dear to my heart, and it came to life through City Owl Press. Thank you for believing not only in the first book, *Waverly Lake*, but in the town and spirit of these books. Thank you to Tee Tate, my editor. It was great fun working with you. I especially looked forward to your reactions in the side comments.

To my agent Amy Brewer, and her team at Metamorphosis. You believed in and championed this small-town romance series, finding the right place for it in the publishing world.

Thank you to all of my readers, especially those who kept with this series from the beginning. Your social media posts, videos, blogs, and word-of-mouth give me much joy and the fuel to write more.

And as always, thanks to my family. From buying my books, actually reading them, and talking about them with friends, to giving me the ability to do what I do, I cannot be grateful enough.

About the Author

MARY SHOTWELL is the author of small-town love stories with happily-ever-afters for all seasons. Her debut romance novel *Christmas Catch* (Carina Press, 2018) was a Golden Leaf Finalist and earned a starred review from Library Journal. She loves incorporating her science and nature background into her fiction. When adulting, she's a wife to husband Matt and mother to three children. She currently resides in Tennessee.

Visit her website to her blog about writing, travels and publication news.

www.maryshotwell.com

 facebook.com/AuthorMaryShotwell

 twitter.com/MaryEShotwell

 instagram.com/authormaryshotwell

 tiktok.com/@authormaryshotwell

About the Publisher

City Owl Press is a cutting edge indie publishing company, bringing the world of romance and speculative fiction to discerning readers.

Escape Your World. Get Lost in Ours!

www.cityowlpress.com

facebook.com/CityOwlPress
twitter.com/cityowlpress
instagram.com/cityowlbooks
pinterest.com/cityowlpress
tiktok.com/@cityowlpress